A lasting impression . . .

His eyes held hers. "Now that you put me in mind of it, Miss Campbell, I agree with you. One does not fall in love with a face. In fact, it is possible for people to fall in love without seeing each other at all. I know a case where a man fell in love with a voice, and a manner, and a tiny glimpse of his beloved's soul."

Her mind went swiftly back to a darkened street and a kiss from an invisible stranger who, even then, felt like no stranger at all. Pain caught at her heart. "They do say love is blind," she said faintly.

Kilverton's eyes still held hers, steadily. "The gentleman I speak of was only blind until he met you, Miss Campbell . . ."

SIGNET REGENCY ROMANCE
Coming in February 1999

Karen Harbaugh
Cupid's Kiss

Patricia Oliver
The Lady in Gray

Emily Hendrickson
Miss Timothy Perseveres

The Nobody

by

Diane Farr

A SIGNET BOOK

SIGNET
Published by the Penguin Group
Penguin Putnam Inc., 375 Hudson Street,
New York, New York 10014, U.S.A.
Penguin Books Ltd, 27 Wrights Lane,
London W8 5TZ, England
Penguin Books Australia Ltd, Ringwood,
Victoria, Australia
Penguin Books Canada Ltd, 10 Alcorn Avenue,
Toronto, Ontario, Canada M4V 3B2
Penguin Books (N.Z.) Ltd, 182-190 Wairau Road,
Auckland 10, New Zealand

Penguin Books Ltd, Registered Offices:
Harmondsworth, Middlesex, England

First published by Signet,
an imprint of Dutton NAL,
a member of Penguin Putnam Inc.

First Printing, January, 1999
10 9 8 7 6 5 4 3 2 1

 REGISTERED TRADEMARK—MARCA REGISTRADA

Printed in the United States of America

TO:

The memory of
THE REV. DR. J. WESLEY FARR
and ESTHER LYNDEN FARR,
who believed I could;

GARY MICHAEL HART,
who dared me to;

and
GAIL EASTWOOD,
who showed me how;

this book is gratefully dedicated.

Chapter I

With an exclamation of pleasure, Mrs. John Campbell snatched up a letter that was waiting beside her breakfast plate. As only her immediate family was present, she did not hesitate to open her letter at the table. Seconds later, she uttered a faint shriek and went into a coughing fit.

Nicholas, a sturdy lad of ten, helpfully pounded his mother on the back until his father requested in no uncertain terms that he stop. When Amabel had somewhat recovered her breath, she announced the contents of her sister's letter in a trembling voice.

"My dears, the most wonderful news! Your Aunt Harriet is inviting one of our girls to London for the Season!"

A stunned silence greeted this proclamation. Caitlin paused in the act of buttering her toast. Her eyes went immediately to her sister Emily, for whom this must be the greatest of all possible news. But Emily, an ethereal blonde of eighteen summers whom one might expect to be overcome by rapture at such a moment, was not alone in her jubilation. To Caitlin's surprise, her entire family was shortly reduced to chaos.

Emily leaped up from her place and executed a neat step dance; John Campbell kissed his wife; little Agnes began tugging on her mother's sleeve, demanding to be told what it all meant; and Nicholas took advantage of the general bedlam to perform a handstand in the dining room—something Caitlin suspected he had always longed to attempt.

Her brother's legs waved precariously in the air. "Mind the dishes, Nicky!" Caitlin cried, as Nicholas's boots clattered down upon the sideboard. This brought the rest of the family more-or-less back to its senses. They resumed their accustomed places round the table to savor their unexpected good fortune.

"London!" breathed Emily. "Oh, Caitie, how envious I am!"

Caitlin paused, toast aloft. "Envious? I thought you would be ecstatic."

Emily blushed. "I do not mean I wish to take your place, of course! But I have longed all my life to go to London for the Season."

"Take my place?" Caitlin, now startled, turned to their mother for enlightenment. "Good heavens, Mama, has Aunt Harriet invited me, rather than Emily? No, no, she could never have made such a mistake! If she meant to invite me, she might have done so any time these four years."

Emily also turned to their mother, her blue eyes wide with anxiety. "But she could not invite me over Caitlin. It would be grossly improper, would it not, Mama? Caitie is the eldest unmarried daughter."

"Your aunt must be the best judge of what is proper, my love," Mrs. Campbell assured her. A slight cough from her husband caused her dimples to appear. "Do not laugh, John! Harriet may not have an extensive education, or an extraordinary degree of native intelligence, but on matters of *ton* she is infallible."

Mrs. Campbell began swiftly reading through her letter. Caitlin saw the painful hope flickering in Emily's eyes, and affectionate amusement lit her own. "Never fear, Emily! Our aunt has sent the invitation to you, now you are turned eighteen. What do I want with a Season? What a figure I would cut, dressing in white and acting the simpering ingenue at two-and-twenty!"

"You look splendid in white," said Emily staunchly. "And you needn't *simper,* just because it is your first Season."

"Well, I hope not, because however shy you may feel, Emily, you certainly never simper. I am persuaded you will do us all great credit."

Emily bit her lip bravely. "It is you, Caitie, who will go to London and do all credit. Indeed, how could you not? You are never at a loss, and always know just what to say. I wish I had your poise. And your height. And your coloring! Blond hair is so insipid."

"Do not talk to me of hair," exclaimed Caitlin, diverted. "Mine is the greatest trial to me!"

"Gibble-gabble, gibble-gabble," mimicked Nicky. "Couple of peahens."

"Eat your breakfast, Nicholas," recommended his father. Nicky subsided.

Agnes leaned in to whisper anxiously to Caitlin: "Is it not the fashion to have red hair?"

Amused, Caitlin tousled her little sister's curls. "Your hair is not red, Agnes, it is auburn. And ringlets are always fashionable."

Mrs. Campbell looked up from her letter, her forehead puckered. "Well, how vexatious! I have read Harriet's letter twice through, and nowhere does she say which one of you she means to invite."

Caitlin munched her toast reflectively. "I daresay she could not recall our names."

The children unsuccessfully stifled their giggles and Mrs. Campbell frowned with mock severity at her unruly brood. Mr. Campbell reached over to his wife, and she relinquished the letter to him.

"I would not be surprised to learn that she is inviting both of you," he remarked. "I suppose that is how it will end." He began methodically studying the letter.

"At any rate, Harriet is the dearest, most wonderful, most generous of sisters!" declared Mrs. Campbell. "She was under no obligation to make such a gesture. Years ago, she must have intended to bring Isabella out—after all, Isabella is her goddaughter—but my other girls have no claim on her whatsoever."

"Why did she not bring Isabella out?" asked Agnes, puzzled.

"Isabella fell in love with Tom," her mother explained.

"Before anyone could stop her," added Caitlin helpfully.

"Caitie, hush!" exclaimed Emily. "We are all very glad that Isabella married Tom."

"Yes, but only think what a splash Isabella would have made in London!" said Caitlin, stirring her tea with a pensive air. "I never considered the matter before. It must have cost you something, Mama, to allow the Beauty of the family to throw herself away on a mere squire's son."

"Why could not Tom have gone to London, too?" pursued Agnes.

John Campbell raised an eyebrow, his eyes twinkling. "Explain it to her, Amabel," he suggested.

His wife fluttered helplessly. "Oh, dear! I never should have begun this conversation at the breakfast table. It is most improper to discuss such matters before Nicky and Agnes."

"Ho!" uttered Nicky scornfully, if indistinctly, through a mouthful of ham. "I know all about it."

"You terrify me," said his father calmly. "What is it that you know?"

Nicky swallowed, and sat up. "They have a Season in London, every spring. And the girls all go to meet the swells and get married."

"Gentlemen, Nicky. Not *swells,*" said Mrs. Campbell firmly. "And there is far more to it than that."

Her husband chuckled. "Is there? Apart from the idiom, I thought his description remarkably apt."

Agnes was still bewildered. "Do they only have one season in London? We have four seasons in Hertfordshire."

"Not with dancing," asserted Nicky.

Agnes brightened. "I would like to see the dancing. Are we all going to London, Mama?"

"Heavens, no, chickie! You won't be ready for balls for another ten years. Only grown-up young ladies may go to London for the Season." Amabel decided the time had come for her to confide her thoughts to her family. She folded her hands and looked earnestly at Caitlin and Emily.

"Well! It wouldn't do to speak of it before, but I confess it *did* give me a pang to see Isabella forego her Season. She is perfectly happy with Tom, for which I am most grateful, but her choosing Tom spoiled my plans—not only for her, but the rest of you as well. Since her marriage I have been more worried about my younger girls than I liked to admit."

"Worried about us? Why, Mama?" inquired Caitlin, throwing her mother temporarily off stride. As Caitlin was no longer in the first blush of youth, Mrs. Campbell might have been pardoned for thinking that Caitlin herself ought to be a bit worried. However, Amabel knew her daughter. It was hopeless to expect cheerful, independent Caitlin to fret about matrimonial prospects. Caitlin was a pretty-enough girl (although she couldn't hold a candle to Isabella or Emily), but she had grown from a rambunctious, lanky, athletic child into a graceful, confident, regrettably headstrong young lady—with a twinkle in her eye that the neighborhood beaux found disconcerting. Several young men called on the Campbells with suspicious frequency, to be sure, but they all seemed to hover around the sweet and fragile Emily.

Amabel looked a little uncomfortable and began to pleat her napkin. "Caitlin dear, I hope I am not a mercenary creature, and I never wanted to be one of those detestable matchmaking mamas—but, you know, I had hoped—foolishly, I am sure!—that Isabella might achieve a little higher worldly position. Oh dear, how dreadful it sounds! But, you know, much as your father and I wish to give our children every advantage, it has not been in our power to—that is, we haven't the means to—oh, dear!"

"What your mother is trying to say," said Mr. Campbell, "is that she could not afford to give her daughters a Season in London because she married a penniless younger son."

"And lived happily ever after!" said Amabel quickly.

He smiled softly at his wife. "Yes, we have had the temerity to be perfectly happy all these years—a solecism for which your father has never quite forgiven us."

Amabel dimpled again. "Pooh! Papa is so stuffy, there's no bearing it. But I don't believe he's any kinder to Harriet, and she married excessively well."

John shook his head with mock gravity. "She did marry a baron, which naturally gratified your father. But then she loved her husband, you know, and he could not approve of that."

"Very true, dearest. That is—oh! You are roasting me!"

"And what is worse, I am interrupting your tale. You were explaining why living on a monkey's allowance made it impossible for you to give your own daughters the come-out you once enjoyed."

"Yes, I see that you are still laughing at me, but I assure you it is no laughing matter! Our girls deserve at least one proper Season, do they not? And when Harriet married Lord Lynwood—all that money, and the title besides—well! I am not proud of it, but I suppose I fell into an absurd way of thinking that her marriage would someday make all our fortunes. After all, Harriet was Isabella's godmother. What could be more natural than for darling Isabella to someday enjoy a Season under her godmother's aegis? And if Isabella had married a gentleman of fashion, she would, in turn, have sponsored her younger sisters into the *ton*." Amabel sighed. "The long and the short of it is, I am afraid I had my hopes for the entire family pinned upon Isabella's chances."

"Ah," said Caitlin thoughtfully. "Poor Isabella! I would have married Tom myself, to escape such a burden."

Mrs. Campbell turned shocked eyes upon her Caitie, but relaxed when she saw the twinkle in Caitlin's own. "Really, Caitlin! I often wish you would try to be a little less *clever*! A burden, indeed! It is no hardship to spend a few weeks in London, enjoying the fashionable life! Of course I would never ask a daughter of mine to marry anyone she did not like, but I *did* want my girls to have the opportunity of meeting—and liking!—gentlemen from—from—well, a wider circle than we have here in Hertfordshire."

Caitlin opened her eyes at this. "Are the Hertfordshire gentlemen inadequate? It never crossed my mind."

"Well, it's very natural that it shouldn't," stated Mrs. Campbell untruthfully, reminding herself, with an inward sigh, that she was *glad* her children had not been reared to concern themselves with worldly matters. "What purpose would it serve for my chickens to worry about their futures, particularly if their circumstances couldn't be helped? But as your mother, I confess it has exercised my mind considerably. I don't have a word to say against dear Tom, of course. But he is simply not in a position to introduce his sisters-in-law to— well, he himself is not acquainted with—oh, dear, how difficult this is! But what in the world will become of you all, if you stay buried here at Rosemeade? I don't worry so much about the boys, because Hector is doing so well at the university, and Nicky has a very good head on his shoulders—"

Caitlin's eyes danced. "I also have a very good head on my shoulders."

Amabel frowned at her daughter with loving exasperation. "Now, Caitlin, you know that is entirely beside the point! No, do not argue with me, dearest. Suffice it to say, I have worried about you, and Emily, and even little Agnes. It is only in the nature of things, after all, that if girls have no opportunity to meet eligible young men, they will fall in love with *ineligible* young men. And I have dreaded the day when one of you takes a fancy to some half-pay officer, or perhaps the curate—"

"Mr. Horton?" gasped gentle Emily, with such honest horror that there was a general shout of laughter. Emily blushed.

"Well, perhaps not Mr. Horton," amended Mrs. Campbell hastily. "But I am afraid there are so many sadly underbred young men in the neighborhood—gracious, how excessively vulgar I sound!"

"Never mind, my pet. We understand you perfectly," said Mr. Campbell, appearing vastly entertained by his wife's discomfiture. "You are not a mercenary person—you merely wish, like any parent, to see that your daughters do not make the same mistake you did."

Mrs. Campbell straightened indignantly and turned a little pink. "Now, that is exactly what I do *not* mean, John, and well you know it!" she cried. "I have never regretted choosing you, although I might have married Mr. Maltby, and he was as rich as a nabob."

"Thank you, my dear," said Mr. Campbell, bowing gravely from his chair.

Mrs. Campbell looked very wise. "It is a mistake to let material considerations outweigh the promptings of one's heart," she pronounced. "I would never dream of urging my girls into loveless marriages, whatever the gentlemen's circumstances. But—but—" She broke off, suddenly confused.

"But," her husband suggested helpfully, "it is just as easy to like a wealthy gentleman as a poor one."

Over her children's laughter Mrs. Campbell, very pink indeed, pretended to rap her husband's knuckles with her teaspoon. "Laugh if you must, but it's perfectly true! Harriet was very happy with Lord Lynwood."

"Yes, but after she married we scarcely saw her," Mr. Campbell reminded his wife. "The disparity in your circumstances led to an estrangement between you."

"Oh, not an estrangement, John!" said Amabel, distressed. "It *has* been difficult to see her as often as I would like, because we never go to Town, and Harriet so rarely comes to the country. And then, she is accustomed to having everything so very grand—armies of servants at her beck and call, and everything of the finest—I can't help feeling a bit awkward, trying to entertain her here at Rosemeade."

Mr. Campbell patted his wife's hand affectionately. "Dear heart, Harriet's life isn't far removed from what you were accustomed to in your father's home."

Amabel frowned. She did not like her darling John to draw unfair comparisons between the life he had given her, and the life her sister led. "Fiddle! My father chooses to ignore it, but his fortune was made in trade, you know. And not a large fortune, at that! You only knew him after he was knighted, dearest; I promise you he never put on such airs when I was a child."

"Well, you mustn't think I don't appreciate the sacrifices you made in marrying me."

Amabel smiled blindingly at her husband. "Sacrifices! How can you, John? I wouldn't trade my life with you for a hundred thousand pounds!"

She glanced proudly around the table, thinking that a finer group of healthy, well-grown offspring could not be found. The Campbell children had not been taught to admire their own appearance, but they were a good-looking family, with regular features, fair skin, and beautiful complexions. The family resemblance was elusive, however. Their father's Scottish ancestors had bequeathed height and red hair to Caitlin, Hector, Nicky, and Agnes, but Amabel was a petite and golden-haired creature who had endowed Isabella and Emily with her flaxen curls and exquisite daintiness.

Mrs. Campbell lost no time in accepting her sister's invitation. Though they had only been half serious at the time, Mr. Campbell and Caitlin had each judged correctly: Lady Lynwood had couched her invitation in vague terms only because she could not recall the names of Amabel's numerous progeny, and once it was made plain to her that the Campbells possessed two eligible daughters she instantly broadened her invitation to include them both.

Chapter II

Caitlin slipped unseen through her hostess's elegant French doors, her face burning with mortification. She took a deep, grateful breath of the crisp night air. Perhaps it could douse the fire in her cheeks before anyone noticed how flushed she had become.

How she wished she could escape! She felt caged. Caitlin crossed the terrace and clutched the balustrade, hard. The coldness of the marble seeped through her gloves and she shivered, welcoming the sensation. She welcomed anything that would distract her at this moment.

She was still unaccustomed to the heat generated by a throng of overdressed people in a salon lit with dozens of candles. In another sense, she was unaccustomed to the coldness that could be generated by these same people. But the spring night was familiar; it smelled fresh and damp and wild. If she closed her eyes, she could almost imagine herself back at Rosemeade.

A wave of homesickness struck her and she opened her eyes again, embarrassed. How idiotish! She would be home again soon enough. And doubtless would remain there forever, thought Caitlin, her mouth twisting wryly. Her London Season was not proving an unqualified success.

A spattering of glove-muffled applause caused her to turn and gaze through the windows behind her. Standing outside in the darkness, Caitlin realized she was invisible to the silk-clad, smiling people surrounding Miss Whitlock's harp. It was a rather lonely sensation. She wondered sadly if she had been invisible to most of them all along. There was more than a pane of glass dividing Caitlin Campbell from the brightly lit room. The *haut ton* suddenly seemed as alien to her as a tribe of Hottentots.

But no; she had it backward, hadn't she? She was the Hottentot. The laughter that was never far from Caitlin's eyes lit them for a moment, as it occurred to her that an actual Hottentot would receive more respect from these aristocrats than John Campbell's daughter. It was a mistake to wear a silk gown and her mother's pearls tonight. Had she donned a grass skirt and tied a bone in her hair, she might have passed for visiting royalty.

The humorous image faded in the face of her agitation, and Caitlin walked the length of the terrace in a vain attempt to recover her spirits. The overheard remark that had driven her onto the terrace haunted her. *The redhead? Oh, she is nobody, my dear* . . . How lightly Lady Elizabeth had said it. How casually she had dismissed Caitlin as a mere tuft-hunter. To Lady Elizabeth Delacourt, born a duke's daughter and recently betrothed to an earl's heir, Caitlin Campbell was an insignificant bumpkin.

Returning to the salon and feigning an interest in Miss Whitlock's harp seemed impossible. Alone on the terrace, Caitlin was in a unique position to slip away. Oh, if only she dared! She stepped to the balustrade again and leaned over it, peering into the gardens beneath the terrace. Why, one could see the square from here. A little path ran right to it. Five minutes of brisk walking would bring her to her aunt's door in Half Moon Street.

Her impulse to escape was so strong, she actually took a step or two toward the garden before catching herself and stopping. Poor Lady Lynwood would swoon if she caught her headstrong niece traipsing down the London streets after dark! Aunt Harriet would not countenance Caitlin's walking alone in London, even in broad daylight. They had already had several "discussions" regarding her impatience with that particular edict.

Still . . . tonight, and only tonight, it was just possible that no one would ever know. Aunt Harriet was not with her, and neither was Emily. Tonight was the night of Emily's formal presentation, and, never having been presented herself, it had not been possible for Caitlin to accompany her sister and aunt to the Queen's drawing rooms. Rather than sit alone at Lynwood House and wait for their return, Caitlin had accompanied her friend Serena to this dreadful party. Lady Serena Kilverton was the only kindred spirit Caitlin had found in London. Serena's mother, Lady Selcroft, was very kind, but most of the extremely select company this evening had treated Caitlin with decided coolness.

She sighed with frustration. The night was calling to her, but this was not rural Hertfordshire. London offered a young lady many delights, but midnight tramps were not among them. Caitlin turned reluctantly to return to the stuffy salon.

Before she could reach the French doors, they opened, throwing a bar of light across the terrace. Two young women walked out. Caitlin caught a glimpse of Lady Elizabeth's elegant profile before Serena blocked her view. Serena's highspirited little face was set in an uncharacteristically mulish expression.

This was awkward indeed! Caitlin hesitated. Should she make her presence known? Or should she turn away and seek another entrance into the house? They had not seen her yet. Caitlin began to step forward, but Lady Elizabeth's first words halted her in her tracks.

"It is a great mistake to encourage persons of that order," said Lady Elizabeth calmly. She sounded kind but firm, as if she were speaking to a wayward child. "Pray do not think that I am criticizing you, my dear Serena, but I consider it my duty to give you a hint. By September I will be in the nature of an older sister to you, you know."

Serena tossed her head with an irritated little laugh. "Thank you, but I have not required a governess for several years now! And if I needed one, I doubt that Mama would consider Richard's fiancée a suitable candidate for the post."

Lady Elizabeth's calm appeared unruffled. "Nevertheless, I have considerably more experience than you in these matters. I cannot stand idly by and watch her encroach upon your good nature."

Serena's reply was quiet, but it carried to Caitlin quite clearly. "In what way do you imagine I am being imposed upon?"

Lady Elizabeth laughed gently. "Oh, I daresay you have no notion of it! But claiming friendship with Lady Serena Kilverton, you know, can add tremendously to the consequence of a mere Miss Campbell. You are furthering her social ambitions by lending her countenance."

Caitlin felt stunned by the unfairness, the sheer meanness, of such a remark. Lady Elizabeth's refined accents droned on, delicately warning Serena against her friend, but Caitlin could not stay to hear more. She turned blindly and walked into the garden. The evening had taken on the odd, sick quality of a nightmare.

Well, the fact that Lady Elizabeth was marrying Serena's brother in September explained a great deal. Caitlin had not thought of that before. No wonder her ladyship was meddling in what otherwise, surely, did not concern her.

Tears of anger and humiliation sprang to Caitlin's eyes. Caitlin was no fool. She knew there were advantages attached to friendship with an earl's daughter. But Caitlin would have befriended Serena if her father had been a bootblack. High-spirited, fun-loving, affectionate Serena! It was impossible to picture any brother of hers choosing Lady Elizabeth for his life's companion! Viscount Kilverton must be very different from his sister.

Caitlin dashed her angry tears away impatiently and tried to steady herself. What did it matter what the *ton* thought of her, after all? She would go home to Rosemeade in a month or two and never see these people again.

Ah, but it did matter. It mattered to Emily. If the *beau monde* thought of the Campbell girls as upstarts trying to climb above their natural station in life, what were Emily's chances of forming an eligible connection? Aunt Harriet had certainly married well, and as the nieces of Lady Lynwood, Caitlin and Emily had the *entrée* almost everywhere, but facts were facts. The Campbell girls might be attractive, they might be well-mannered, they might be anything you choose, but they had neither rank nor fortune to recommend them.

She suddenly became aware that her restless feet had taken her, unbidden, to the edge of the garden. She stopped. One or two more steps would bring her onto the pavement that lined

the square. The street, for some reason, was much lighter than
the garden. Caitlin placed one hand against the stone wall beside her and, taking care to remain in shadow, leaned round
the corner of the house to investigate this phenomenon.

Stone-faced mansions lined the square, their manicured en-
tries illuminated by flambeaux and their windows blazing
with light. Linkboys and liveried coachmen stood idly about,
waiting for highly polished doors to open and guests to depart
from their evening's engagements. The picture of stately,
well-lit respectability was dazzling to Caitlin's country-bred
eyes.

Her earlier fantasy of walking home returned to tantalize
her. Her heart beat a little faster at the thought. It would be
shockingly unconventional, but what did that matter? It was
absurd to follow the rules when the rules were both inconvenient and unnecessary! There could not be anything dangerous about walking a few short blocks in this elegant
neighborhood. And a brisk walk would do much to restore the
tone of her mind.

Very well, she would do it! She would not stop to scold
herself back into submission; she would not stop for anything!
She stepped into the light with every appearance of poise and
assurance, left a brief message for Lady Selcroft with the
nearest linkboy, and was off.

By the time this daring plan had been put into execution,
Caitlin was feeling much more cheerful. Action had an elevating effect on her spirits. She crossed the square briskly, turned
the corner onto Curzon Street, and soon left the clusters of
linkboys and coaches behind.

It seemed strange to see Curzon Street with all the shops
closed and the street completely empty. Were it not for the
marvelous new streetlights, she would never have recognized
it. Her footsteps echoed strangely, and she found it necessary
to step carefully in these dimly lit, unfamiliar surroundings.
Still, the night was lovely, and the solitude refreshing.

As she walked, she became aware of a commotion of people running and shouting somewhere in the distance. This did
not concern her unduly—until she realized the sounds were

coming nearer. The streetlights suddenly seemed less bright. Her heart beat a little faster, and she quickened her steps.

A sudden cry of "Hi! There he goes!" in a thick Cockney baritone came from round the corner just behind her. Alarmed, Caitlin shrank back toward the doorway of the shop she was passing and turned to discover the cause of the disturbance.

There was just enough light to discern a tall man, who appeared to be in evening clothes, running toward her at top speed. She caught a glimpse of a gleaming white shirtfront and flying cape before he caromed into her with an exclamation, grabbing her arms to steady himself. Quick as thought, he pulled her with him into the recessed doorway, swinging her body in front of him so her back blocked all view of him from the street.

"Forgive me!" he uttered, and immediately pressed his lips to hers.

Too startled to protest, too amazed to think, Caitlin simply froze. She had never felt a man's lips against her own, never felt a man's arms hold her in just such a way. This forced intimacy with a complete stranger, a man whose face she had not even seen, was the single most astonishing event of her life.

Through her confusion, she could hear the sound of several pairs of running feet slowing as they approached. The stranger's arms tightened around her, and as she tried to utter a muffled protest, he pressed his mouth even more firmly against hers. She heard a guffaw behind her, a rough voice sneering, "Love's young dream!" and a smothered curse.

" 'E must've gone round the corner, lads!" shouted another voice. And the feet ran on.

When the clatter of running boots on cobblestones began to fade, the stranger pulled his face away from hers. Caitlin's eyes flew open with a shock of mortification, as she suddenly realized she had shut them like a swooning adolescent during his kiss. She raised a shaking hand to smooth her hair, and took a deep breath. Among her many conflicting emotions—anger, humiliation, fright, and, yes, a bubble of amusement—struggled for supremacy. She didn't know whether to slap the stranger, hide her face and run away in shame, scream for help, or laugh out loud.

The light from the street was far too dim and wavering to make out his features. She wondered, in a dazed sort of way, if she might actually be in danger from this person. It was impossible to know whose booted feet she had heard pursuing him; perhaps it had been the Watch. For all she knew, this man was a criminal flying from the scene of his crime.

"Mademoiselle, you have probably saved my life," whispered the stranger.

His accents were those of a gentleman. One heard stories of well-bred young men playing stupid pranks for amusement. Perhaps he was one of these nincompoops.

"How gratifying!" Caitlin replied, with icy politeness. "Please don't thank me; it has always been my ambition to rescue a gentleman in distress. And I warn you, if you beg my pardon I shall go into strong hysterics. My nerves cannot sustain another shock!"

"But I do thank you, and I do beg your pardon," he said—although, to Caitlin's annoyance, his voice quivered with amusement. She stiffened, and he quickly added, "Infamous, I know! But there was no time to think of another ruse. Those ruffians were hard on my heels."

"Oh, *pray* do not give it another thought! I am refining too much upon what is, after all, the merest commonplace. I daresay a lady in London may expect to be accosted in this fashion a dozen times a day. I am persuaded I shall grow accustomed to it."

"Ah, so you are new to London?" he inquired.

"If you *dare* to ask me how I am enjoying my stay—"

"I wouldn't presume!" he interrupted, with a low laugh.

"Would you not? How very odd!" retorted Caitlin. "I had thought there was no end to your presumption."

"You must think me a complete villain," he remarked, but without a trace of embarrassment. "I really have nothing to say in my own defense—unless, of course, it is to point out that young women of virtue are not generally found alone and unprotected on the streets of London. And never, I might add, after dark."

"One immediately perceives why!" Caitlin countered, flushing in the darkness. "Tell me, sir, are you in my aunt's employ? One might almost suppose she had set you on—" But she stopped short, vexed at having said so much. Unfortunately, the stranger was too perceptive to let this pass.

"You have exactly hit it," he said, mendaciously. "You clearly need to be taught more circumspect behavior. As you say, your aunt set me on." The amusement crept back into his voice. "It only remains to discover—who is your aunt?"

Caitlin bit her lip with vexation. Heavens! Here she was, actually conversing with the wretch, when any lady should have screamed for assistance and brought down all of London on his head! Whatever possessed her? She was suddenly aware that his hands were still lightly gripping her arms, and was furious. Giving herself a mental shake, she pulled out of his grip and clutched the remaining shreds of her dignity around her, continuing to address him with the frostiness he deserved.

"Sir, if you feel yourself to be out of danger now, perhaps you will be good enough to let me go?"

"Not only a villain, but a coward! Mademoiselle, you mortify me." But he glanced swiftly up and down the street, which appeared deserted except for the two of them. There were no sounds of running feet; the city was oddly still. He looked back down at Caitlin. She lifted her chin and gave him stare for stare, although she knew he could not see her expression.

"The ruse worked, at any rate. They are gone." In the dimness she sensed, rather than saw, his frown. "Now what am I to do with you? You cannot walk about the streets of London in the middle of the night unescorted."

"Are you about to offer me your protection?" demanded the outraged Caitlin. "I *shall* have hysterics!"

His teeth flashed white in a sudden grin. "What? And you so fearless! I'd like to see it."

"Well, you won't," said Caitlin crossly. A new difficulty presented itself to her. She was very close to Half Moon Street. Unless this insufferable man chose to leave her, he would discover where she lived. She stood for a moment, irresolute, and he seemed to read her thoughts.

"What will you do, I wonder?" he asked, in a tone of great interest. "You are in a rare pickle, ma'am! If you allow me to escort you home, you shall make a present of your identity to me. That will never do. On the other hand, if you refuse my escort, honor will oblige me to follow you anyway, you know, to protect you from all the *other* scoundrels who may be prowling the London streets. The only way to prevent my assistance is to summon the Watch—in which case I will doubtless be hauled before a magistrate. Inconvenient for me, of course, but only think how embarrassing for you! You would have to give your evidence."

This was too much. Caitlin's annoyance immediately flamed into anger. "I shall be delighted to give my evidence! If you do not remove yourself immediately, I will scream my lungs out and you will be apprehended—probably by the same watchmen who were pursuing you a moment ago!"

"A villain, a coward, and a *felon*! Alas, you cut me to the quick!" came the outrageous reply. He was still laughing at her, the cad! "Permit me to point out to you, ma'am, that although your voice and manners both are those of a lady of quality, your presence in the street at such an hour might have deceived anyone. Now, come—may we not call a truce? You really cannot proceed alone, and my protection, however ironic it may appear to you, is better than none."

"Thank you! But as it appears *you* are the person I most need to be protected from, I believe I can dispense with your escort."

"Nevertheless, you shall have it," calmly asserted the stranger. Then, as if he sensed her impotent fury, his voice softened. "May we be serious for a moment? I am deeply in your debt, ma'am—and you have, indeed, been shamefully used. As I can see no other way of making amends, pray allow me to offer you the only assistance that lies within my power."

Caitlin glanced doubtfully up at his shadowed face, her anger fading. His words and manner still struck her, against her will, as gentlemanly. He had certainly laughed at her, and seemed to take an annoying degree of pleasure in her embarrassment, but he had taken no other advantage of her. She knew that if he had been another sort of man, her situation might have proved truly dangerous. If only it were possible to read his expression!

He seemed to feel her hesitation and stepped back from her, bowing, and offering his arm. He did this with such an air of respectful courtesy, she bit back a laugh. How ridiculous it was! She started to take his proffered arm, but hesitated again. Nothing in life had ever prepared her for such an occurrence.

"Oh, if only I knew what to do!" she exclaimed. "Really, sir, I cannot put myself under obligation to you. Intolerable! Do you not perceive the quandary I am in?"

"I do, indeed. Let us stand here and discuss it. Eventually the sun will rise, and you may continue your walk in safety."

She choked on another laugh. "No, let us go our separate ways! That would also enable me to continue my walk in safety."

He flung up his hand in mock salute. "Touché!"

"Please, sir, I assure you I am entirely in earnest. Let me go, and do me the courtesy of not following me." He began to speak, but she hurried on. "You must appreciate how impossible this is! I really cannot have you escort me, or worse yet, follow me to my door."

She sensed his frown returning. "There is much in what you say. After all, you have no assurance that I am what I seem."

She almost gasped at his unconscious arrogance. "I rather hope you are *not* what you seem!"

This seemed to finally take him down a peg, she noted with satisfaction. There was a grim pause. "I deserved that, I suppose," he said then, wryly. "I can only beg your pardon yet again. Tell me this: you need not say in which direction, but how far do you live from here?"

"Only a step, I assure you."

Now it was his turn to hesitate. "Well, ma'am, I can find it within me to sympathize with your point of view. On the other hand, should any further adventure befall you between here and your door, I would indeed consider myself the villain

you think me for abandoning you to your fate. What is the solution to this puzzle?"

"My fate, sir, is no concern of yours."

"Nonsense! It became my concern the instant I embroiled
you in my affairs." His grin flashed again. "And so reprehen-
sibly, too!"

She was thankful the night hid her blush.

"Perhaps," he continued, "I might stay here in this doorway
while you walk to your house. I will engage myself to fly to
your rescue if you cry out any time in the next—five minutes,
shall we say? If you indeed live so near, I imagine I would
hear you quite well if you were to—what was it? Ah, yes—
scream your lungs out."

Was he still laughing at her? Caitlin peered up at him suspiciously, but the darkness gave her no clue to his expression
and his voice was quite bland. If it was offered to her in an
unexceptionable manner, she realized she would be glad now
to know protection, of a sort, was at hand. As she could think
of no dignified alternative, she decided to give him the benefit
of the doubt. "Thank you," she said stiffly. "I will be home
within five minutes—and I do think I will be within earshot
the entire time."

"Hush! No more!" he said. "Next you will be giving me
your address after all."

She could not repress a tiny gurgle of laughter. "You are
absurd!" she said. "Promise me you will not remark which direction I travel."

"You have my hand on it," he replied warmly, and she
found herself actually shaking the hand of this audacious
stranger in the friendliest manner and going on her way.

Half Moon Street was indeed just round the corner, and the
lamps outside No. 14 were lit. She was never so glad to see
the front door of a house in her life, and fairly ran up the
steps. The door opened immediately, and the butler gazed at
her in ill-concealed astonishment.

"All alone, miss?"

She tried to give her voice a note of airy unconcern, and
smiled carelessly at him. "As you see, Stubbs," she replied
cheerfully, pulling off her gloves. "How good of you to meet

me with a candle! I wish you a very good night," and she hastily took the candle from his outraged hand and started up the stairs.

"Good night, miss," came the wooden reply as Stubbs, stiff with disapproval, closed the door behind her.

In the safety of her room, she suddenly realized she was shaking. What an extraordinary thing to have happened in the middle of Curzon Street! Her nerves were completely overset, and she had always thought she didn't have a nerve in her body. Unconsciously, she scrubbed the back of her hand across her mouth as if to erase the memory of those hard, insistent lips against hers. She had always supposed that if and when she experienced her first kiss, it would be under very different circumstances—very different indeed! How infamous of that vile man to steal something so precious from her! Although, she scolded herself, she had no one to blame but herself. She would not flout the conventions quite so blithely in future.

She lit her bedside candles with a hand that trembled a bit, and turned to cast her gloves and reticule onto a chair. It was then she caught sight of herself in the pier glass. Her cheeks were flushed, her eyes unnaturally bright, her hair slightly disarrayed, her general appearance distraught and strange. But what caused her to gasp was the sight of the stains on her gown. Unbelieving, she walked closer to the glass and stared, picking up a fold of the diaphanous stuff and spreading it with her fingers.

Blood. It was definitely blood. Blood in streaks above her elbow where he had gripped her, blood in drips on her skirt where it had fallen, and—turning to check—blood across the back of her gown where his arms had held her.

What kind of an adventure had she just had?! The flush in her cheeks disappeared as she went white and sat rather suddenly on the bench before the mirror.

Chapter III

By the time the Honorable Edward Montague's man admitted Lord Kilverton to Mr. Montague's lodgings in Clarges Street, his lordship was beginning to feel just a trifle out of frame.

Kilverton felt no need to stand on ceremony with Ned Montague. Mr. Montague's ancestral acres lay less than ten miles from his, and they had been friends from boyhood on. Ned's graceful person could generally be found at this hour gladdening the heart of some fashionable hostess. However, Kilverton knew Mr. Montague had contracted a nasty head cold and trusted that tonight Ned would be spending a rare evening at home.

Sure enough, Lord Kilverton discovered Mr. Montague lounging before his fire, sneezing and yawning over a steaming bowl of punch. He was attired in a dressing gown of startling hue. Ned's heavy eyes brightened at the unexpected sight of his friend.

"Kilverton, by all that's wonderful! What brings you to Clarges Street in the middle of—" he broke off as he saw Kilverton sink, wincing, into a deep armchair. "Good God! What's amiss?"

Lord Kilverton gingerly felt his shoulder and winced again. "That dressing gown, Neddie. Gave me quite a turn," he replied. "What the devil do you mean by receiving visitors in it? Should have had Farley say you weren't at home."

Mr. Montague grinned and smoothed a satin sleeve. His slender frame and dark coloring would have accorded well with the brilliant purple, had he lived in a more flamboyant age. "Born too late!" he mourned. "Now, m'grandfather used to go peacocking all over the town in purple satin. Don't you care for it? I was sure you'd be green with envy—rush out to purchase some—and between the two of us, we'd bring it back into fashion." He looked more closely at his friend, and the laughter left his eyes. Mr. Montague reached to turn up the lamp. "You needn't pitch any more of your gammon, Richard," he said grimly. "You're wounded."

"A scratch," corrected Kilverton. "Nothing to signify. But I should be glad of a glass of your punch."

Mr. Montague strode to the door and unceremoniously shouted for Farley. Farley, who had been a military man, not only brought Lord Kilverton an extra punch glass, but also a bowl of water and some linen which he began efficiently tearing into strips. Lord Kilverton's objections were overruled, his formerly elegant coat was removed, and an ugly shoulder gash laid bare. Farley bathed and dressed the wound swiftly and capably, dipped his lordship a glass of punch, bowed impassively, and left the room.

Kilverton grinned ruefully over the rim of his punch glass at his friend, who was frowning very seriously at him. "Come now, Neddie! It's not as bad as that."

Mr. Montague sneezed indignantly and took a revivifying sip of punch. "It's every bit as bad as that! You really can't come in and bleed all over my second-best armchair and then behave as if nothing out of the ordinary has happened."

Lord Kilverton meekly begged pardon.

"And don't try to bamboozle me into thinking it was an accident! You tried that the last time and I wasn't more than half convinced. If you ask me to believe in a second accident within a month of the first, that's coming it a bit too strong."

"You are very severe, Ned," complained Lord Kilverton. "An ambush may happen to anyone."

"Not to you! Why, you're handier with your fives than anyone I know, you're a dead shot, and there's not many would care to cross swords with you. You have the reflexes of a panther. I would have thought you were the last man in London to be taken unawares."

Lord Kilverton grimaced. "Apparently not. Thank you for your touching, if misplaced, confidence in my fighting prowess, but I was indeed taken unawares. I was set upon by a pack of footpads in Trebeck Street and rather hopelessly outnumbered."

Mr. Montague's mobile eyebrows shot up. He dipped himself another glass of punch, carefully fishing out a lemon slice to float on top. "Footpads?" he repeated. There was an odd gleam in his eyes, but his voice remained neutral. "Last time it was highwaymen or some such thing, was it not?"

Kilverton groaned, covering his eyes with his hand. "It was indeed highwaymen, and I promise you these were not the same men, so you may stop weaving conspiracy theories! You see, I forestall you."

Mr. Montague's odd expression vanished and he grinned reluctantly. "Yes, but—"

"But nothing!" said Kilverton firmly. "I am greatly obliged to you for loaning me Farley to minister to my hurts, and I will be even more obliged to you if you do not spread this extremely embarrassing tale around town."

"Mum as an oyster!" Mr. Montague assured him. "But what happened, Kilverton? You say you were outnumbered?"

"Yes, I was set upon by half a dozen burly individuals. Some with cudgels, and at least one—as you can see—with a sword stick."

"Good God! You are fortunate to have escaped with your life!"

Lord Kilverton nodded pensively. "Yes, I rather fancy I am. I'll admit those reflexes you so generously complimented a moment ago stood me in good stead. And I had my stick with me—although I seem to have lost it now. I was fighting with my back to a wall, Ned, and there wasn't another soul in sight. I can tell you, there were a couple of moments when I thought . . ." His voice trailed off as he looked meditatively into the fire and sipped his punch. "But all's well that ends well, in fact."

Mr. Montague was much moved. "By Jove, Kilverton! What a lucky escape! How many did you have to kill?"

"None, I think, although I certainly gave as good as I got."

"Did they take anything from you?"

"No, nothing," A faint crease appeared in Kilverton's brow.

"Odd. They had every opportunity to rob me. I wonder why they did not?"

"Thank God they did not! How did you get away?"

"Fought my way through their guard and ran like the devil was on my heels."

Mr. Montague sat a little straighter in his chair. "You out-ran them?"

"Not exactly." An odd little smile flickered across Kilverton's face. They ran past me."

Mr. Montague was amazed. "They ran *past* you?"

"I was in disguise," Lord Kilverton explained.

Mr. Montague choked on his punch. When he had some-what recovered, he gasped, "In disguise! You're bamming me."

"Not at all. I disguised myself as Romeo, stealing a mid-night stroll with his Juliet."

Mr. Montague set his glass carefully on the tray beside him, and looked at his friend very hard. "I hope you are about to explain to me how one disguises oneself—as Romeo or any-one else—while being hotly pursued by a gang of cutthroats."

Lord Kilverton laughed softly. "I wonder?" he mused. "Would it betray a lady's confidence? An interesting problem. I am rather inclined to believe that since I am unaware of the lady's identity, I am at liberty to describe the incident. After all, I can hardly compromise her if I can't tell you her name, can I? I can't even tell you what she looked like."

Lord Kilverton then described to his friend how he had lit-erally run into a lone female in Curzon Street, grabbed her, and cold-bloodedly used her to shield himself from his attack-ers. Mr. Montague, scenting an intrigue, was delighted.

"Well, what a romance! You really have no clue to her identity? Come now, Kilverton—let us approach the problem scientifically. We know, for example, the neighborhood in which she resides—now think! Was she tall or short?"

Kilverton stared into the fire and thought, smiling reminis-cently. "Tall. And slender." The smile grew. "But not *too* slender. A cozy armful, in fact." He thought again, still smil-ing into the fire. "Unquestionably a lady. And innocent. I'd stake my last groat she'd never been kissed before."

Mr. Montague gave a crack of laughter. "Yes, one can usually tell! Anything else?"

"Intelligent. Well-bred. Sense of humor. Pleasant voice, rather low-pitched. Forthright. And utterly fearless."

"Fearless?"

"Consider, Ned: she was accosted on the street by a perfect stranger under circumstances that should have been terrifying to an unescorted female. She was manhandled in a most reprehensible fashion; for all she knew, I could have been as dangerous as the fellows I was running from. To her, in fact, I was! And yet she handled the situation with perfect sangfroid; took me to task very soundly, and walked off by herself without turning a hair."

Mr. Montague was unconvinced. "Perhaps she recognized you."

Kilverton shook his head. "No, I am positive I have never met the lady. She mentioned she was new to London." The smile flickered again. "And somehow I feel sure I would remember this girl if I had ever met her before."

This was disturbing, but Mr. Montague kept his inevitable reflections to himself. He was aware that Kilverton, after searching in vain for a bride who could stir stronger emotions in him than respect and liking, had recently contracted an extremely eligible engagement. Although the ceremony was not to take place for some months yet, Richard Kilverton was as good as married. Under the circumstances, it was fortunate that he was unlikely to discover the identity of his mysterious charmer. She seemed to be firing his imagination in a rather dangerous way.

Mr. Montague decided his friend needed to take a damper. He assumed a gloomy tone, shaking his head pessimistically. "Sounds to me like some dashed governess, Kilverton. Probably forty if she's a day, and hatchet-faced. If you saw her in the daylight, she'd more than likely be covered in spots, or bucktoothed. Mark my words; only a dragon could come through an experience like that without having the vapors."

But Kilverton only laughed, stretching his long legs out before him. "Not bucktoothed, Neddie! Of that, at least, I am sure!"

His shoulder was beginning to pain him, and Ned looked as if he should be in bed, so his lordship soon called for a hackney to take him to his family's residence in Mount Street. It was late; that was good. No fear of his disheveled appearance alarming anyone. His valet could discreetly dispose of the ruined coat, and no one need know of his adventure.

He caught himself staring out the windows as the jarvey drove past Curzon Street, trying to calculate the possible direction of a certain young lady's footsteps, and frowned. What nonsense!

Lord Kilverton sank back against the squabs and ruefully pondered the fickleness of fate. However silly it undoubtedly was, and however fleeting his interest would no doubt have proved, he felt a pang at finding himself for the first time unable to follow his inclination. If he were unattached, he realized, he would have tried to solve the mystery and find that girl.

Of course, Ned was right. Once found, she would no doubt prove as insipid as every other female of his acquaintance. But at the moment, it seemed a rather cruel joke that after years of searching, he had finally located a female he felt at least a passing interest in—and it was too late.

Chapter IV

It was long before Caitlin could fall asleep that night, and she awakened the next morning feeling little refreshed. One of the housemaids had brought her a pot of morning chocolate, but even this agreeable luxury failed to raise Caitlin's spirits. She sat up in bed, sipping the hot, sweet liquid gloomily.

She was in the suds, and no mistake. The more she considered the previous evening, the worse it appeared to her. It was bad enough to have been snubbed by Lady Elizabeth Delacourt, but Caitlin's cheeks grew hot when she recalled her own behavior. Leaving the party early—and unescorted! With only a *message* to Lady Selcroft! Oh, she had definitely crossed the line. She had committed an unforgivable solecism, and her unknown assailant had given her her just desserts.

She frowned, unseeing, at the bedpost. It was absurd the way her mind kept returning to that man. No amount of self-scolding succeeded in banishing him from her imagination. Despite the evidence of the bloodstains he had left on her gown, she could not convince herself he was a sinister individual whom she was fortunate to have escaped. It was maddening to think she would probably never discover his identity.

On the other hand, she reminded herself with a shudder, I am excessively glad that he will probably never discover mine!

It would have relieved her considerably to confide the story to a sympathetic listener, but that was out of the question. If any part of the tale came to Lady Lynwood's ears, Aunt Harriet would probably wash her hands of her hoydenish niece and send her back to Hertfordshire without more ado. And Emily would be scarcely less shocked than Aunt Harriet at Caitlin's wanton disregard of the proprieties.

Serena might understand—but then a dreadful thought occurred. Caitlin had stupidly seconded Lady Elizabeth's advice with her own shocking conduct. The next time she saw Serena, she would probably receive a crushing snub. Caitlin had alienated her only friend in London, and she had no one to blame but herself. Her eyes suddenly filled with remorseful tears.

Caitlin set her chocolate cup down, dashed the tears from her eyes, and resolutely scrambled out of bed. If it killed her, she would go down to breakfast with a semblance of her usual cheerful calm. Emily would be longing to confide the story of her presentation. Caitlin hoped fervently that the *ton* had given Emily a warmer welcome last night than her sister had experienced.

She would not wait for Jane to come and help her dress. Besides, she must not grow accustomed to the life of luxury she was leading at Lynwood House. Caitlin had waited on herself all her life, and since she was doubtless returning to Rosemeade in disgrace in the near future, she would probably wait on herself forever. She dressed hastily and dragged a comb through her hair, trying to arrange the copper-colored tresses as Emily had taught her, then grimaced at her reflection. In her white muslin morning dress, she looked like nothing so much as a—a lit candle!

She hurried downstairs, dreading what she might find there; she could not help fearing that sensitive Emily had been slighted as she had been. But when she stepped through the breakfast room door Emily flew out of her chair with a cry of joy.

"Caitie! How I wish you had been with us last night!"

Caitlin laughed, and hugged her younger sister. "Indeed, Emily, I wish I had been," she replied, thinking Emily could little know how heartfelt that sentiment was. "Did you enjoy yourself? Was it everything you hoped?"

Emily's soft blue eyes glowed, and her cheeks were more than usually pink. "Oh, it was lovely! Everyone was so kind."

Caitlin sent up a silent prayer of thanksgiving. If Emily succeeded in joining their aunt's world, Caitlin felt she herself could happily return to obscurity in Hertfordshire. "But this is excellent!" she remarked, her eyes twinkling. "If everyone was kind to you, Emily, you must have been a great success."

This brought a chuckle from Aunt Harriet, sitting at the head of the table with the morning post scattered beside her breakfast plate. "A portionless girl from the country cannot expect to cause a sensation, Caitlin!" she announced, her satisfied expression belying the admonition. "But on the whole, our little Emily did very well. Very well indeed."

Lady Lynwood was a plump little woman who retained much of her youth's prettiness, and almost all of its giddiness. With her correspondence and tea things heaped about her like a nest, she reminded Caitlin of a contented little hen, preening and clucking over last night's success.

Feeling immensely relieved, Caitlin seated herself and shook out her napkin. "There was never a doubt in my mind that Emily had only to be seen to be appreciated. Once we removed her from the backwater and brought her into the world, it was only a matter of time before all of London fell at her feet."

Her sister's blond curls danced as she shook her head earnestly. "Caitie, I'm sure it is wicked to say such things, or even to think them."

"She doesn't think them," proclaimed Aunt Harriet with conviction. "Pray do not exaggerate, Caitlin! You are distressing your sister."

Caitlin laughed, one auburn brow arching quizzically. "Have I put you out of countenance, my dear? Never mind! Levity, you know, was always my besetting sin. Tell me about last night!"

Emily turned beseeching eyes upon her aunt, and Lady Lynwood patted her hand comfortingly. "Emily dear, you conducted yourself with perfect propriety. And I must say, that silk we chose made up beautifully. A lucky chance we stopped at Lisette's that day, wasn't it? I was beginning to think we would never find anything suitable, and although I am as fond of shopping as anyone—or *fonder!*—I really thought I had reached my last possible hour of looking at dress-patterns. Well, we had been doing so for days! They all begin to look alike, and one's head goes round and round! But that pattern she found gave you just the right touch. What a fortunate circumstance that white becomes you! You cast them all into the shade. Did you see that Lady Mary Ellersbee? Haggish! Her mother was just such another; put her into pastels and she instantly appears ten years older. I don't know why it should be so, but there it is. And it was clear from the outset Miss Emmons would trip on her train. La! The poor girl was quite out of her element. Gawky!"

Caitlin felt the story was straying rather far from the point. "But, Aunt, do you think Emily will—"

"Oh!" Lady Lynwood threw her hands into the air rapturously. "It could not have been better! So graceful and poised, and she looked such a picture! I was most pleased. And do you know"—she leaned forward impressively—"no less a personage than the *Duke of Severn* told me she was prettybehaved. Pretty-behaved! His very words, I promise you."

Caitlin saw that Emily was now quite scarlet, and laughed. "An encomium, indeed!"

"Well, so it was," said Lady Lynwood happily. Her eyes brightened. "Bless me if I haven't forgotten to tell you the best part! The most fortunate coincidence! Mrs. Drummond-Burrell was present. Only fancy! The woman always puts me in a quake, but I vow, I never saw her in better humor. And as luck would have it, she spoke to Emily. Well! Emily had no notion who she was, of course, or she might have gone into one of her tongue-tied fits, but by the luckiest chance Emily did not catch her name."

Lady Lynwood beamed at her nieces triumphantly. "She told me, Emily-love, that she thought you *unexceptionable*."

The color drained from Emily's face. She looked as if she were about to faint. "Mrs. Drummond-Burrell said *that*?"

Caitlin choked on her toast, then burst out laughing. "Oh, I am sorry!" she gasped. "But surely such a mild compliment is not enough to overset you, Emily?"

Lady Lynwood was indignant. "Mild compliment? No such thing! I have every hope that we will secure vouchers for Almack's now. And that is no small feat, let me tell you!"

Caitlin was impressed despite herself. "Vouchers for Almack's! So Emily is to parade her wares in the marriage mart. I congratulate you, Aunt."

Emily uttered a faint protest. Lady Lynwood chuckled. "Only vulgar persons refer to Almack's as the marriage mart, Caitlin. Pray do not do so again! And I have every hope that you are *both* to 'parade your wares' there, so you may stop quizzing your sister."

Caitlin set her teacup down and stared at her aunt. "Now it is you who are quizzing me! I cannot go to Almack's. I have never even been presented."

She instantly regretted her remark. Just as she feared, Emily began reproaching herself—for the hundredth time. "Oh, Caitie!" she mourned. "I feel dreadful whenever I think of you giving up your place so that I might be presented. I cannot think it right. I know the family could not afford to present us both, but why should I have been presented rather than you? After all—"

Caitlin pretended to place her hands over her ears, and appealed to the head of the table. "Aunt Harriet, I implore you—! Convince Emily that she is distressing herself to no purpose!"

"Do not place your elbows on the table, Caitlin," said Lady Lynwood placidly, applying a generous portion of jam to a crumpet. "And, Emily, your sister is quite right! There is no need for these lamentations. You are eighteen, and that is the perfect age for a first Season. I could not convince your mother to let me bring you both out, since Amabel did not wish me to go out of pocket—such stuff! A choice had to be made, and even Caitlin believed that you should be the one chosen."

"Yes," agreed Caitlin firmly. "I never stirred the slightest interest among the Hertfordshire beaux, so there seemed little point in exhibiting me to the *ton.*"

Emily cried out again at this, and Lady Lynwood pointed her jam-slathered knife at Caitlin. "Caitlin, really! We are going to exhibit you to the *ton,* and you may stop rolling your eyes at me, for I won't change my mind! No, now really, Caitlin—there is simply no more to be said on the subject! You are an excessively pretty girl—yes, you are!—and although your hair is very red indeed, I think we need not despair. It is not a *carroty* red, you know, and you are not, thank Heaven, bran-faced—now, whatever have I said to send you into whoops?"

"I beg your pardon!" gasped Caitlin. "Pray continue. Besides my lack of freckles, what else have we to thank heaven for?"

"Your height," replied Lady Lynwood promptly. "You wear clothes very gracefully, Caitlin, and there is much to be said for an elegant air! Of course there are many gentlemen who dislike tallness in a female, but on the whole, I think it rather an advantage. And as for worrying about Almack's, pooh! An almond for a parrot! How are people to know you have not been presented? Since you are a bit older, it will be assumed you have been 'out' for some time. And so you have! Though only in Hertfordshire, of course."

Lady Lynwood munched her crumpet reflectively. "We must not become discouraged if you are not an immediate success, my love. In my view, it will be an excellent thing if we do not secure respectable alliances for both of you at once. In fact, I would dislike it excessively! For then I would not be able to invite you next year, you know, and of course it will be *years* before Agnes is old enough. I cannot begin to express to you, my dears, how much I enjoy having you here! I cannot imagine why I never thought of inviting you before."

Caitlin hid a smile. She had often heard Mama express that very sentiment! Now that Caitlin was better acquainted with her loveable but scatterbrained aunt, she suspected that Lady Lynwood had remembered her nieces' existence only because she was moped to death, all alone at Lynwood House. The baronness had been widowed two years ago, and now both her sons were from home; James was off enjoying whatever advantages a very limited Grand Tour could provide a young gentleman in these dangerous times, and little Harry was away at school. Aunt Harriet was far too gregarious to live alone, and Caitlin suspected that putting on her blacks and foregoing the pleasures of last year's Season had been a severe punishment for her widowed aunt.

After breakfast, Lady Lynwood and Emily went on a shopping expedition. Caitlin, declining the treat, escaped to the morning room. She needed to write a long-overdue letter to Mama. She also needed to cudgel her brain to come up with a way to neutralize the effects of her social ostracism. For surely, once Serena cut her acquaintance, Caitlin would find herself on the fringes of Society. She was certain that she, at least, would never cross the sacred threshold of Almack's. Would Emily be exiled with her? She was staring sadly out the window with the ink drying on her pen when, to her astonishment, Stubbs announced Lady Serena Kilverton.

Chapter V

Serena rushed impetuously into the morning room, barely waiting until Stubbs had shut the door before casting herself into Caitlin's arms and giving her a quick, fierce hug. She burst out in her honest, unaffected way with: "Caitlin, you heard her, didn't you? I shall never forgive Elizabeth. Never!"

Caitlin felt tears of mingled relief and shame springing to her eyes. She had underestimated her friend. She gave a shaky little laugh and tried to speak lightly. "Serena, you goose! I might have known you would fly in the face of anyone's advice, however well-intentioned it was."

Serena sniffed disdainfully. "You certainly might have known I would fly in the face of *that* advice, at any rate. Did you think I would tamely agree to distance myself from you? I am not so henhearted!" She tossed her muff and reticule onto a nearby sofa and flung herself into its cushioned depths. "Now, Caitlin, confess: you did not expect to see me today."

"Well, no," admitted Caitlin. She sank onto a chair across from her friend, and managed a wavering smile. "But I must say, Serena—I am very glad to see you!"

Serena's eyes snapped dangerously. Her face was too pretty and mischievous to achieve malevolence, but she did acquire something like the aspect of a fierce kitten. "That—that *shrew*! How could you believe I would listen to her? Really, Caitlin, I don't know what you deserve!"

"I would not have blamed you for cutting the connection, so do not eat me!" Caitlin found she could not meet her friend's gaze and looked down at her hands, forcing her words past a sudden constriction in her throat. "It's all very well to say you cannot forgive Lady Elizabeth, but according to her own lights she was quite right. I'm sure she meant nothing but kindness in warning you away."

"Elizabeth is an ill-natured harpy!" declared Serena, bouncing indignantly upright on the sofa. "And I won't have you defending her!"

Caitlin's cheeks grew hot. "But my behavior last night was enough to give any well-bred person a disgust of me. I walked off without a word to anyone—left your mother a *message*—oh, I am covered with shame whenever I think of it!"

"Nonsense. You behaved beautifully until Elizabeth uttered those unhandsome remarks. And you needn't tell me you overheard them by accident!"

"Thank you," said Caitlin, with difficulty. "But really, Serena, you must not encourage me in such shocking impropriety! I don't wonder at it that Lady Elizabeth thought me a vulgar upstart. After all, she is the Lady Elizabeth Delacourt, and I am the veriest nobody."

Serena's eyes flashed. "Fiddle! You are a niece of Lady Lynwood and cousin to Baron Lynwood. A nobody, indeed! I defy anyone to call you so in my presence!"

Warmhearted Serena was clearly ready to do battle for her friend. Caitlin was touched. Trying for a lighter note, she responded, "What a pity I did not stay on the terrace long enough to hear your response to Lady Elizabeth's amiable warnings! Once you had proved you were as rag-mannered as I, I would have been quite comfortable again."

Serena giggled. "Well, she is enough to try the patience of a saint! I do wish Richard had offered for Maria Carleton, or Anne Markham. Heaven knows they threw out enough lures! And although poor Maria is sadly fat, and Anne has more hair than wit, at least they are both pleasant and kind."

This puzzled Caitlin. "I don't mean to sound vulgarly inquisitive, Serena, but why did your brother offer for Lady Elizabeth? Is it not a question of—well, of love?"

Serena pulled a face. "With Miss Prunes and Prisms? Love! Certainly not." Seeing Caitlin's bewildered expression, Serena burst out laughing. "Oh, Caitlin! I wish you would pop on your bonnet and walk with me. I have been having the most *unchristian* thoughts about my future sister-in-law, and until today there was not a soul I could tell!"

Caitlin assumed an air of exaggerated interest. "How excessively fortunate that she behaved scaly to me!"

Serena's eyes danced. "Yes, indeed! I can unburden myself to someone at last! But not here—I always have the most dreadful suspicion that Stubbs is listening at the door."

Soon the two girls were walking briskly down Half Moon Street. Caitlin, with a newborn appreciation for propriety, rather halfheartedly suggested that they ask Jane to follow in their wake, but Serena spurned this poor-spirited suggestion. So Caitlin allowed herself to be persuaded that such a precaution was unnecessary if the two girls walked only as far as the Green Park. The morning was sunny, but a spanking breeze rattled their bonnets as they walked.

"Now then—where was I?" Serena demanded.

Caitlin smiled. "You were about to explain why your brother offered for Lady Elizabeth, I believe."

Serena tucked a hand confidingly into Caitlin's elbow. "Yes, but if you knew our family's situation, you wouldn't wonder at it. My unfortunate brother! He is Papa's only son, you know, and must marry as soon as he may. Papa—" Serena hesitated, and her voice softened. "Papa isn't well. I daresay you have wondered why Mama and I go alone to parties, but he insists we not deprive ourselves of pleasure merely because he isn't strong enough to join us. Papa suffered an attack several years ago that almost carried him off. His health has been declining again of late, and Richard is determined to ease Papa's mind by setting up his nursery as soon as possible. It will do poor Papa a world of good to see Richard safely married before he—well, before—"

Caitlin nodded sympathetically, and Serena continued. "It is of the first importance to the family that the line continue through Richard, you see. And the sooner the better! The entire Selcroft fortune goes with the title, and as things stand if anything happened to Richard both the title and the fortune would go to Papa's brother Oswald—a dreadful fellow, I promise you! He and Papa have been at odds for as long as I can remember, and it would be nothing short of a calamity to see Oswald Kilverton in Papa's shoes. The more so because he has been so maddeningly sure it would come to him one day! He made ducks and drakes of his own fortune, I believe, thinking the family inheritance would eventually be his."

Caitlin raised an eyebrow. "An optimistic gentleman!" she observed. "It is natural to assume one will inherit a title from a parent, but from a brother—?"

A spurt of laughter escaped Serena. "Oh! You must understand that Uncle Oswald is many years younger than Papa—he is the child of my grandpapa's second wife. And Papa did marry rather late in life, you know, and then my parents were married years and years before Richard arrived. Papa had quite given up hope! So you see, all that time it seemed perfectly reasonable to suppose my father's half brother would succeed to the title—and, of course, the fortune."

"Do you mean to tell me your uncle has lived his entire life eagerly anticipating your father's demise?" Caitlin demanded, astonished. "He sounds positively ghoulish!"

Serena gave a little skip, and pulled her hands free so she could clap them. "Excellent, Caitlin! *Ghoulish* is an extremely apt description of my deplorable Uncle Oswald! A smooth-tongued, cold-blooded scoundrel, in fact! There is not much one would put beyond him."

Caitlin protested this startling exaggeration, but Serena peeped up from beneath the brim of her bonnet, her eyes dancing. "You may ask anyone. He is a most reprehensible character, but so fascinating! I am afraid he is sadly extravagant, too. Isn't it shocking? As near as anyone can tell, his fortune is nearly all gone and the estate he inherited from my grandfather is mortgaged to the hilt. They say every family has at least one dirty dish! Uncle Oswald is ours."

Caitlin pondered this information. "Your brother's arrival must have been a severe blow to your uncle."

"Oh, monstrous!" agreed Serena cheerfully. "I am not supposed to know this, but I believe Uncle Oswald was so certain he would one day be the Earl of Selcroft, he lived for years by borrowing against his expectations. You may imagine the row that ensued when that was discovered! At any rate, he and my father could not be more different from one another, and I am afraid there is no love lost between them. Since Richard is the only person standing between my uncle and the title, Papa would be extremely glad to see Richard married."

This seemed eminently reasonable to Caitlin. The girls slowed their pace as they entered the park and headed down a path. The park seemed very full of nursemaids, and most were shepherding excessively noisy children. The girls walked carefully, mindful that one of the park's attractions was a small herd of dairy cattle.

"Is your brother much older than you?" asked Caitlin, lowering her voice as they passed an infant sleeping in a perambulator.

"A little more than seven years," Serena replied. "Richard is eight-and-twenty now. He has been determinedly seeking a bride for the past three Seasons—and very diverting it has been!" She gave a spirited description of the various caps that had been set at her brother, and the discomfiture of the matchmaking mamas when it became clear that Lord Kilverton fancied no female above another.

"For you must know, Caitlin, my brother is held to be the most shocking flirt! He never meant to encourage anyone's expectations, but of course he is such a matrimonial prize that the tongues began to wag if he so much as waltzed with a girl. It was excessively uncomfortable for him. And the end of it was, he couldn't find any female he *particularly* liked. I promise you, under the circumstances he is blessing his good fortune to have secured an alliance with Arnsford's eldest."

Caitlin bit back a smile at Serena's disgruntled expression. "You don't agree that he should be blessing his good fortune?"

Serena shook her head dolefully. "I cannot rejoice, however hard I try! Although I seem to be alone in my dismay. My parents are *aux anges,* and the betrothal caused great satisfaction among the *ton.* If you had come to town only a few weeks earlier, you would have seen that for yourself. It was quite a seven-day wonder! Everyone except myself seems to believe it is an ideal match."

Caitlin laughed. "Then let us hope they are right. Perhaps Lady Elizabeth is perfectly amiable once one comes to know her."

Serena looked skeptical. "I fancy that is not how the world judges these matters. If she were the worst harridan imaginable, people would still congratulate my brother! By allying himself to Lady Elizabeth, he is establishing a connection with an extremely exalted branch of the peerage, you know. Both families will be forever after connected to nearly every great house in England. And I daresay Lady Elizabeth's personal fortune, once the Selcroft fortune is added to it, will make Richard one of the wealthiest men in Europe. One is not supposed to mention such matters, of course—so silly, when one knows that is *exactly* what everyone is thinking when they call it a 'great match'!"

Caitlin felt a tug of sympathy, but thought she ought not to encourage Serena's pessimism. "It may be that they are well-matched in other areas, too. We must wish them the best, Serena, and hope they will be happy together."

"Yes, of course," said Serena, with a marked lack of enthusiasm. "If they are not, it will not be Richard's fault. I must say, even Elizabeth seems to realize that. She has been more puffed up than ever lately—now that she has secured the hand of one of the most sought-after prizes on the marriage mart! At five-and-twenty, even a duke's daughter can hardly expect to do better."

Caitlin laughed out loud. "I make every allowance for the fondness of a sister, Serena, but do try for a *little* even-handedness! You know I did not enjoy my own encounter with Lady Elizabeth, but to do her justice, I believe she has more to recommend her than fortune and breeding. She is a good-looking woman, do you not think? And she will know exactly how to manage a large estate. Your brother's home will be well-run, his guests flawlessly entertained, and his wife will never cause him any embarrassment. There is much to be said for that."

Serena sniffed. "Is there? It sounds very dull."

"Well, such a marriage would not suit everyone," conceded Caitlin. "But many persons feel that an unexciting but well-ordered life is actually *preferable* to a love match. Perhaps your brother is among them. If Lord Kilverton is not in love with any particular lady, and yet is determined to marry, I believe he has done very well for himself."

It was clear that Serena's opinions on the subject were not easily swayed. She wrinkled her nose in disgust at Caitlin's portrait of domestic serenity. "Pooh! Our parents enjoy a warm regard for one another, and I feel sure Richard hoped to find someone he could love."

"And who are we, pray, to say that he cannot love Lady Elizabeth? You know, Serena, it is not unusual for a sister to find her brother's choice unfathomable. In fact, sisters-in-law frequently have little in common. That does not mean, however, that the man is unhappy in his choice."

Serena looked thoughtful. Then her troubled expression lightened a little. "You are right!" she exclaimed. "Why, I can think of a dozen examples among my own acquaintance."

"There, then!" cried Caitlin, triumphant. "I refuse to let you despair."

Serena's eyes twinkled. "I will be delighted to be proved wrong, you know. I hope Richard will be delirious with joy on his wedding day, and live in untrammeled bliss forever after. But between ourselves, Caitlin—I would not wager a groat on it!"

They were brought up short by a toddler who ran, shrieking, after a ball and collided with Serena's legs. Serena disentangled herself and announced that she had had quite enough of the Green Park for the moment. "I say, Caitlin," she said, her eyes brightening, "I saw the loveliest bonnet the other day. Do walk as far as Curzon Street with me and let me show it to you—why, whatever is the matter?"

At the mention of Curzon Street, Caitlin had turned the most extraordinary shade of pink. "Nothing!" she stammered hastily. "But I think I had rather not—just now!" And using the excuse of her unfinished letter, she succeeded in returning to Lynwood House without any dangerous detours.

Chapter VI

Lady Elizabeth's attempt to curtail Serena's association with Caitlin only resulted in strengthening the bond between the two girls. Serena even coaxed her mama into securing an invitation for Lady Lynwood and her nieces to a select reception being held by Lady Dassinghurst in honor of a visiting Bohemian princess. When this harbinger of delight arrived in the morning post, Lady Lynwood clasped it rapturously to her plump bosom.

"Only fancy, my loves! Elvira Dassinghurst! What a stroke of good fortune! Not that I have ever cared for her, of course—in fact, I think her a pompous old crow—but nothing could be more flattering than to receive an invitation from her! She doted on my poor Charles, as I am sure everyone did, but she has never accorded me more than the barest civility. I don't believe I have exchanged three words with her since Charles passed away. We must owe this invitation entirely to Lady Selcroft's good graces. How glad I am that you can call Lady Serena your friend, Caitlin dear!"

Caitlin was a little embarrassed by her aunt's tangled speech and even more tangled motives, but at least she could wholeheartedly agree that she was glad to call Serena her friend.

On the night of Lady Dassinghurst's reception, Lady Lynwood insisted that the girls dress with extra care. She reserved for herself the right to inspect their appearance before allowing them out the door. They waited rather nervously in the drawing room until Aunt Harriet bustled in to scrutinize her nieces.

Emily was in high bloom, as always, and presented a lovely

picture in pink and white with her soft gold curls dressed fashionably high. Caitlin had donned an elegantly simple silk of pale yellow trimmed with buttercup satin. Matching yellow primroses adorned her fan and crowned her hair, which was piled softly on her head; a few coppery tendrils had been pulled free and curled with hot irons.

The baroness ran a practiced eye over her protégées, and reached out to flick a curl into place here, a ribbon into place there. "Now let me see you, Emily love! Yes, yes, it is just how I knew it would be. You will break hearts, I vow! And, Caitlin, that silk becomes you to admiration. I hope you are not fretting, my dears. Everything will go very well, I promise you."

She cocked her head, birdlike, and her eyes twinkled as she beheld her nieces' stunned expressions; they were taking in the glory of their aunt's appearance. Her dress, as always, was extremely expensive, became her well, and suited a widow's dignity. But tonight Lady Lynwood's plump bodice was engulfed in a sea of flashing jewels.

"Good heavens, Aunt!" said Caitlin faintly. "We are blinded."

Lady Lynwood chuckled, and tapped the enormous necklace with a gloved forefinger. "Isn't it dreadful? Elizabethan, of course, so I am sure all this hideous chase-work is the purest gold. I am simply *staggering* under the weight. So tiresome! But that is the way of these heirlooms; one daren't have the stones reset."

Caitlin's eyes widened. "Do you mean—Aunt, are those the *Lynwood Diamonds*?"

"Yes, love. I believe they are quite famous," replied Aunt Harriet brightly. "I am expected to trot them out from time to time, you know. Well! I thought it would do my nieces no harm to be seen in their company."

As Caitlin was still staring, fascinated, at the jewels, another chuckle shook Lady Lynwood. "Now, Caitlin, pray remember that only a yokel appears amazed! Besides, I am not wearing *all* the Lynwood Diamonds. There is a coronet, naturally, and two brooches, and a ring, and a scepter—of all things! You can't imagine how cumbersome. I am so thankful when I consider that by the time our dear Regent is crowned, my James will probably have married. His bride will have to wear them to the coronation, not I. I hope, for her sake, he chooses a *sturdy* sort of girl. La! I wore the coronet to a reception once, and had the headache for a week!"

By this time, Lady Lynwood had bundled her charges out the door and into a waiting carriage. Her nervous excitement was contagious, and Emily's eyes were growing round as saucers. Caitlin could not help wondering what all the fuss was about, but when they alighted at the Dassinghurst mansion she began to perceive that this invitation was, indeed, something out of the ordinary. A massive stone facade greeted her astonished gaze as she was handed down from the carriage, with rows of liveried footmen lining an imposing flight of marble steps.

"Good gracious!" murmured Caitlin. Lady Lynwood threw her a speaking glance, and they processed solemnly up to the portico. Bowing lackeys divested them of their cloaks, and Lady Lynwood handed their invitation to a wigged, gloved, gorgeously arrayed individual who paced slowly before them to an overheated foyer.

"Baroness Lynwood! Miss Campbell! Miss Emily Campbell!" this personage bawled in stentorian tones as they stepped across the threshold. They entered a vast, brightly lit hall thronged with glittering people, and joined a rather loosely organized receiving line. Lady Lynwood immediately began chatting with a hawk-nosed lady in purple sarcenet, so Caitlin and Emily were deeply thankful when Lady Serena rushed up and greeted them affectionately. Serena looked very pretty in her pomona green crepe, and her light brown curls had been coaxed into modish ringlets on either side of her face. She seemed to be in unusually high spirits, and her eyes sparkled with mischief.

"So! You *did* receive the coveted invitation! Have you come to court the society of your betters? Or merely to ape their manners?"

Emily's soft eyes dilated with alarm, but Caitlin rapped Serena with her fan. "If we ape *your* manners, Serena, Lady Dassinghurst will show us the door!"

Serena gave a choke of laughter. "Much you would care! Do try to acquire a little ambition, Caitlin."

Caitlin pulled a face. "And toad-eat every titled dowager who crosses my path? No, thank you."

"Well, it's a pity you are not inclined to study the art, because you will find any number of instructive examples tonight. Lady Dassinghurst is continually surrounded by—" But Serena broke off, perceiving her brother escorting her mother and Lady Elizabeth in from the hall. "Never mind that! You must all come and say how-do-you-do to my brother. I want to see Elizabeth's face when she finds you hobnobbing with the Dassinghurst set!"

"Serena, you are incorrigible!" exclaimed Caitlin, and turned in time to see Lady Elizabeth entering the room on the arm of a tall gentleman dressed in the height of elegance, but with none of the extremes of fashion. There seemed to Caitlin to be something arresting about him that immediately drew, then held, her attention.

Serena's brother has a distinguished air, she thought approvingly. It was due more to his bearing and manner than his exquisite tailoring. Caitlin could not immediately see his face. He was bending his head attentively to hear what his fiancée was saying.

"The Countess of Selcroft! Lady Elizabeth Delacourt! Viscount Kilverton!" came the announcement from the portal. Serena pulled Lady Lynwood's party back to the entrance to introduce Caitlin and Emily to Lord Kilverton. Lady Serena had spoken of him so frequently, and with such affection, Caitlin had a great curiosity to meet this paragon of brothers who had unaccountably offered marriage to a prig.

While Emily was murmuring a shy greeting to his lordship, and Lady Lynwood was reminding him of certain exploits he had shared with her son James, Caitlin was at leisure to observe Richard Kilverton. He was a good-looking man, with a rather aquiline cast of countenance, a lean, athletic build, and a marked resemblance to Serena. His air of quiet elegance, however, differed from his sister's lively mischievousness. He had her coloring, and something of her manner; the appreciative gleam in his eye when he looked at Emily lent a good deal of humor to his expression and brought an involuntary smile to Caitlin's face. Then he turned to meet Caitlin—and she had the oddest sensation that the breath had been knocked out of her.

Her opinion that Lord Kilverton was a good-looking man was instantly forgotten. Caitlin could no longer tell whether he was handsome or plain, and had she been asked she could not have described a single feature of his face. He simply struck her as the embodiment of an ideal. Had she met him before? she wondered dazedly. It must be the resemblance to Serena, she decided, as her hand was taken in a cool, firm clasp and they exchanged bows and pleasantries.

Lord Kilverton, bowing to Miss Campbell, was experiencing a similar impact. Because he had so obviously admired her sister, he turned to catch Caitlin smiling humorously up at him in an irresistibly frank and friendly way; one couldn't help but return such a smile. He found himself shaking hands with a girl whose flaming hair and creamy skin was gorgeously set off by the primrose silk of her gown. A few bright curls dropped across her shoulders and softly framed her face. It was a face he somehow felt he knew. The slant of her auburn brows, the laughter in the depths of her eyes, the smile on her generous mouth, all seemed oddly familiar to him. He had heard Miss Emily Campbell described as the Beauty of the two, and could only wonder at the perversity of people's taste. His instant and overwhelming impression was that once one beheld Miss Campbell's brilliant coloring, dazzling smile, and air of well-bred elegance, the other girls in the room faded like candles in the sunshine. He found it difficult to take his eyes off her. But where on earth could he have seen her before?

The group stayed and chatted a few minutes, and as Caitlin was speaking with Lady Selcroft she felt Lord Kilverton's eyes on her. She finally turned to him inquiringly, and caught him regarding her with a slight, puzzled frown. Seeing her raised eyebrow, he laughed and begged pardon.

"Am I staring at you, Miss Campbell? You will hardly be appeased when you hear my excuse. I have a strong impression that we have met before, and I am trying to recall where or when that may have been."

"How very original!" observed Miss Campbell in a congratulatory tone, surprising a snort of laughter from his lordship. Unfortunately, this drew Lady Elizabeth's attention.

"May I share the joke?" she inquired archly, taking Kilverton's arm with a proprietary air. He turned courteously to include her in the conversation, but the laughter left his eyes.

"I am afraid Miss Campbell caught me staring at her rather rudely, and has given me a well-deserved set-down," he said lightly. "Behold my discomfiture!"

"Indeed?" said Elizabeth frostily. She was clearly offended. It was unclear, however, whether she was offended more by the idea of the plebeian Miss Campbell giving a set-down to one so far above her, or by the unwelcome picture of her fiancé staring at another woman. "And what is there to laugh at in that? Whether you have been rude to Miss Campbell or she has, in fact, been rude to you, I see nothing humorous in either event." Elizabeth smiled thinly. "You will think me old-fashioned in my notions, I suppose. I do not find modern banter amusing."

There seemed to be nothing to say to this. Kilverton bowed, and Caitlin bit her tongue to keep from uttering a crushing retort. Her aunt then claimed her attention and drew her off to present her to other acquaintances. Caitlin gratefully escaped before she could be betrayed yet again into unladylike conduct by Lady Elizabeth's condescension.

Lord Kilverton watched her walk away. He was struck anew by something familiar in Miss Campbell's graceful carriage. He frowned in an effort of memory.

Suddenly his expression changed to one of startled speculation. "Good God!" uttered Richard Kilverton, raising his quizzing glass and staring after Miss Campbell's departing figure. Could it be possible—?

Chapter VII

Throughout the evening, Caitlin was aware from time to time of Lord Kilverton watching her, and was puzzled and astonished to find herself so aware of him. It was completely unlike her to notice a man's eyes upon her. When she glanced up to find her eyes meeting his across the room for perhaps the fourth or fifth time, she deliberately held his gaze, with so much reproof in her expression that he colored slightly and looked away.

There! she thought triumphantly. At least he won't stare at me again! She wondered fleetingly what he meant by it, but it wasn't until the party was going in to a very late buffet that she had leisure to reflect on Lord Kilverton's strange behavior.

What ails the fellow? she wondered crossly, helping herself to lobster patties. It is impossible that we have met before this evening. And even if we had, why should he stare so? Unless—

A ghastly suspicion assailed her.

Unless when we met before, he could not see me!

With an exclamation of horror, Caitlin turned involuntarily to look at Lord Kilverton, and her eyes, wide with dismay, met his yet again. He was *still* watching her! And even as her eyes met his, she knew her expression of shocked realization was confirming his own suspicions. The interest in his gaze sharpened into triumph, and his eyes danced with unholy amusement. At her expense! She immediately looked away, covered with confusion and blushing scarlet.

"No! Oh, no!" she whispered. Hardly recalling where she was, she turned blindly with some vague notion of escaping the room. Emily, however, was at her side and touched her arm with timid concern.

"Caitie, are you ill? What is amiss?"

Caitlin stared unseeingly at her sister, her thoughts in turmoil, her color fluctuating alarmingly, and her expression quite distracted. "Ill?" she repeated numbly. "No, I am not ill. I merely—that is—oh, this is dreadful!"

"Dreadful? What is dreadful?"

Caitlin, becoming aware of Emily's anxiety and the curious gaze of an inquisitive woman nearby, made an effort to control her rising sense of panic and appear more normal. She took a deep breath, and schooled her features into a calm and rational expression. After all, she was at Lady Dassinghurst's reception! Nothing untoward could occur. But as she was opening her mouth to reassure Emily, a dreaded voice was heard behind her.

"Miss Campbell, we meet again! Allow me to recommend the trifle, which has apparently escaped your notice."

Lord Kilverton audaciously slapped a spoonful of trifle onto the plate trembling in Caitlin's hand. She did not dare look up at him, but ventured to respond in a voice that shook only slightly.

"I dislike trifle!"

Emily's sweet, worried gaze turned to Lord Kilverton. "I am afraid my sister is not feeling quite the thing."

"Very understandable," replied Lord Kilverton, with quick sympathy. "Such a press of people round the table! I feel it myself."

"The heat is a little oppressive," agreed Emily innocently. "We did not look for such warm weather in May. One feels it more when it is unexpected."

While her sister spoke, Caitlin cast a mute, but agonized, glance up at her tormentor. She immediately looked away again, but she knew her expression had been eloquent of horror and embarrassment. Even a heart of stone must feel compassion for such distress! Lord Kilverton, however, appeared unmoved.

"Yes, indeed!" he agreed blandly. "Even the strongest person can be overpowered by"—his eyes flicked toward Caitlin—"unexpected heat."

Caitlin almost gasped aloud at this astonishing piece of insolence. She glared indignantly up at his lordship and found herself confronting such laughing eyes, in such a solemn face, she had to look hastily away again. How appalling to discover within herself a temptation to *laugh* at this hair-raising situation! What was wrong with her? She bit her lip, and achieved an icy politeness.

"It is somehow impossible to believe you know the first thing about it, my lord. You certainly do not have the appearance of one who is easily overpowered." She dared to look challengingly at him, but was immediately sorry she had done so. He was smiling softly down at her, with laughter still in his eyes, and something else as well. Something that sent a fresh wave of color to Caitlin's cheeks and brought her heart into her throat.

"I assure you, Miss Campbell, I am extremely conscious of the heat surrounding us," he said softly. "It is only by the strongest effort of will that I am not at this very moment succumbing to it."

Caitlin was thrown into such confusion she hardly knew where to look. Terrified, she took refuge in impertinence.

"If that is the case, I wonder you do not quit the room! Most *gentlemen in distress* are capable of rescuing themselves!"

Emily was shocked by her sister's extraordinary rudeness, but Lord Kilverton actually laughed out loud. As if Caitie had said something witty! thought Emily, bewildered but relieved.

"I will rescue us both," announced Lord Kilverton with unimpaired good humor. "Shall we take a turn round Lady Dassinghurst's admirable gardens? I am persuaded the fresh air will do us a world of good."

Caitlin uttered a strangled syllable which Emily thought must signify assent. Lord Kilverton did not fall into this error, however. As Emily turned back to the buffet table, he lowered his voice confidentially.

"Come, Miss Campbell, why do you spurn my escort? You will give me a very odd opinion of you, you know. Do you always walk unattended?"

Caitlin addressed his lordship in an agitated whisper, stammering a little in her distress. "Certainly not. That is—I mean—why, it's none of your affair!"

"I hope you do not expect me to stand by the buffet table and listen for your screams, while you walk round the garden alone. I cannot be certain I would hear a cry for help in all this hubbub."

Anger suddenly stiffened her spine and banished all desire to laugh. She turned to face him, her eyes blazing. "How *dare* you accost me in this fashion? This is the greatest piece of rudeness I have ever encountered!"

Kilverton chuckled. "Is it?"

Caitlin flushed scarlet. "No—it is the second-greatest piece of rudeness! But you are responsible for the first, as well! I must tell you I am shocked—deeply shocked!—by your conduct, my lord. You must be perfectly aware that our first meeting shamed me to the core—and through no fault of my own!"

"Yes, I thought it was you," remarked Lord Kilverton in a tone of great satisfaction, which caught Caitlin up short.

She instantly realized that it was only her last speech that had actually given her away. He had succeeded in putting her to the blush without ever mentioning their first meeting in so many words. Had Caitlin held her tongue, she might yet have pretended not to recognize him. If only she had had the presence of mind to ignore his ill-bred innuendos! She could have blamed her agitation on—oh, anything! How pleasant it would be to stare uncomprehendingly into his handsome face and tell him freezingly that she did not understand his manner or his remarks! Too late now! Her seething silence allowed him to continue urbanely.

"You will recall my earlier observation that I thought we had met before. How gratifying it is to have one's intuition confirmed by subsequent revelations! I am most eager to renew our acquaintance, Miss Campbell. Do let me take you round the gardens—at once!"

Caitlin's voice shook with outrage and mortification. "It is a wonder I did not recognize you instantly, for no one else could be so dead to shame! Round the gardens, indeed! I would not willingly walk across the room with you!"

"Well, you're out, there," replied Lord Kilverton affably, "because if I'm not mistaken, my sister means to invite you to eat supper with our party. Unless you wish to appear nohow, you must, in fact, walk across the room with me. I am glad of it. It has become something of an ambition of mine to tuck your hand into my elbow."

She stared at him in wrathful astonishment, furious that he had somehow invested his words with such intimacy that she felt her cheeks growing hot. "This is beyond anything!" she choked. "I will thank you, my lord, to remember your surroundings! This is no darkened street, and I am no longer a stranger to you. There is no excuse for your effrontery!"

But in fulfillment of his prophecy Serena suddenly appeared, chattering cheerfully, taking Caitlin and Emily firmly by their elbows and ushering them over to the table where her brother, herself, Lady Elizabeth, and a certain Captain Talgarth had established places. Caitlin helplessly allowed herself to be propelled to the table by Serena, with Lord Kilverton following in their wake. Her only consolation was the thought that she had not, after all, been forced to take Lord Kilverton's arm.

With a heightened color and wooden expression, Caitlin seated herself stiffly at the small table. She eyed her plate resentfully. It contained nothing but two lobster patties and an enormous spoonful of trifle.

Caitlin's agitation was such that she could neither eat nor attend to the chatter and laughter surrounding her. The sound seemed to wash over her in meaningless waves while her mind worked furiously to hit on an escape. It occurred to her that she and Emily might excuse themselves on the grounds of seeking their aunt. Caitlin tried in vain, however, to catch her sister's eye. Serena had placed herself and Captain Talgarth between them, and Emily, overwhelmed at finding herself in such exalted company, seemed unable to lift her eyes from her plate.

Caitlin was still trying to draw Emily's attention when she suddenly became aware that Serena had laid an insistent hand upon her wrist. "Do say you'll come!" exclaimed Serena.

Caitlin blinked at her friend, momentarily confused. "I'm sorry, Serena, I—"

She felt Serena's fingers tighten, and a slippered foot

pressed Caitlin's toes beneath the table. Serena was sending what was obviously meant to be an urgent signal. Even more confused, Caitlin halted her apology. Serena, her eyes overbright and her laughter a little breathless, rushed into speech.

"It is a bit sudden, but you cannot possibly have plans for tomorrow morning, Caitlin—you know you were to have gone riding with me. Well, I simply forgot to tell you about the Richmond drive—so silly, but quite my own fault! Now, do say you'll accompany us, or I'll believe you've taken offense at my carelessness."

"Well, I—"

"And Miss Emily Campbell, too, of course!" cried Serena, swiftly turning to include Emily in her invitation. "Are you free tomorrow morning, Miss Campbell?"

"Oh, yes!" said Emily, her soft eyes glowing. "I would like it of all things."

"Then it is settled!" cried Serena gaily. Caitlin managed a rather weak smile as she wondered what had just been arranged for her morning's entertainment. She would have to discover their plans from Emily later. And what was the meaning of that extraordinary expression on Lady Elizabeth's face? She looked as if she had just swallowed a lemon. Caitlin, preoccupied with her own thoughts, had clearly missed something important.

Lady Elizabeth, however, was far too well-bred to parade her annoyance in public. It was not until she was alone with Lord Kilverton in the carriage as he escorted her to her home that she allowed herself to express her views.

"What do you think of your sister's new friends?" she began, with a playful little smile. "For myself, I do not quite like to see our dear Serena encouraging such persons to think themselves at home among the *beau monde*."

Kilverton was mildly surprised at her tone. "Do you mean the Campbell girls? What's wrong with them?"

"Oh, nothing at all. I'm sure they are both very good sorts of girls—in their proper sphere. The younger one seems to be an innocent, at least—although appearances can be deceptive, of course. But the elder!" She laughed gently. "I do not think

there is any scheme too base for that girl's effrontery. I fear
poor Serena is being sadly taken in."

Kilverton's brows snapped together. In addition to the as-
persion cast on his sister's judgment, he found himself dispro-
portionately annoyed with Elizabeth for criticizing the elder
Miss Campbell. "If you have any reason to suspect my sister
is deceived in Miss Campbell, you had better address your remarks to her. I warn you, however, that I have never known
Serena's instincts to err when it comes to judging character,
and you will have a difficult time persuading her she has been
mistaken in her friend."

"I have already spoken to her, Richard, and I fear it is just
as you say. Serena has disregarded my advice in what I can
only consider to be a reckless and headstrong manner. She insists on continuing her sponsorship of these Campbells. I hope
she may not live to regret it. There is a streak of stubbornness
in dear Serena that I fear I must deplore. I hope in time to
teach her to respect the counsel of those older and wiser than
she, but as yet I see no signs of her heeding me. I fancy it is
because your dear papa has been weak for so long, and your
mother, you know, never asserts her authority. As the
youngest child, and the only girl, it is perhaps natural that Serena has grown up a trifle *spoilt*."

Kilverton listened to her in gathering wrath. "Let me advise
you, Elizabeth, not to attempt to correct Serena! She is a
young woman, not a child, and any influence you may gain
over her can only be won through befriending her. I hope you
did not try to preach to her, or, God forbid, assert your imaginary 'authority' over her."

Elizabeth stiffened. "In what way, pray, can my authority
be considered imaginary? I will be an older sister to her."

Kilverton gave a crack of laughter. "You may keep your
own sisters firmly under your thumb, but you won't do so
with mine! Lord! I'd give a monkey to have seen her face
when you tried to induce Serena—*Serena!*—to abandon her
friends! She must have flown up into the boughs."

Elizabeth's chagrined expression confirmed the accuracy of
Kilverton's guess. Her lips compressed into a thin line and her
voice sharpened angrily. "I did not realize how cavalierly you

would regard your sister's behavior, or that you would show so little regard for her reputation. Foisting a—a *mushroom*—onto the *ton* will not endear her to the likes of Lady Dassinghurst! Serena has reached an age when she must court influential hostesses, not alienate them. If she has a preference for low company, she would do well to hide it until she has contracted an unexceptionable alliance."

Kilverton could scarcely believe his ears. "Have you run mad?" he demanded. "Serena is in no danger of finding herself on the shelf! And as for the Misses Campbell, they are nieces of Lady Lynwood. They do not require Serena's sponsorship to achieve the *entrée* to the polite world."

Lady Elizabeth's sneer became marked. "And who is Lady Lynwood, pray? The daughter of a mere knight! I understand Mr. Campbell is nobody at all—a gentleman farmer, in fact! Not even a fortune to recommend him! You are mistaken in thinking the Campbells have the *entrée* anywhere they choose. Your precious Lady Lynwood hasn't crossed the Dassinghurst threshold since her husband died, and you wouldn't have seen her there tonight if not for your sister's misguided efforts."

"You are singularly well-informed, Elizabeth," said Kilverton grimly. "Do you have a taste for gossip? I would not have believed it."

Elizabeth gasped. "Gossip! By no means! I have naturally made it my business to discover what I could about the bosom friend of one who will be a near relation of mine. I would greatly dislike to see my sister-in-law drawn into a set of company I believe to be beneath her."

"If that is so," remarked Kilverton dryly, "I cannot conceive why you provoked her into including those girls in my driving party tomorrow."

"In what way did I provoke her?"

"By announcing you had taken it upon yourself to invite Sir Egbert Kilverton, Serena's least favorite cousin! As you apparently made it your business to invite people on my behalf, Serena felt she could do so as well. Needless to say, she made a point of inviting the very people she believed you would least enjoy."

At this, Lady Elizabeth's fury betrayed her into an unwise speech. "Sir Egbert Kilverton is a most respectable man! A man of sober judgment and high principles! I daresay he will be the only man present tomorrow who could be described as such! Sir Egbert will add a welcome note of propriety to a party which, I fear, will otherwise prove to be extremely *rackety*."

The carriage drew up before His Grace of Arnsford's elegant town house. As his coachman threw open the door, Kilverton had the last word. "A defense of Sir Egbert is not a defense of your conduct in inviting him, Elizabeth. I'll thank you not to meddle with my rackety parties in future—and I'll take care not to include you in them. Good night!"

Elizabeth swept out of the carriage without another word, and Kilverton signaled the coachman to drive on. He was deeply perturbed by this exchange with his fiancée. It seemed his affianced wife, among her many sterling qualities, possessed a snobbery and meanness of spirit that he had not glimpsed in her before. Coupled with her desire to control those around her, her lack of humor, and an apparently deep-seated belief in her own infallibility, these were qualities which Kilverton foresaw could make his future life miserable indeed. The prospect of marrying Lady Elizabeth, which he had heretofore contemplated with satisfaction, suddenly struck dismay into his heart. Odd that he had never been conscious of these misgivings before tonight.

He spent the rest of his short journey home in trying *not* to think that there might be other reasons for this new reluctance to embark upon married life with Lady Elizabeth. No, the root of his unhappiness must surely be these revelations about Elizabeth's temperament and character—not this sudden, irrational dissatisfaction with the color of her hair, or this vague wish that she were not so dull.

Strange! Why had it not occurred to him before? Elizabeth was actually a rather boring person. He found himself shuddering at the thought of spending his life with a woman who never put a foot wrong, never breached her own strict code of behavior—and never made him laugh.

Chapter VIII

The day of Lord Kilverton's driving party dawned bright and fair, dashing Caitlin's hopes that the excursion might be postponed. She supposed it would be cowardly to cry off from Lord Kilverton's projected expedition to Richmond. But she did wish she had had the presence of mind to refuse when Serena issued her artless invitation. How disastrous it would be for her to court Lord Kilverton's company! She turned quite pink with embarrassment just imagining it. What was she to say to the man? How could she defuse the situation so he would not feel he had an advantage over her? It was dismally clear to her that breaking the code of propriety carried its own penalty; one then had no guide for how to deal with the consequences.

But (she reminded herself) since he was Serena's brother, there was no help for it. She must, perforce, become acquainted with Lord Kilverton. She must overcome the unfamiliar and alarming emotions churning within her at the prospect, and steel herself to remain unaffected by his disturbing presence.

What was the matter with her? She was startled and confused by the rush of feelings that set her restlessly pacing in her bedroom and robbed her of her appetite at breakfast. Certainly embarrassment and chagrin were enough to explain the panicky sensation she felt, but how to explain the strange exhilaration that came over her at the prospect of seeing Richard Kilverton again? How to explain the reckless and giddy excitement underlying her panic? Wherefore this compulsion to dress with extra care this morning?

She pushed the unwelcome thoughts aside and dealt sternly with the only emotion she recognized in herself that made sense—embarrassment, pure and simple, at having to publicly face a man who had kissed her against her will.

I am being stupidly missish! she chided herself. It was my own fault for walking home from that party alone, and it is absurd to fret over the consequences now. It was a meaningless little encounter which I would do better to forget, as no doubt Lord Kilverton has done. Or *would,* she amended (recalling certain portions of the previous evening which proved he had obviously *not* forgotten), if my blushes weren't keeping the memory fresh! As he is Serena's brother, I can neither cut his acquaintance nor become tongue-tied every time I am in his company. I may as well start sooner than later; today will be a very good opportunity to become accustomed to treating him just as I would anyone else. However much it goes against the grain, I *must* carry this off with a high hand! If I behave as if our first meeting was an unremarkable occurrence, he will very soon forget about it and we may be friends.

With this admirable resolve, she eventually departed for Richmond feeling tolerably composed. Most of the party had already assembled when they stopped by Lynwood House to take up Caitlin and Emily. The Campbell girls made a charming picture in matching sprig muslin, Caitlin in green and white and Emily in pink and white, with chip straw hats, fluttering ribbons, and dainty parasols. Lord Kilverton, in a very natty driving coat, was driving Lady Elizabeth in his curricle behind a gorgeous pair of matched bays. Serena, quite dashing in a blue velvet habit, was riding her lovely little mare, Nellie. Kilverton had secured his mother's barouche to transport the rest of the party. Lord Kilverton's friend, Mr. Montague, noticeably brightened when the Campbell sisters joined the party. He fairly leaped out of Lady Selcroft's barouche to make their acquaintance.

Caitlin was disappointed that Serena would not ride with her and Emily in the barouche, but when it became apparent that Captain Talgarth was riding, Serena's reasons for choosing Nellie over the barouche were obvious to Caitlin. It was clear that since Serena's invitation to the Campbell girls had increased the party by two, two persons would now need to ride—and Serena had carefully arranged who those two persons would be.

Captain Philip Talgarth was an excessively handsome young man. He made an imposing figure in the saddle. His blond hair gleamed in the sunlight; with his military bearing and dashing mustache he looked every inch the conquering hero. Caitlin was amused to see Serena so dazzled. From what she had observed, Lady Serena was being hotly pursued by several extremely eligible young men (in addition to several not-so-eligible fortune hunters), and had been kindly, but firmly, discouraging them all. Caitlin wondered how long her friend had known Captain Talgarth, and if he was the reason she kept other young men at arms' length.

Emily and Caitlin were gallantly handed into the barouche by Mr. Montague, who scrambled up after them with alacrity, and the party set off for its last stop, Sir Egbert Kilverton's apartments in Courtfield Road. Mr. Montague protested against the necessity of adding Sir Egbert to the party at all. "Nothing could be more snug than our present company," he declared, roguishly eyeing the Campbell girls seated opposite him in the barouche. "I am persuaded that adding to the party will only diminish our comfort. Miss Campbell, do you not agree with me? A fourth person in this barouche will be one too many."

Emily blushed adorably, but Caitlin fell into the spirit of this at once, and replied with mock severity: "If the barouche becomes too crowded, Mr. Montague, you may ride on the box with the coachman."

Mr. Montague sat up indignantly. "I? Ride on the box?" He gasped, apparently affronted. "My dear young lady, you cannot have considered! You would be left to the mercies of Sir Egbert Kilverton. I could not abandon you to such a fate."

This sounded alarming. Emily looked as if she would gladly learn more about Sir Egbert prior to meeting him, but Caitlin, interestedly looking about her, was too busy noting the sights of London to attend further to Mr. Montague's raillery. They were passing through parts of town she had not seen. "I never imagined anything could be so large and bewildering!" she exclaimed. "And how does one ever accustom oneself to so much noise?"

"My sentiments exactly. But how is this? I thought you were unacquainted with Sir Egbert!" cried Mr. Montague outrageously. Serena and Captain Talgarth were riding close enough to overhear this sally, and Serena laughed aloud. As Mr. Montague was not above laughing at his own joke, their joined merriment and choked repetitions of *"Large!"* and *"Bewildering!"* and *"So much noise!"* drew the attention of several passers-by. Their laughter was infectious, and Caitlin bit her lip to contain her amusement, but Captain Talgarth and Emily turned shocked and reproachful eyes upon the pair.

"Lady Serena, I am sure you do not wish to laugh at someone else's expense," said Captain Talgarth quietly. This instantly silenced Serena and caused Mr. Montague to turn his laughter into a kind of cough. "And you forget, Mr. Montague, that several of us do not have the pleasure of Sir Egbert's acquaintance and cannot share your joke."

"Hm! Yes! Beg pardon, I'm sure," muttered the abashed Mr. Montague, rolling an anguished eye toward his accomplice, Serena. Serena spiritedly came to his aid.

"You will share the joke soon enough, Captain Talgarth—if I am not mistaken, we are approaching my cousin's residence. The pleasure, as you call it, of his acquaintance will immediately be followed by the pleasure of his company for the reminder of the day—*ergo,* farewell pleasure!"

Captain Talgarth looked very grave at this sample of Lady Serena's wit, but when Sir Egbert Kilverton appeared and climbed ponderously into the barouche, Caitlin soon found herself in sympathy with Serena and Mr. Montague. Sir Egbert proved to be a stout and self-important young man of thirty or so, dressed meticulously, but extremely conservatively, in a style that made him appear older than his years and could not be said to flatter his girth. Seated beside the elegant Mr. Montague, Sir Egbert did not appear to advantage. Mr. Montague's lithe frame and mobile, good-humored countenance made it possible for him to affect a rather dandified style of dress without appearing either ridiculous or effeminate. Lounging gracefully against the squabs, not a hair out of place, he made Sir Egbert appear even more stodgy than he otherwise would have.

Sir Egbert had grown up under the stigma (he felt) of having an unscrupulous and rake-hellish father, and determinedly sought to cultivate a reputation as far removed from Oswald Kilverton's as possible. He had taken such pains, indeed, that although he was neither charming nor clever he had been knighted at the age of twenty-seven and was bidding fair to become the very image of respectability. This was all commendable, of course, but extremely dull, and Sir Egbert combined his dullness with a habit of monopolizing the conversation to paralyzing effect. This paralysis was occasionally enlivened by Sir Egbert's flashes of unintentional humor, but as he became most comical whenever he was most in earnest, polite persons could not openly enjoy this aspect of his society.

It was not every day that Sir Egbert had the opportunity to show off his rather pedestrian knowledge to pretty girls. The presence of Mr. Montague was not felt by him to be an impediment. Edward Montague was nothing but a rattle and would benefit a great deal by learning to take an interest in something other than the cut of a coat or the fall of a pair of dice. Reveling in his captive audience, Sir Egbert held forth on a variety of uninteresting subjects during the drive to Richmond, lecturing the company in the barouche on the history and horticulture of various places they passed until Mr. Montague was frankly yawning and even Emily's eyes glazed over. Caitlin, Emily, and Mr. Montague were very glad to escape when the carriages finally pulled to a halt.

The party disembarked before a pretty little inn where they were to partake of a light nuncheon prior to exploring Richmond Park. Mr. Montague handed the Campbell girls out of the barouche just as Lord Kilverton drove smartly up in his curricle. Lady Serena and Captain Talgarth had ridden ahead, and Serena hailed them cheerily from the door of the inn.

"I thought you had all been lost, and Captain Talgarth and I would have to explore the park without you!"

Lord Kilverton jumped lightly from the curricle and turned to hand Lady Elizabeth down. "You would have found it dif-

ficult, Serena, since I hold the tickets of admission," he said
shortly.

This was not like her usually sunny-tempered brother. Serena raised an eyebrow at Richard's grim expression and the crease of annoyance between Lady Elizabeth's brows, and drew her own fairly accurate conclusions. Her sharp eyes also noted that Lady Elizabeth did not touch her brother's hand longer than was absolutely necessary to descend from the high perch she occupied, but although Elizabeth immediately walked away from Richard she pinned a smile to her lips when she turned to greet the others. Sir Egbert, unable to exit the barouche with any degree of agility, was still clambering down as he spoke.

"A charming spot, Kilverton! Charming!" he puffed. Reaching the ground at last, he beamed genially at the entire company. "A typical English country inn, what? Couldn't be better! Just a little cold meat, and perhaps a smidgeon of cheese, and we shall all be set to rights."

Lady Elizabeth glanced round the inn's small yard with disfavor. "I hope the parlor may be found to be reasonably clean. I believe country inns are not kept as carefully as those in town."

"I trust you will not insult the landlady by voicing your opinion within her hearing, Elizabeth." Lord Kilverton's tone was polite, but an uncomfortable pause ensued. Elizabeth shrugged, and, with a visible effort, forced herself to speak lightly.

"If the landlady knows how to make a decent pot of tea I shall own myself satisfied. I will be extremely glad to be out of the sun for half an hour. I do not know how it is, but strong sunlight always gives me the headache."

"It is often so!" assented Sir Egbert earnestly, taking Lady Elizabeth's arm and escorting her indoors with great solicitude. "I believe sunlight to be most injurious to ladies. You are too delicate, Lady Elizabeth, too fragile to withstand the ferocity of Apollo's rays! I cannot think it advisable for ladies to be abroad in the strongest light of day. The heat is withering, the burning brightness far too powerful! No, no! They must be sheltered, they must be hidden from Phoebus's wrath!"

"How fortunate that these particular ladies reside in England, and may safely count on gloomy weather six days out of seven," cried Mr. Montague, escaping Sir Egbert's monologue and the apparently grim mood of his host by entering the coolness of the inn with Emily on his arm.

Caitlin, overhearing, could not hide a smile at picturing a wrathful Phoebus overpowering Lady Elizabeth, and at the soft English sunlight being described so wildly, but as Sir Egbert seemed to be warming to his theme she took care to place herself in the rear of the procession, hoping to escape being seated near him. This placed her next to Lord Kilverton, whose forbidding expression had vanished in amusement at Sir Egbert's unconscious absurdity. He turned to her and gravely offered his arm.

"Miss Campbell, allow me to remove you from Phoebus's wrath!" he recommended, surprising a choke of laughter out of her.

"Pray remove me from your amiable cousin—as far as the table will allow!"

"How uncivil of you," observed Lord Kilverton blandly, tucking Miss Campbell's hand into his elbow. She tried very hard to read nothing into this action. He began slowly leading her to the parlor. "Do you make a habit of sneering at your host's family members?" he inquired conversationally. "It will make severe inroads in your social life, you know."

Caitlin bit her lip. "You cannot accuse me of sneering, Lord Kilverton, when I only described your cousin as *amiable*."

"Yes, an amiable dolt!" he agreed. "No matter what encomium you used to describe him, I am not deceived. It is useless to prevaricate, Miss Campbell—my cousin has failed to fascinate you. Despite his best efforts, you think him a pompous nodcock. Poor Egbert! He has his uses, of course. A half hour of his company makes you glad to take my arm."

Caitlin stiffened and he grinned, covering her hand firmly with his own. "Now, how can you be offended when I have agreed with you so wholeheartedly? My cousin is an intolerable jaw-me-dead."

"Your cousin, however, is a pattern-card of respectability," she said severely, trying unsuccessfully to pull her hand out of Lord Kilverton's grasp.

"Unlike myself, I take it? Pray do not remove your hand, Miss Campbell! Having achieved my ambition at last, I am loath to relinquish it."

She immediately pulled free and clutched her parasol with both hands. "Your ambition, Lord Kilverton, is obviously to put me to the blush as frequently as possible, and *I* am loath to understand why!"

"Really? That is easily explained. The temptation to provoke you is, unfortunately, irresistible. You have a singularly transparent face, Miss Campbell. Your thoughts are written plainly there for all to read."

"Oh, I sincerely hope not!" she gasped, dismayed. This caused Lord Kilverton to laugh out loud, and Caitlin to blush rosily. She hastened to take a place beside Mr. Montague at the table, but Lord Kilverton took the place opposite her and continued to regard her with enjoyment throughout the meal, with the result that Caitlin once again ate very little and hardly knew where to look. She could not remember ever feeling so flustered by anyone as she was by Richard Kilverton. Caitlin had been used to think of herself as a poised and self-assured young woman, never at a loss. It was most unsettling, and extremely annoying, to find herself rattled whenever Lord Kilverton was present.

Once Sir Egbert was occupied in enthusiastically consuming a substantial luncheon, his tongue was stilled and the group was able to converse normally. Sunshine and a light breeze poured through the inn's small windows, bringing the scent of flowers and the merry song of a lark. The atmosphere of unpleasantness that had begun to descend on the party outside the inn quickly evaporated.

It was fortunate for Serena that Lord Kilverton's attention was focused on Caitlin throughout the meal. This distracted him from the spectacle of his sister making sheep's eyes at the handsome Captain Talgarth. Lady Elizabeth, however (once her attention was no longer claimed by the busy Sir Egbert), was all too aware of her future sister-in-law's fixation. Serena showed every disposition to sit in Captain Talgarth's pocket to the exclusion of the rest of the company, and only the captain's calm good manners prevented her from exposing her infatuation even more than she did. What was particularly vexing about this was that Lady Elizabeth's quarrel with her fiancé, far from being forgotten, had continued throughout the drive to Richmond. She knew he would be in no humor to hear strictures from her on his sister's behavior. Nevertheless, Lady Elizabeth was not one to shrink from an unpleasant duty. She determined to speak to Richard on this subject again, the instant they were alone.

Chapter IX

After lunch Lord Kilverton shepherded his party to Richmond Park and produced his tickets of admission. The group prepared for a walking tour. The weather could not have been prettier, and the air was scented with all the perfumes of spring. Casting an appraising glance at the sun, Caitlin tugged her gloves securely over her wrists and unfurled her parasol to protect her complexion before starting out. By the time she had completed these necessary precautions Serena had seized Captain Talgarth's arm and was far down the path. Mr. Montague had Emily on his arm, and Lady Elizabeth had claimed Lord Kilverton, which left Caitlin with Sir Egbert for an escort. She turned to find him beaming fatly at her with great good humor, and smiled back at him with as much good grace as she could muster.

"Are you familiar with Richmond Park, sir?" she asked politely, hoping devoutly he would say no. The prospect of an afternoon spent listening helplessly to Sir Egbert's instructive oratory was more than she could bear.

"I have not had the pleasure of finding myself within the grounds before today, ma'am," replied Sir Egbert with obvious regret. "However, I have heard—"

Caitlin interrupted him hastily. "Then how pleasant it will be to discover the various points of interest for ourselves. Do let us join some of the others!" And she fairly dragged him on to where Mr. Montague was attempting to make her sister laugh. Judging by the bewildered expression on Emily's face, his humor was going over her head. Lord Kilverton and Lady Elizabeth were walking some ways apart, in close conversation.

"Mr. Montague, we depend on you to direct us," cried Caitlin merrily. "Which path are we to take for the best views?"

"How can you ask? Any path the Misses Campbell take is sure to provide the best views!" replied Mr. Montague promptly, covering Emily with confusion and causing Caitlin to glare at him with mock severity.

"Mr. Montague, does this style of conversation generally recommend you to the ladies of your acquaintance?"

He feigned ignorance. "What style do you mean?"

"I mean your uninterrupted flow of humbuggery."

"Miss Campbell, you wrong me! I am completely sincere."

Caitlin looked at him very hard. "Mr. Montague," she asked innocently, "have you ever been to Ireland?"

His eyes gleamed. "Aha! You are thinking of the Blarney stone. Now, really, Miss Campbell, that is too bad! What is the world coming to when a pretty girl is so suspicious? Can you not accept my honest admiration as your due?"

Caitlin laughed, but shook her head. "Worse and worse! I am silenced. Let us take the path that seems shadiest, since it is plain none of us has the least notion where we are. What a pretty wood it is, to be sure."

They could have applied to Lord Kilverton for guidance, but he and Lady Elizabeth had drawn apart and stopped under a nearby oak, to all appearances engaged in a heated discussion. The other four tactfully forbore to interrupt. They turned to the right and began walking up a gentle incline. Overarching boughs from a line of trees on their right shaded the path without obscuring the view to their left, and the prospect was charming.

Sir Egbert's share in the conversation was minimal. It lessened as the walk continued upward. His large luncheon, high cravat, and tight waistcoat were evidently making him extremely uncomfortable. He began to puff a bit with exertion, and frequently mopped his face with a handkerchief. When they reached a grassy plateau with a lovely grove of trees and several benches overlooking the view, he sank onto a bench and mopped his face again.

"Delightful!" he gasped. "Don't know when I've enjoyed myself more." As he appeared acutely miserable, Caitlin found herself forced to turn away to keep her countenance.

"Such lovely weather," agreed innocent Emily. "I was sure we would be chilled under these trees, but it is no such thing."

"No, indeed!" responded Sir Egbert feelingly. This was too much for Caitlin, who had to pretend to be taken with a coughing fit. She did not hoodwink Mr. Montague, however. He spuriously rushed to her assistance.

"It seems Miss Campbell has taken a chill after all! There is no help for it; we must walk in the sun from now on."

Sir Egbert's look of dismay was so ludicrous, it completely overset Caitlin's gravity. "Mr. Montague, you are shameless!" she choked. "No, no, do not offer to pound me between the shoulder blades! I shall be better directly."

Emily turned inquiring eyes upon her sister. "Do you feel cold, Caitie? I vow it is quite comfortable here in the shade."

"I am perfectly comfortable! And if Mr. Montague will stop talking nonsense I shall be more comfortable still."

Lady Serena and Captain Talgarth suddenly appeared around the bend of the path before them, walking back toward the others. Serena had the train of her riding habit looped over one arm and a hand laid upon Captain Talgarth's sleeve. Despite her proximity to the captain, she looked none-too pleased. It was clearly Captain Talgarth's idea, not Serena's, that they should rejoin the party.

Far too soon for Sir Egbert's comfort they all set off again in the direction Captain Talgarth and Lady Serena had already traversed, and since Captain Talgarth had politely drawn Sir Egbert into conversation the party regrouped slightly. Emily again took Mr. Montague's arm and Caitlin and Serena walked a little way apart. Caitlin did not like to see Serena's brow clouded, and wished very much that she could coax her friend back into a sunny humor. She began by quizzing her a little.

"Serena, how long have you known the gallant Captain Talgarth? You've kept him very dark."

Serena did smile a little at that. "Would not you?" she asked saucily. Then she sighed. "For all the good it's done me! I have known him any time these eighteen months, and he has yet to speak. What am I to do, Caitlin?"

"Eighteen months! That is certainly a period. Why did you never mention him to me?"

"Well, he was in the action at Mahidput last year, you know, and only recently returned to England. When I first became acquainted with him he was not a captain, and I was only eighteen, so he told me I must not think of him. He has the noblest nature!"

"Would your family have disapproved?"

"Oh, I daresay they would have disapproved of anyone at that time—I had seen so little of the world, you know, and wasn't precisely 'out' yet. He is the third son of Sir Humphrey Talgarth, and his mother was Lady Caroline Jevinghurst. It is a pity he is a younger son, of course, but there is nothing to object to in his birth—and he is certainly not hanging out for a rich wife, as they say. I believe his fortune to be in the neighborhood of four thousand a year, which is not contemptible."

Caitlin was aware that four thousand a year did not compare to Lady Serena's fortune, but she had to agree that Captain Talgarth could not be thought ineligible by the most exacting parent. "How long did you know him before he went to India?"

"Only six weeks. We met while he was stationed near Selcroft Hall during the autumn of 1816. And then he was away so long! I began to think I had mistaken my heart—but when I saw him again he was even handsomer than I remembered. I am sure no man could equal him. Every inch the gentleman! Why, one has only to *look* at him." Which Serena did, smiling mistily.

"Does he return your regard, do you think?"

Serena hesitated. "I was sure of it when we first knew one another—and when he returned to England he certainly lost no time in renewing our acquaintance—but lately I cannot help wondering if—well, I cannot tell! His notions of propriety are so very strict. I had hoped to coax him into walking alone with me today, but no such thing. As soon as he perceived we were out of view of the rest of the party, he insisted we walk back. He told me we would not wish to present 'too particular an appearance'—such fustian! We could hardly present too particular an appearance to suit *me*."

Caitlin was thoughtful. "On first impression, Serena, he does strike one as an extremely conscientious young man."

"Oh, yes! A very high stickler. And so *serious*! I am in despair. The more he is around me, the more I shock him, Caitlin. I cannot seem to mind my tongue, and he thinks *levity,* you know, to be so very bad. Many people feel that way, I fear. And I cannot help myself! When I laugh out loud, or make some silly jest, he often looks at me so gravely I am ready to sink with mortification."

"But your sunny nature and vivacity are exactly what one most admires in you!" Caitlin exclaimed indignantly. "You cannot wish to ally yourself with a man who would *squelch* you."

Serena sighed. "He does not seek to squelch me, precisely—just check me a little. There is nothing strange in that. I had a governess once who was forever telling me my exuberance went beyond the line of being pleasing."

"Very likely! I make no doubt you were a giggling and bumptious child! But, Serena, you are no longer a schoolroom miss. I am sure you will find a man who loves and appreciates your animation for the attractive quality it is."

Serena looked doubtful. "Do you think so? I cannot credit it! Captain Talgarth is one of those men who are drawn to timid, die-away creatures requiring guidance and support— and I will never be among them."

"Nonsense, Serena, he must admire you!" Caitlin said firmly. She could not resist adding, "Such a punctilious young man would not otherwise allow you to hang on his sleeve."

Serena brightened. "Then perhaps if I am able to school myself into more circumspect behavior, and mind my tongue, his affections will reanimate toward me."

This was disturbing. Caitlin squeezed Serena's elbow earnestly. "Do not alter yourself one jot. If a deception is necessary to attract Captain Talgarth, I promise you you will never find happiness with him."

"At any rate," declared Serena with spirit, "I shall not hang on his sleeve anymore today!" She then ruined the effect by adding: "Perhaps he will pursue me if I hold a little aloof."

The path widened as it dipped slightly downhill toward a grassy area lined with elms, and Mr. Montague strode up to join Lady Serena and Caitlin. Caitlin glanced back to see Emily walking between Sir Egbert and Captain Talgarth, who had politely slowed his steps to suit his companions' sedate pace. Sir Egbert and Emily both appeared glad to dispense with Mr. Montague's lead, whose idea of a comfortable stroll was much brisker than theirs. His energy exactly suited Serena and Caitlin, however, and as he seemed delighted to have a pretty girl on each arm the three of them were very well satisfied and soon drew far ahead of the rest of the party. Mr. Montague's high spirits restored Serena's ebullience faster than Caitlin's sympathy had been able to, and the three of them were so merry that they hardly noticed the passage of time until a clock was heard striking three in the distance.

"Good heavens!" exclaimed Serena. "Whatever became of my brother? We haven't seen him for an age."

Mr. Montague shook his head disapprovingly. "Shabby, I call it," he said severely. "Not at all the thing to abandon one's guests in the middle of a party. After driving them out of town, too! Shocking bad *ton*."

Serena had known Mr. Montague all her life and refused to stand on ceremony with him. "Do be quiet, Ned!" she begged. "You never say anything to the purpose! We will have to go in search of the others."

Mr. Montague nudged Caitlin. "Runs in the family, you see," he explained. "Rag-mannered, these Kilvertons. Pack of barbarians. I have meant to speak to them about it, but from one cause or another it never seemed to be the right moment."

"I daresay your natural delicacy makes you too shy, Mr. Montague," replied Caitlin kindly. "You lack the necessary forcefulness that would make such Philistines attend to you."

Mr. Montague seemed much struck. "There is a great deal in what you say, Miss Campbell," he announced gravely. "I don't know when I've met a woman with a better understanding! Between the two of us, do you think we might bring Serena to a sense of—"

"Oh, hush, Ned, for pity's sake!" cried Serena, between laughter and exasperation. "It is past three o'clock, and you know we were to start back to London by three-thirty. We shall have to turn round."

But no sooner had they turned than they perceived Lord Kilverton waving to them from the edge of another wooded area to the south. When they joined him he announced he had left the others resting in the shade and come to fetch the energetic threesome back to the rest of the party. Serena and Mr. Montague had begun a mock argument on the rival merits of elms and beeches, so Lord Kilverton and Miss Campbell fell into step together. This caused Caitlin's heart to beat uncomfortably fast, but as he seemed a trifle preoccupied she plucked up her courage and reminded herself of her earlier determination to treat him just as she would anyone else, thus demonstrating her complete indifference to his company. Time to begin.

She tilted her head up, regarding him from under the brim of her chip-straw hat. He was gazing abstractedly ahead with a slight crease between his brows. "I haven't thanked you, Lord Kilverton, for including me in your delightful driving party," she began politely.

He immediately came back from wherever his thoughts had taken him, and looked down into the face turned up to his. Amusement lit his eyes. "You forget, Miss Campbell, that I did not include you in my party."

Nonplussed, she returned her attention to the path and sought in vain for a suitable reply. "I beg your pardon!" she said stiffly.

"Oh, no need!" he replied kindly. "It is Serena who owes me the apology." Indignation rose in her, and she did not trust her voice. This allowed him to blandly continue.

"Do you admire Richmond Park, Miss Campbell?"

"Yes!" she replied shortly, in a suffocated voice. "I have enjoyed myself very much—until now!"

His shoulders shook. "I wonder why it gives me such pleasure to goad you?" he mused.

"Perhaps it is your overbearing disposition, Lord Kilverton!

Or a natural meanness of spirit that leads you to take pleasure in others' discomfiture."

"No, I don't think so," he replied, with unimpaired calm. "For I do not generally take pleasure in others' discomfiture. It is only *your* discomfiture, Miss Campbell, that I find so irresistible."

At this, all her resolve vanished, and with it her composure. Impossible to behave with indifference! Impossible to pretend their first meeting never happened! Her eyes flashed and her voice shook.

"As you hardly know me, Lord Kilverton, I can only ascribe your intolerable manners, and the disgusting familiarity of your language, to a desire to rub my nose in an incident I wish with all my heart could be forgotten. Such unhandsome conduct does you no credit, believe me! A gentleman would never take such advantage of a lady unless he held her in the greatest contempt imaginable. But I have done nothing to earn your contempt! The liberties you took with me were—as you must know!—taken without my consent. I did not encourage you! I did not assist you! I did not welcome your advances! It is grossly unfair for you to—to *leer* at me in this insufferable fashion. To shame me, and press your advantage, when every advantage you have you took from me by force!" Her voice broke, and she angrily dashed tears from her eyes. "But it does not signify talking, after all."

She would have walked away from him at this, but he caught her arm and addressed her in a completely altered tone. "No, do not run away from me!"

She jerked her arm out of his clasp with an angry little cry, but he caught it again. "Please, Miss Campbell, you must compose yourself. You do not wish to join the others in a state that will excite comment."

She hesitated, irresolute. "Please," he said again quietly, and she allowed him to lead her a little way off the path as if to admire the view. He then produced a handkerchief and would have dried her tears for her, but she snatched it out of his hand. He said nothing, but stood quietly by as she dabbed her eyes and gave a disconsolate sniff.

"Miss Campbell, I beg your pardon from the bottom of my heart. I never meant to make you cry."

"I am not crying!" she announced, in a voice of loathing. "That is a weakness I despise! It is just that I am so angry!"

"You have every reason to be angry."

"Your conduct toward me, Lord Kilverton, has been reprehensible from the instant you encountered me!"

"Yes, it has."

"I cannot imagine what possessed you, to seize a stranger in the middle of the street and use her so."

"Shocking!"

"And then when you encountered me again, to pursue your advantage so rudely! You should have pretended not to recognize me."

"Very true! My conduct was most ungentlemanly. I am a monster."

"Well," she continued in a more mollified tone, "it may have been merely thoughtlessness on your part. I daresay you did not stop to consider what my feelings must be."

"No, Miss Campbell, do not let me off so lightly—for I *should* have considered what your feelings must be! There is no acceptable excuse for my behavior. Let us agree I am the greatest beast in nature and you have suffered Turkish treatment at my hands for no reason whatsoever."

He looked so contrite she was obliged to give a watery chuckle. She handed his handkerchief back to him. "Agreed, Lord Kilverton!"

"I am relieved," he said gravely, accepting the handkerchief and offering his arm.

She took it, somewhat warily. "I do not see why you should feel relieved! I have expressed the lowest possible opinion of you."

"Yes, but I am relieved to find us in such perfect accord," he explained, leading her back to the path. She peeped up at him uncertainly, but he appeared absolutely serious. This wrung an unwilling smile from her.

"You are the strangest creature!" she remarked.

He smiled at her. "What, for enjoying harmony? Or merely for acknowledging myself to be in the wrong?" His face hardened a little, and he glanced away. "After today's experiences, it is greatly refreshing to find myself in agreement with a lady."

She thought she understood, and felt a twinge of compassion for him. "Even at the price of disparaging yourself?" she inquired lightly.

He gave a short laugh. "At any price! But you misunderstand, Miss Campbell. It is one thing to be raked deservedly over the coals by someone you have genuinely wronged, and quite another to listen to several hours of uninterrupted hogwash."

He caught himself then, coloring slightly as he realized he had said too much, but her expression was so sympathetic he gave her a slightly twisted smile. "Do not heed me, Miss Campbell. I am talking a great deal of nonsense."

"Now, how am I to take that?" she demanded in a rallying tone. "And after I very nearly accepted your apology!"

He laughed and disclaimed, but they were coming to the grove where he had left the rest of the party. Sir Egbert was seated with Lady Elizabeth, and Captain Talgarth and Emily were standing apart, conversing together with absorbed interest. Serena's peace had all-too obviously been quite cut up by this. She threw an anguished look at Caitlin and deserted Mr. Montague to run to her friend as she arrived.

"Caitlin, what am I to do?" she whispered, with an agonized look at Captain Talgarth. Her brother was uncomfortably reminded of certain criticisms expressed by Lady Elizabeth not an hour since.

"The best plan, I think, would be to stop making a cake of yourself," he recommended under his breath, and walked away to join Elizabeth and his cousin.

Caitlin could not help thinking that was very good advice, but did not wish to ruffle Serena any more than Lord Kilverton had already done. She took Serena firmly by the arm. "Now, Serena, you are making a great piece of work about nothing," she said bracingly. "If you are thrown into torment every time Captain Talgarth converses with another lady, your life will be a misery. Recollect that he has not declared himself to you. Until he does, you must not expose yourself in this fashion."

Serena took a deep breath. "You are right," she said with difficulty, and returned to Mr. Montague with a great show of gaiety. She surprised that gentleman a good deal by clinging affectionately to his arm all the way back to where the carriages were waiting, and allowing him to throw her up into her saddle. Unfortunately, her little charade was quite wasted on Captain Talgarth. She turned to discover him resting one arm on the barouche, animatedly describing some military adventure to Emily. Emily was hanging breathlessly on the captain's every word.

Serena found herself possessed by a very unladylike impulse to scratch Miss Emily Campbell's eyes out. Fortunately she controlled this natural desire and maintained a rather forced air of unconcern. Mr. Montague, however, was not deceived. He leaned confidentially against her knee as she gathered the reins purposefully in her competent hands.

"Dished, Serena?" he murmured provocatively, his eyes twinkling. She flushed to the roots of her hair.

"I don't know what you mean!" she snapped. Knowing he was all too ready to explain, she hastily urged Nellie into a trot and left him laughing softly behind her.

Caitlin and Sir Egbert slowly approached the barouche, she listening politely to his ponderous description of a topiary he had once seen, but when Kilverton's groom brought the curricle round she was distracted. One of the high-stepping bays reached out his long neck as if inviting her to stroke his glossy face. "Oh, you beauty!" she cooed to him as he nibbled delicately on her glove. Lord Kilverton strolled up, raising an eyebrow.

"Admiring my cattle, Miss Campbell?" he inquired pleasantly.

"Oh, yes!" she exclaimed. "I never saw a pair of bays more beautifully matched, sir."

"Very pretty! Very pretty indeed!" agreed Sir Egbert affably. "There are few sights so agreeable as a well-matched team of English horses."

Kilverton wanted very much to ask what attributes Sir Egbert considered peculiar to English horses, but resisted the temptation. "Would you care to try their paces, Miss Campbell? I would be honored to take you up in my curricle."

She turned to him, surprised. "I would like it above all things. But—do you mean now?"

"Why not?"

"Well, surely—Lady Elizabeth—"

"You need not consider Lady Elizabeth. She has ridden in my curricle any number of times. No one will object to your riding back to London with me."

Sir Egbert goggled a little, and proved Kilverton wrong by expostulating feebly. "Richard, dear boy, you cannot have considered! I am persuaded Lady Elizabeth is expecting you to drive her. You do not wish to slight your fiancée!"

A shade of annoyance crossed Lord Kilverton's face. Slighting his fiancée was, in fact, exactly what he wished to do. He hoped it might teach Lady Elizabeth a much-needed lesson.

"Lady Elizabeth has said she has the headache. I will be grateful to Miss Campbell if she gives up her seat in the barouche so my fiancée may ride home in greater comfort."

"Oh, poor Lady Elizabeth!" cried Emily, overhearing. "Caitie, you must ride with Lord Kilverton in the curricle. You know you are never ill."

Lady Elizabeth had come up by this time, and was furious to learn of the way she was being summarily disposed of. Before she could command herself enough to protest, she was handed solicitously into the barouche by Captain Talgarth, who then pressed Emily's hand in parting and swung into the saddle. It was fortunate Serena was no longer present to behold Captain Talgarth's unconscious gesture and the starry-eyed smile lighting Emily's face at that moment. Sir Egbert climbed ponderously after Lady Elizabeth, still clucking and muttering, Mr. Montague took the place next to Emily, and before she knew it Caitlin was being lifted up into his lordship's curricle. Kilverton took the reins, his groom sprang up behind, and they were off at a smart trot, passing the barouche with a salute and drawing well on ahead. Captain Talgarth, meanwhile, rode off at a canter in search of Lady Serena, and Caitlin soon found herself—but for the presence of an expressionless groom—completely alone with Lord Kilverton.

Chapter X

The first mile or more was traveled in silence save for the sound of two wheels crunching on the road, a pair of horses trotting, harness creaking, and bits jingling. Caitlin kept her gaze carefully turned to the left, her hat obscuring her face so the man sitting so closely on her right could not see her color fluctuating. Absurd! she scolded herself. As if I never sat beside a man before! She wondered with a kind of feverish confusion why she was so aware of the proximity of this particular man, why the occasional brush of his coat sleeve or brief contact with the edge of his knee sent fresh waves of color to her burning cheeks. She cast about wildly in her mind for some topic of conversation that would break the awkward silence, but could not still her whirling thoughts long enough to gather her wits. As Kilverton was experiencing a similar reaction to her nearness, and was even more astonished and perplexed by his reaction than Caitlin was by hers, the silence remained unbroken for some time. Eventually Kilverton spoke, with an effort.

"Are you comfortable, Miss Campbell?"

"Oh, yes indeed!" she assured him brightly, thinking she had seldom felt less comfortable in her life. He was not to know that, however. She thankfully pursued the line of small talk he had opened. "How very well sprung this curricle is. And—and your bays are indeed beautifully matched. I had thought they matched only in appearance, but—how strongly they pull together! One is scarcely aware of the speed at which we must be traveling." She stopped abruptly, afraid she was chattering like a nervous schoolgirl.

"Thank you," he said, "I rather fancy they are a well-

matched pair." His voice was strained. They had now ex-
hausted the topic of his well-matched horses, he thought. Another pause ensued. Kilverton cleared his throat, painfully
aware—as Miss Campbell could not be—of the probable
emotions of Mullins, the groom riding behind them. Mullins
had served the Earl of Selcroft's household for nearly thirty
years and had never known the Young Master to be tongue-
tied in the presence of any lady. Mullins, of course, was far
too well-trained to smile—but his wooden countenance did
not deceive Lord Kilverton. Kilverton was fairly certain a grin
would appear and Mullins' comments would be forthcoming
the instant Miss Campbell was set down at Lynwood House.
That was the trouble with servants who had known one since
one wore short coats, he thought wryly. They could never be
induced to show a proper degree of respect!

His reflections were abruptly cut short by a loud report that
seemed to come from the woods close on their right. The shot
whistled directly over the horses' heads. One of the horses
gave a terrified scream and the animals jumped forward, trying to bolt. Kilverton reacted immediately, and would have
succeeded in holding them had a second shot not sounded.
The second shot catapulted the horses into headlong flight,
galloping wildly down the road.

Caitlin clung to the seat as the curricle rocked and jolted
and Mullins and Kilverton shouted unintelligibly to one another. Kilverton fought grimly to regain control, and even in
her terror, part of her mind was grateful to have a man of his
skill and strength at the reins. He was succeeding—the horses
were still galloping, but clearly were responding to his mas-
tery—the curricle was slowing—when suddenly it gave a peculiar lurch. Time slowed to a dreamy crawl as Caitlin saw
the wheel beneath her disconnect from the vehicle and fantas-
tically, incredibly, spin away and roll toward the fields like a
child's hoop.

The carriage seemed to be tipping in slow motion, dipping
her toward the ground. The road looked to her to be inex-
orably rising up to meet her, and simultaneously flying along
beneath her at a dizzying rate. With a cry of fear and horror,

Caitlin began to climb up the crazily tipping curricle, instinctively trying to shift her weight to the higher side.

Mullins' strong arm reached down and grabbed her from the right, and Kilverton, still fighting with the reins, was reaching for her left hand when the now-wheelless left side of the curricle touched down. The carriage immediately spun sideways and began to drag. There was a sound of splintering wood, a hoarse shout from Kilverton, a despairing cry from Caitlin, and as Mullins' hand slipped from her arm she felt herself flung from the carriage.

The force of the curricle's sideways snap hurled her into the neat hedgerows bordering the road. The jar was sickening and she cried out in pain as the bushes broke beneath her, stabbing her in several places and badly tearing the delicate muslin of her gown. Her senses swam momentarily while she regained her breath. She was afraid to move. She heard the horses plunging to a standstill and watched dazedly as the broken curricle dragged to a halt not far from her.

Mullins had also apparently fallen from the curricle, for she saw him scrambling to his feet in the road. To her helpless horror, Mullins swayed for a moment in the center of the road, then collapsed back down into the dust. She saw Kilverton sprawled across the top of the curricle—what had been its right side panel—still clutching the reins and hanging on somehow by gripping with his knees. The instant the curricle stopped moving he twisted to look behind him, slid off the side, abandoned the horses, and hastened back to Mullins and Miss Campbell. It was clear the horses were unlikely to go anywhere whether their heads were held or not. Caitlin struggled to free herself so she could also run to Mullins but cried out as the bushes stabbed her anew, and Kilverton, with a cursory glance at the prostrate groom, ran to her.

"Do not move, Miss Campbell!" he ordered, his voice sharp with anxiety. She obeyed him and he bent over her, still gasping from his exertions and his face white with strain. "Are you badly hurt?"

"I think not," she replied uncertainly. "But I cannot get out of these bushes." Kilverton disengaged the worst of the brambles, pulled her free, and helped her stand. There was a wrenching pain in her left wrist where she had tried to break her fall, and there scarcely seemed to be an inch of her that was not scratched or bruised, but she knew there were no bones broken and she had somehow escaped serious injury. Had she been thrown onto the surface of the road, or if this portion of the road had been walled with stone rather than lined with greenery, she supposed she might have been killed. The thought made her feel rather sick.

Their first concern was to discover what had happened to Mullins. They limped to where Mullins lay and found he was unconscious, with a dreadful pallor that struck fear into Caitlin's heart.

"Oh, the poor man!" she cried. "Ought we to move him, do you think? Would it hurt him?" She shaded her eyes with her hand—her hat had disappeared—and looked frantically about them for help. Not a soul was to be seen; beyond the hedgerows the fields and woods stretched peacefully in every direction.

Kilverton's look of strain deepened. "We cannot leave him in the road," he replied. He knelt beside the inert groom and examined him with deft fingers. "I cannot find a head injury, but as I am not a surgeon that means little," he said finally. "He has certainly injured his right leg and perhaps—I cannot tell—his left arm."

"Oh!" whispered Caitlin remorsefully. "He was pulling me with his left arm!"

"Do not distress yourself, Miss Campbell," said Kilverton quickly. "If there is blame to be assigned here, it is mine. I was driving." He struggled to his feet and Caitlin noticed for the first time a red stain spreading on his left shoulder.

"You are hurt!" she exclaimed. He glanced briefly down and frowned with annoyance.

"It's nothing," he said shortly. "But the devil of it is, I shan't be able to move Mullins without assistance."

"I will move him," said Caitlin stoutly. He looked her over doubtfully, and a reluctant grin momentarily dispelled the grimness of his expression. Miss Campbell had lost her hat, her parasol, and one shoe, and stood before him in a torn and dusty gown. She was bleeding from a dozen scratches and her bright hair, tangled with leaves and twigs, was tumbling in a heap around her dirty face. Despite the determination blazing in her eyes, hers was a pale and woebegone figure. One had to admire her spunk, but she did not present the appearance of one who was capable of moving a cat, let alone a well-grown man, to the side of the road.

"Unnecessary!" he told her. "If no other travelers pass us, the barouche will arrive in a few minutes. I only hope Mullins remains unconscious until he can be moved. I am sure it will hurt him very much to be lifted. His leg is swelling fast. If it is not broken, it is very badly sprained." Kilverton loosened Mullins' neckcloth as he spoke, and tried to dispose his limbs more comfortably.

"Do you think we should remove his boot?" asked Caitlin.

"I think not, unless we can find something to use as a splint."

"Then if there is nothing further we can do for him, we ought to do something for that shoulder of yours."

"Nonsense! Stay here a moment with Mullins. I am going to look at my horses," stated Kilverton. She stopped him by the simple expedient of catching his left sleeve, which caused him to halt in his tracks, wincing with pain.

"Your horses can wait, sir," she said quietly. "If the blood has seeped through your driving coat, your injury is bleeding very freely. It must be looked at and bandaged as best we can." The look of impatient dismissal on his face caused her to lift her chin at him. "If you do not wish to oblige me in this, I hope you mean to stretch out next to Mullins! I cannot be expected to tend two insensible men lying at opposite ends of the road."

He laughed unwillingly. "All right, ma'am, we shall see what needs to be done." They sat on a grassy space at the side of the road and she helped him to gingerly remove his driving coat and the morning coat beneath it, exposing a blood-soaked shirt. Worried, she discarded her ruined gloves and tore with frantic fingers at his beautifully tied cravat.

"Here! What are you doing?" he demanded indignantly.

"Sir, we must remove your shirt from this shoulder! It is the strangest thing, for there is no tear whatsoever in the shirt and yet your flesh is torn beneath it. What can it mean?"

"It only means that I have reinjured a wound I thought was healing nicely." He sighed, reluctantly helping her to unwrap the cravat and open his shirt. "I am not surprised. I had expected it to ache a bit after such a long drive, but I own I did not allow for the additional stresses involved in fighting a runaway team, ditching my curricle, and pulling my companion out of a shrubbery."

When Caitlin saw the gash she was appalled. "My lord, you must sit perfectly still," she urged. "I don't know what you were about, to run all over the road and offer assistance to me. Why, my hurts are nothing to this!"

She picked up and discarded his mangled cravat as too dirty, then hunted swiftly through the pockets of his morning coat for a handkerchief. The only one she found was the one she had used to dry her tears at Richmond Park. How long ago that seemed! When she saw there was no other clean cloth anywhere to hand, she unhesitatingly lifted the torn flounce of her gown and began to tear her gauze petticoat into strips. Kilverton was touched, but protested.

"Miss Campbell! You really must not! Stop that at once!" he ordered, trying to struggle upright. She placed her hand firmly on his chest.

"I must and shall. If you are not to bleed to death before my eyes, we must staunch the blood somehow."

"But you will ruin your petticoat!"

Caitlin shot him a look of exasperation, then returned to her task. "If you have a better suggestion I will be glad to hear it! If you do not, pray do not hinder me."

He did not have a better suggestion, so reluctantly surrendered. She ripped and tore at her expensive petticoat in a very businesslike manner, evidently not stopping to think how she was exposing her shapely ankles to his interested gaze. With some difficulty, for she could not turn her left wrist, she packed the wound with the clean gauze and bound it firmly with his handkerchief. He watched her, a strange little half smile on his face. The sunlight behind her made a nimbus of her hair. She was so beautiful, he thought, she would have looked like a vision from heaven—had it not been for the smudges on her face, and the look of fierce concentration that clenched her soft mouth into a thin line and drew her brows straightly over her worried eyes.

"You are a heroine, Miss Campbell," he murmured ruefully. "Now let us tear up something of mine, to fashion a sling for that wrist of yours."

She laughed a little, pushing the hair back from her brow. "We will do no such thing." She stood and walked back to where Mullins still lay. "Thank God!" she cried eagerly. "His color is returning."

"Unlucky for Mullins," observed Kilverton. "The poor fellow must be coming round."

As if to prove this, Mullins gave a soft groan and his brows contracted in pain. Caitlin moved swiftly to shield his face from the sun, and bent softly over him. She spoke with a note of gentle authority.

"You must not try to move, Mr. Mullins. There has been an accident with the curricle. You have only to lie quietly for a few minutes and not trouble yourself."

"What happened?" he inquired dazedly.

Kilverton rose and came to him, ignoring the pain in his shoulder and Caitlin's minatory frown. "Some fool of a hunter let off a shot too near the road," he said cheerfully. "The horses bolted, and a wheel came off. That is all."

For the first time, it occurred to Caitlin to wonder what did, in fact, happen. She felt a faint prickle of fear as she remembered there were not one, but two shots. Her troubled gaze met Kilverton's, but he shook his head warningly at her and returned his attention to his groom. Clearly their task at the moment was to bring Mullins whatever ease they could.

"The horses?" Mullins said faintly.

"Strained fetlock. Nothing serious," Kilverton assured him. Caitlin knew he had not had an opportunity to examine the horses, but held her tongue when she saw some of the worry leave Mullins' face.

The sound of an approaching carriage heralded the barouche's arrival and Caitlin turned eagerly to greet its appearance around the last bend in the road. It was coming on as fast as the coachman dared drive it, and all the occupants were leaning anxiously forward, Emily half standing and clinging to the side in her apprehension. Some way back they had come upon Caitlin's parasol lying in the dust and Kilverton's curly-brimmed beaver rolling along the side of the road, and for the past half mile they had been fearing a hideous sight round every bend.

When they arrived at the actual scene of the accident Emily instantly burst into tears of mingled distress and relief. Lord Kilverton and Miss Campbell certainly appeared battered, but both were on their feet, and although the curricle was smashed the horses had survived. Mullins was in a great deal of pain, but clearly not in mortal danger. Both horses were lame, but although they would have to be led there seemed to be no permanent damage done. Everyone was quick to agree that their escape from a worse fate was miraculous.

Lady Selcroft's coachman saw to Kilverton's horses while Emily spread the coachman's driving coat on the grassy bank to receive Mullins. Mr. Montague and Sir Egbert carried Mullins to the side of the road to dispose him as comfortably as they could on the driving coat. At this point, Captain Talgarth and Serena arrived on the scene, having ridden back to discover what had become of the party. Captain Talgarth immediately rode off to the nearest inn to summon help and a surgeon for Mullins. Serena offered to ride back and retrieve whatever property she could find that had been lost in the horses' flight, and triumphantly returned with everything except for Caitlin's missing sandal.

During all the commotion, Lady Elizabeth maintained a rigid silence and did not budge from her seat in the barouche.

It was decided that Lady Selcroft's coachman would stay with Mullins and Lord Kilverton's horses until Captain Talgarth returned with help, while Lord Kilverton and Miss Campbell should be conveyed back to town as quickly as possible in the barouche. Kilverton thought he also ought to stay with Mullins, but after a short argument he finally consented to take a place in the barouche next to Miss Campbell. They were seated together so they might both face forward, which Emily insisted would be more comfortable for them. This finally displaced Lady Elizabeth, who now had to sit beside

Emily in the backward-facing seats. The barouche was to be driven to London by Mr. Montague, with Sir Egbert riding next to him on the box and Serena keeping Nellie close beside them. And as soon as they were under way Mr. Montague demanded to know what had happened.

Now that the shock of the accident was over, Caitlin was beginning to feel very stiff, sore, and ill, and Kilverton also looked as though he would be glad to rest instead of talk. She did not wonder at it that he answered his friend in as few words as possible, using much the same language he had used to Mullins.

"Someone hunting in the woods too close to the road. He let off a round just as we drove past, my bays bolted, and a wheel came off."

Mr. Montague slewed round on the box to regard his friend for a moment. Kilverton returned his gaze blandly enough, but Caitlin, her nerves on the stretch, thought there was some message being passed between the two men. Mr. Montague turned to the front again, replying in a gruff tone that sounded to Caitlin as if he was hiding some strong emotion.

"Oh, aye! Could have happened to anyone!" was all he said. She could make nothing of this, but something was clearly troubling Mr. Montague and she suddenly realized something was troubling her as well.

"There were two shots," she said faintly. "And they were fired across the road, my lord. How are we to account for that?"

The barouche lurched as Mr. Montague unaccountably dropped his hands. "Mind your team, Neddie," recommended Kilverton affably. "I've no wish to repeat today's experience."

Mr. Montague recovered the reins, muttering something under his breath, but Emily reached out comforting hands to Caitlin. "Oh, Caitie, how dreadful!" she cried. "How frightened you must have been! I would have fainted dead away."

Caitlin smiled affectionately at her sister. "I should have fainted, of course, but I did not wish to put Lord Kilverton to additional trouble," she explained. "He seemed to have quite enough on his hands."

"Thank you," said Kilverton with an appreciative grin, and Caitlin bowed politely.

It was Sir Egbert's turn to slew round on the box, which he did with difficulty. "Did you say two shots, Miss Campbell?" he inquired, a note of indignation in his voice. Upon her assenting, he faced forward again, continuing in tones of strong disapproval. "Demmed careless! I never heard of such a thing. D'you mean to tell me this fellow made off afterwards with nary a word to you? Never came forward to offer assistance? Bless my soul! These poachers! Something ought to be done about 'em."

Caitlin seized gratefully on Sir Egbert's interpretation of the events. "Yes, it must have been a poacher! That would account for his not coming forward," she said, relieved. Her brows puckered again. "But surely any game would be in the wood. Why do you suppose he fired across the road?"

"Trying to bag my horses, perhaps," murmured Kilverton. "After all, several disinterested persons have complimented me on those bays. I would have thought they were worth more alive than dead—so that trapping them would be preferable to shooting them—but I daresay he was hungry."

Caitlin choked, then winced as the laughter hurt her bruised ribs. She regarded Lord Kilverton with a fulminating eye. "Lord Kilverton!" she chided him. "Are you able to find humor in *every* situation?"

He appeared to think deeply for a moment. "Only the humorous ones," he explained. This silly remark caused Caitlin Campbell and Richard Kilverton to smile at each other, and a strange phenomenon immediately occurred. The rest of the party, the events of the day, and the entire world seemed to swiftly recede, leaving them completely alone together in some far-off place. They floated there for a timeless and dangerous moment.

"Disgraceful!" ejaculated Lady Elizabeth, suddenly recalling them to the planet by breaking her long silence. Her voice shook with suppressed passion. She was sitting rigidly upright, averting her eyes to stare determinedly past Kilverton at the road unwinding behind them. Kilverton, Caitlin, and even

Emily blinked at her in surprise. She seemed to be laboring under a great deal of emotion.

Lady Elizabeth had had a trying day. She had spent most of it in fruitless argument with her fiancé, and had been deeply dismayed to discover how completely incompatible their views were on almost every subject. On the return to London, Richard had humiliated her by rejecting her company in favor of Miss Campbell's. Next she had very nearly witnessed a shocking curricle accident, and had been forced to behold a repulsive scene involving a quantity of blood, which was naturally upsetting to a delicately nurtured female. But the crowning moment of horror had come when the barouche pulled up to the scene of the accident and Lady Elizabeth had had to avert her eyes from the sight of Richard's bare neck and partially exposed shoulder. Not only was the exhibition of so much male skin extremely embarrassing, it was all too obvious whose shameless hands had bared her fiancé's shoulder, whose hands had bandaged that wound! Mullins was prostrate on the ground; it positively *leaped* to the understanding that Miss Campbell had taken it upon herself to minister to Richard's hurts. Also, that brazen young woman was unblushingly wearing a gown that was practically cut to ribbons in the back—and the sunlight shining through the muslin had made it all too clear that her petticoat was torn off below the knees. One had only to notice the edging of lace fluttering incongruously on Richard's bandage to instantly perceive what had become of Miss Campbell's missing petticoat. Every feeling was offended! And even though it was Lady Elizabeth's very own fiancé who had been injured, no one had stopped to consider her feelings or expressed any sympathy for her at all. The headache she had developed earlier was not improved by riding backward in the barouche, and having to give up her place to Miss Campbell—of all people!—had exacerbated her temper. Fury, chagrin, and outraged modesty had kept Lady Elizabeth silent, though stiff and white-faced, but now it seemed she was going to be treated to the spectacle of her fiancé flirting—yes, *flirting!*—with Miss Campbell, and she could remain silent no longer.

"Only a lunatic could find anything to laugh at in this intolerable situation!" Lady Elizabeth announced wrathfully. "What does it matter whether there were two shots or a dozen? The only thing that signifies now is that we are obliged to drive through town in an open carriage, to be gawked at by every fool in London. And the state your clothing is in—! Your appearance is not only bizarre, it is positively *indecent.* We will be an object of interest to everyone we pass! Under the circumstances, I consider *jocularity* to be completely uncalled-for. Really, in the worst of bad taste!"

This aspect of the situation had not occurred to Caitlin. For the first time, she looked down at herself and was appalled. One shoe and both gloves were missing, her frock was ruined, her hair had fallen down, she was hatless, scratched, and bleeding, and she could tell by Lord Kilverton's disheveled appearance that her own must be as bad or worse. "Merciful heavens!" she said faintly. "Lady Elizabeth is quite right; it is no joking matter. We must stop somewhere and tidy ourselves."

Mr. Montague was moved to expostulate. "You cannot be serious!" he exclaimed. "This is no time to consider appearances!"

"Hear, hear!" cried Serena, perched above them on her mare. "If people stare, what of it? We must get Richard home! Emily, lend Caitlin your parasol so she can hide her face if she wishes."

"Oh, of course!" agreed Emily, immediately handing it to her sister while Caitlin attempted to push her hair into some semblance of order. "What a pity your hat is torn. You may wear mine if you like, Caitie. No one will notice anything out of the ordinary."

"Perhaps my mother has a loo-mask hidden somewhere in the barouche," suggested Kilverton helpfully.

Caitlin gave a little spurt of laughter. "If so, you must wear it, not I!" she retorted. "Your bandaged shoulder is a far more spectacular sight than all my dirt and disarray. And how we are to hide that, I'm sure I don't know!"

"If my spectacular appearance begins to draw a crowd, lend me the parasol and I will engage to duck beneath it."

"Oh, do be serious, Richard!" snapped Lady Elizabeth. "If

you are all determined to proceed directly to town, we must contrive to cover that shoulder somehow." She inadvertently glanced at his half-bared shoulder as she spoke and instantly averted her eyes again, turning a little pink with embarrassment.

Sir Egbert entered unexpectedly into the discussion. "Lady Elizabeth, your concern is justified!" he declared earnestly. "Whatever adventures have befallen us this day, we must contrive, for your sake, to achieve a respectable and unremarkable appearance. We cannot expose you to the comments of the vulgar! We cannot expect you to face with equanimity the rude stares of a plebeian horde! And Miss Campbell, of course. I am sure any female would shrink from such an ordeal."

Serena interrupted him impatiently. "Pooh! Caitlin, at least, is not such a paltry creature. And, Richard, you have only to pull the lap robe up over you and pretend you are asleep. No one will see your shoulder."

This proposal generally met with favor, as Lord Kilverton was already half-reclined against the squabs and, if the truth be known, feeling unwell enough to be glad of a reason to remain there. Sir Egbert was a trifle dissatisfied, but finally pronounced it to be the best possible solution. "It may seem a bit unusual—ill-bred, you know, with ladies present—but I fancy no one will wonder excessively at it."

Kilverton drew the robe up and Caitlin reached over to tuck it round his injured shoulder. Her fingers brushed his neck, and their eyes met. She hastily returned to her seat, blushing vividly, and was careful not to look in his direction again for the remainder of the journey. She was stunned and appalled at the turn her thoughts were taking, and seized upon the hope that her state of mind was merely a reaction to the curricle accident. She had heard it said that people's thoughts and feelings often were disordered by shocks of this kind. She devoutly hoped her unruly emotions would return to her control when she recovered.

Upon returning to Lynwood House, she was very glad to go directly to bed and allow Aunt Harriet and Emily to cosset her for a day or two. Her bruises stiffened painfully overnight, and all efforts to banish thoughts of Richard Kilverton were exhausting—and unavailing. She thought of him frequently. In fact, she thought of him almost continually. And the more she thought, the lower her spirits sank.

Chapter XI

The day after the ill-fated Richmond excursion, Mr. Montague arrived on the Earl of Selcroft's doorstep at what was, for him, an unusually early hour. When ushered into Lord Kilverton's presence he found his friend lounging more-or-less comfortably in a wing chair in his father's library, engaged in looking over his morning's correspondence. At the sight of him, Kilverton glanced at the clock on the library mantelpiece and gave an exaggerated start. Mr. Montague grinned.

"Yes, you may well stare. A quarter past ten, and here I am! Nothing but the greatest concern for you, old man, could have roused me at this hour."

"I assumed, when Bradshaw announced you, that you had not yet been to bed," said Kilverton. "But as you are not in evening dress, it must be that our clock has stopped."

"Wrong on both counts!" Mr. Montague assured him, dropping onto a sofa and giving a prodigious yawn. "Had to see you," he explained.

"I perceive you have spent a sleepless night tossing on your pallet, a prey to doubts and fears, and have rushed to Mount Street at the crack of dawn to reassure yourself of my safety. Touching, Neddie! I am deeply moved."

"Stow it!" recommended Mr. Montague. He crossed one leg gracefully over the other. "By the by, I am glad to see you up and about. You must be feeling better this morning than I thought you would be."

Kilverton grinned wryly. "I am on the mend again, thank you. But my shoulder aches damnably, and the truth is I was too uncomfortable to stay in bed."

"Well, what the devil were you about, driving your curricle all over the kingdom yesterday?" Ned pointed out reasonably. "It hasn't been more than three weeks since you fought off those footpads. Might have known you'd be knocked into horsenails."

Kilverton made as if to struggle upright. "Look here, Ned!" he warned. "If you mean to read me a lecture, Bradshaw can show you the door! How the deuce was I to know there would be an accident? I was in a capital way until the horses bolted—and if you can tell me how I might have prevented that—"

"What kind of chaw-bacon do you take me for?" demanded Mr. Montague, aggrieved. "Is it likely I'd ring a peal over you? Now, Kilverton, take a damper! Here I am on an errand of mercy, visiting the invalid, and you get on your high ropes the instant I express my concern for your welfare! You must be in pretty queer stirrups after all."

"I am, a bit," admitted Kilverton, sinking back into the chair.

Ned regarded him shrewdly. "Hm! It's all very well for you to talk of me tossing on my pallet, but if you ask me, it's you who looks as if he hadn't slept. Are you going to tell me some hoaxing tale about being kept awake on a bed of pain, or shall we talk about what's really bothering you? Aye, and bothering me as well!"

For a startled moment, Kilverton wondered how his friend knew about his sudden and overwhelming desire to terminate his betrothal to Lady Elizabeth. Then he realized Ned had something quite different on his mind. "Ah," he said quietly. He set down the packet of letters and invitations in his hand, and looked quizzically at his companion. "I believe I can guess what you are about to say."

"I imagine you can," said Mr. Montague grimly. "I would be interested to know what your family makes of this shocking run of ill-luck that has been dogging you lately."

"What do you make of it?" countered Kilverton.

Mr. Montague shrugged impatiently. "I told you three weeks ago what I made of it! Good God, man, only a mutton-head could fail to see what is in the wind."

Kilverton was amused. "Yes, you were full of hints and dark warnings, as I recall. On the strength of two completely separate attacks by obvious criminals—and despite no discernible connection between the incidents—you have leapt to the conclusion that a plot exists against my life. Now I see you have come here this morning to convince me my curricle accident was somehow engineered—doubtless by the same mastermind who failed in his other two attempts! Much obliged to you, Neddie, but we do not dwell between the covers of one of Mrs. Radcliffe's romances."

Mr. Montague did not smile. "And you, on the other hand, will try to convince me such a suspicion has never crossed your mind. You won't succeed."

He watched with narrowed eyes as Lord Kilverton opened his mouth, and then shut it again. "Just so!" said Mr. Montague grimly. "You, too, have wondered."

Kilverton spread his hands deprecatingly. "But, Ned, I am the best of good fellows! Who would want to see me dead? I protest, I haven't an enemy in the world."

Ned snorted derisively. "Yes, I know you expect me to contradict you! But it's because you are, in fact, the best of good fellows that we needn't look far for a suspect. Had you pursued a more ramshackle way of life, dear boy, we might have had to sift through a dozen possibilities. As it is, only one name occurs to me. I am a little acquainted with your uncle, Kilverton—a curst rum touch! And there's nothing he'd like better than to see you underground."

Lord Kilverton sighed. "Let us have this in plain English, if you please," he said. "You are of the opinion that my Uncle Oswald would like to have me—er—removed from his path."

"Naturally. You are very much in his way."

"I have been in his way for eight-and-twenty years, but let us, by all means, agree to overlook that! You are here to tell me my uncle has been rendered desperate by the news of my impending nuptials, and is attempting to arrange a fatal accident for me before I am able to marry and produce—ah—additional impediments."

"Not to wrap it up in clean linen—yes!"

Mr. Montague appeared perfectly serious. Kilverton could

not repress a chuckle. "It won't fadge, Ned! My death does nothing for my uncle while my father is alive. Or do you suppose he means to play the same trick on both of us? Even my enterprising Uncle Oswald might find it difficult to leapfrog into the title through *two* accidental deaths. Too smoky by half!"

Mr. Montague hesitated, glancing doubtfully at his friend. He seemed to be searching for the most delicate way to voice his opinion. "I don't suppose he would go so far as to plot Lord Selcroft's death," he said finally. "But, Richard," he added gently, "do you think he would need to?"

Kilverton pondered this for a moment. "I see. You believe the shock of my death is meant to drive my father into his grave as well."

"I know you don't like to think so, but I'm afraid your sudden death might have that effect, Richard. And even if it did not—" Mr. Montague broke off, looking uncomfortable.

Kilverton quietly finished the sentence for him. "Even if the shock did not immediately carry my father off, Uncle Oswald would not have long to wait. It is common knowledge that my father's health is failing, and he cannot be expected to live many years more."

Mr. Montague nodded. "And in the meantime, with you out of the way, your uncle would be established unshakably as Selcroft's heir. His creditors would once again smile upon him, I daresay. If one were reasonably certain of inheriting the Selcroft fortune within a few years, it would be possible to live quite handsomely upon the expectation. Quite a tidy little scheme, in fact."

Kilverton frowned. "It is preposterous!"

Ned leaned forward earnestly. "Let us say, rather, it is monstrous! He may have been contemplating something of this kind for years, you know, hoping that fate would intervene on his behalf and it would not be necessary for him to act. Your betrothal has forced his hand."

Kilverton settled back in his chair as if preparing to listen to an agreeable tale. "Well, you are clearly agog to share your insights with me, and I would be loath to deprive you of any pleasure, Ned. I am willing to be entertained." His voice lowered to a conspiratorial whisper. "Pray illuminate for me the dark forces your powerful intellect detected at work during yesterday's curricle accident—but of course I must not refer to it as an 'accident'—yesterday's sinister attempt on my life, rather! I depend on you to unmask the evil machinations of my wicked uncle."

Mr. Montague grinned, but refused to be dissuaded by his friend's theatrics. "I own it doesn't sound as likely at ten o'clock in the morning as it did at dead of night!" he admitted. "But I mean to tell you what I think, and if you choose to laugh, you may. If I cannot convince you to have a care, I hope you will convince me there is no need. Either way, I'll rest easier."

Kilverton waved a languid hand. "Tell me, then. You plainly doubted my account of yesterday's events. Did my cousin's theory fail to quiet your alarms?"

"Poachers!" Mr. Montague snorted derisively. "A likely story! A dashed chuckleheaded poacher, I must say! He fires not once, but twice—in the clear light of day, within a stone's throw of the King's Road, and barely outside the grounds of a royal park. And we're to believe this fatwit is a curst bad shot, too, for instead of aiming at his game he fires across the road—again, not once, but twice! Oh, and he's also the kind of ugly customer who funks it when he's caused an accident, and leaves his victims to bleed in the road."

"Yes, a clumsy individual," agreed Kilverton meditatively. "I fancy such a man's efforts to poach are not generally crowned with success. One wonders why he did not come forth, while we were distracted with our hurts, and steal the horses. It seems absurd for him to take such pains and then leave with nothing in his sack."

Mr. Montague could not repress a grin at the picture of a rustic in gaiters stuffing Kilverton's bays into a leather sack, but again refused to be drawn from his point. "I do consider it fortunate, you know, that he did not come out to finish what he had begun. I suppose his orders did not include actually putting a bullet through your head."

"Either that, or he is a delicate, well-bred fellow; perhaps he did not care to shoot me in the presence of Miss Campbell."

"Now, that reminds me of another point I wish to make!" Mr. Montague exclaimed, again leaning forward eagerly. "It strikes me, Richard, that if the rogue had been hired in London and told to lie in ambush for a party of persons he did not know, he must have been furnished with a description of you, and Mullins, and the curricle, and the horses—but *not* Miss Campbell!"

For the first time, an arrested expression crossed Kilverton's face, and he swore softly. Mr. Montague nodded with satisfaction. "Yes, I rather thought that hadn't occurred to you!" he said, pleased. "The fellow may have had any number of instructions, but he was not absolutely certain he had the right party! Imagine his consternation when he peeked out from his hiding place and got a good look at the scene. He was told there would be a brunette beside you on the box."

Lord Kilverton stared unseeingly out the window, his mind moving swiftly. "Then once again I find myself indebted to Miss Campbell for preserving my life," he said softly. "Really, it becomes almost embarrassing."

Mr. Montague was not attending. "Richard! I say!" he exclaimed, as a sudden thought occurred to him. "If Lady Elizabeth had been riding with you, she might also have been targeted."

"Almost certainly, if we are supposing your theory about my uncle to be correct," replied Kilverton calmly. "If Uncle Oswald failed to remove me, but succeeded in removing my fiancée, his purpose would be equally well-served. Either way, my marriage is postponed indefinitely." He thought for a moment, and smiled to himself. "As far as my uncle knows, at any rate."

"Good God!" cried Mr. Montague, too much shocked by the idea of Oswald Kilverton plotting the death of Lady Elizabeth Delacourt to puzzle out the meaning of this last cryptic remark.

"But you know, Ned—again, just indulging your theory—I don't think the accomplice necessarily bungled the job. After all, had a bullet killed me there would certainly have been an inquest, and all sorts of dust kicked up. It's possible he was instructed only to frighten my horses, and was not aiming at either myself or my companion."

"He fired two shots."

"Yes, but now I recall the second shot was fired just as I was beginning to get my horses in hand. So if his purpose was to make them bolt, the first shot did not succeed. Once the second shot was fired, of course, I had no hope of controlling them."

Mr. Montague frowned over this for a moment, then shook his head. "I don't see it, Richard," he argued. "That might serve if the purpose were to frighten you, or injure you, but how could it be expected to kill you? Your uncle must know you are no mere whipster. To a man of your skill and strength, a runaway team would not guarantee an accident. And it surely would not guarantee an accident severe enough to jeopardize your life."

"You are overlooking two important points," said Kilverton thoughtfully. "If you are right that the attack on me a few weeks ago was also arranged by my uncle, he would be aware that I suffered a fairly severe shoulder injury at that time."

"By Jove, yes!" cried Mr. Montague, leaping up in his excitement. "He had good reason to believe you couldn't hold a bolting team! That also explains why he arranged the accident for the end of the day. He made sure you were already tired from a day of driving!"

While his friend took a hasty turn around the room, Kilverton placed his fingertips together and addressed his next remark to his hands. "That brings me to my second point. It was safe to assume he could frighten my horses, but he could not be sure how long it would take me to get them back under control—supposing I could control them at all. If I happened to be stronger than he bargained for, his scheme would come to nothing." He kept his voice carefully neutral. "Perhaps, under the circumstances, he took steps to ensure that my curricle could not withstand more than a few seconds of high speed."

Mr. Montague halted in his perambulations. "The wheel!" he gasped.

Lord Kilverton nodded pensively. "The wheel," he agreed softly. "I own, I feel rather uncomfortable about that wheel. I am not a fanciful fellow, Ned, but I am almost tempted to suspect foul play."

"I should jolly well think you might!" exclaimed Mr. Montague, appalled. He sank back onto the sofa and stared, unseeing, into the fire. "I can't imagine why it didn't strike me before! A dashed unlikely thing to happen of itself, by Jove! He must have hired this fellow to loosen the nuts while we were at Richmond Park, then lie in wait for your curricle, and—why, this is beyond everything!" Ned struck a fist fiercely into the palm of his hand. "If you are not convinced, Kilverton, I am. Your uncle must be brought to book."

Kilverton shook his head, smiling faintly. "We have no evidence."

"Rot! Send someone to examine the curricle. You'll have your precious evidence soon enough."

"Evidence of what? That the wheel came off? It will be difficult to prove the nuts were loosened, and impossible to bring it home to my uncle! What a fool I would look, hurling such an ill-founded accusation at him! I don't propose to make such a cake of myself."

"But you are in danger, do you not agree?"

Kilverton frowned wearily. "No," he replied quietly. "I have wondered, of course—but I tell myself it is absurd. I ask you, Ned, even if my uncle wished my death—a most uncomfortable supposition—how could he ever bring it off without suspicion falling upon himself?"

"He couldn't!" said Ned positively, ticking the facts off on his fingers. "His reputation is unscrupulous, he is generally more feared than liked around town, it is common knowledge he is estranged from every other member of your family, it is also common knowledge he has been under the hatches for years, and your death puts him next in line for both title and fortune. His name will be the first on everyone's lips if it comes to light you have been murdered. But, you know, if he succeeds in making your death appear accidental, or the result of a random crime, it will never be investigated as a murder. People may suspect whatever they wish—he will still inherit."

Kilverton's brows climbed, and he laughed unwillingly. "You are very persuasive! Now if you will tell me how my uncle knew I would be driving my curricle to Richmond yesterday, I will congratulate you! He couldn't possibly have had a hand in yesterday's adventure. Do you suppose Sir Egbert divulged the details of my party to his father? That's a bird that won't fly, Ned! My cousin and my uncle are far from intimate—in fact, I believe they would not be on speaking terms if my cousin did not have such a pious regard for filial obligation. Sir Egbert's father is a constant thorn in his puritanical flesh! I have often thought he would dearly love to cut my uncle's acquaintance—but alas, the idea offends Egbert's strict notions of propriety. Can one imagine the respectable Egbert eagerly helping his detestable father to acquire a title through fair means or foul?"

"It's a title he would eventually inherit, remember." But Mr. Montague looked doubtful even as he spoke.

A gleam of speculative interest lit Kilverton's face for a moment; then he sighed regretfully. "No, I'm afraid I must acquit my worthy cousin of conspiring with his father to bring about my demise. Not even for the sake of his own inheritance! A pity—the picture it conjures up is almost irresistible. But the thought of Oswald Kilverton as the Earl of Selcroft would be nearly as repugnant to Egbert as it is to me. Vice rewarded, in fact! Every feeling revolts!" He laughed ruefully. "You see where this leaves your theory, Ned? My uncle did not know about my expedition to Richmond yesterday. So how could he have planned an ambush?"

Mr. Montague looked uncomfortable. "Well, I'm afraid this is the very thing I came to tell you," he explained. "Just as I was falling asleep last night, it hit me. No need for Sir Egbert to divulge anything about your driving party. Your Uncle Oswald had it from me!"

Kilverton closed his eyes for a pregnant moment. "Ned!" he uttered faintly. "Can it be possible? Have I been mistaken in you all these years?"

"Very likely!" retorted Ned. "Now stop blathering and listen to me, for I was never more serious in my life! I was in White's the other day and someone happened to invite me to some rubbishing breakfast or other, and the date fixed for it was yesterday. Well, I told him I was engaged to drive to Richmond with a party, and I'm dashed certain I mentioned the party was of your devising. I may have said more; I don't precisely recall. And what occurred to me as I was dropping off last night was that your uncle had been standing with a party of his cronies just behind me at the time. That fairly flummoxed me, you can imagine! I don't know how I can have been so careless."

"I daresay you are not much in the habit yet of suspecting murderous plots being hatched everywhere you go," said Kilverton soothingly. "Pray do not blame yourself! I am sure you will approach even the sacrosanct portals of White's with the deepest caution and cunning from now on."

"Well, you may choose to laugh, but I cannot! He may have been listening, you know—he was with that prosy old bore, Omberfield, and it would not be wonderful if his attention had wandered. Besides, if it has become an object with him to plot against your life, he must be on the lookout for information about your movements. Now, consider, Richard! He knows I would be the very person most likely to drop such information—so he places himself behind me expressly to overhear just such a tidbit—nothing easier! Your uncle probably knew all about your precious scheme to drive to Richmond, and once he knew that, it was obvious you'd take your curricle. The matter then arranges itself—d'you see?"

"No, I do not see! My dear Ned, it cannot be a simple matter to arrange the details of a murder attempt in two or three days."

"You forget that if he has attempted it twice before, he already has accomplices in his employ. I expect having them ready to hand saves one a great deal of time," Mr. Montague argued. "And you should be jolly glad he had to act in a hurry! If he'd been able to plan more carefully, or find a more skillful hireling, we might not be having this conversation."

"A pleasant thought!" remarked Kilverton. "How kind of you to stop by when I am not feeling well, and cheer me in this fashion."

Mr. Montague gave a short laugh. "Yes, I know you are a hen-hearted creature whose spirits are constantly in need of support! Now, Kilverton, I wish you will heed me. You must be more careful, dear fellow, you really must."

Kilverton regarded his friend with tolerant amusement. "What do you suggest I do, Ned?" he inquired. "Surround myself with bodyguards? Never step out of the house? Have all my dishes tasted before I touch them? Be reasonable, man, be reasonable! I have no real grounds to suspect anything, you know—I have merely suffered a series of stupid accidents."

Mr. Montague wasted the next half hour in a vain attempt to convince his friend to take their suspicions seriously. Kilverton alternately indulged him, argued with him, and laughed at him, and the end of it was that Ned departed in a mood of extreme dissatisfaction.

He hesitated for a moment outside Lord Selcroft's door. Mr. Montague was a creature of impulse. He suddenly recalled Oswald's proclivity for the old-fashioned art of the duel, and inspiration seized him.

He did not stop to consider the consequences; he suffered no qualm of conscience; it did not even occur to him to be afraid. He was convinced that Oswald Kilverton cherished murderous designs on his nephew's life, and if Richard Kilverton would not put a stop to his uncle's plots, by God, Edward Montague would! In fact, ridding the world of Oswald Kilverton appeared to him in the light of a public service.

Mr. Montague set out with a purposeful stride toward White's.

Chapter XII

Before the astonished gaze of several fashionable gentlemen, Mr. Montague was attempting to offend the Honorable Oswald Kilverton by insulting him in every way his fertile imagination suggested.

Edward Montague was known to be a sunny-tempered, easygoing fellow, not in the least quarrelsome. This rendered his behavior so baffling that it gave even Oswald Kilverton pause. In short, Mr. Montague—unused to picking fights with anyone—overplayed his part. Oswald, watching Mr. Montague with a detached and bemused air, gently and skillfully deflected every affront. Ned, frustrated, eventually announced a spurious belief that Mr. Kilverton had won his last rubber of whist through somehow fuzzing the cards.

This caused a general exclamation of disapproval, exasperation, and protest. Several members suggested in no uncertain terms that Montague be encouraged to go somewhere and sleep it off. Lord Omberfield, much shocked, objected feebly. "Really, Montague, you go too far. This is no backstreet hell. You're at *White's,* dear boy! The best of good company! What are you about?"

Mr. Montague then folded his arms across his chest with what he hoped was a sneer. "Does Mr. Kilverton deny it?" he demanded.

Oswald Kilverton stood calmly in the center of a knot of excited persons gesticulating and arguing around him with varying degrees of heat. He was a tall, saturnine gentleman who retained a definite air of the previous century in his elegant languor and meticulous dress. Preserving his haughty detachment, he closed his eyes for a moment as if pained. He opened them again.

"Naturally I deny it, Mr. Montague," he said gently. "And I would be very much interested in hearing your response to Lord Omberfield's uncharacteristically intelligent question. What, in fact, are you about?"

This threw Mr. Montague momentarily off his stride. He resorted to bluster. "I suppose a man may take exception to the presence of a *sharpster* in his club!"

Mr. Kilverton appeared bored. "Undoubtedly. Just as a man may take exception to the presence in his club of an ill-conditioned, boisterous puppy possessing neither manners nor sense."

Mr. Montague pounced eagerly. "I take your meaning, Kilverton!" he exclaimed. "You refer to me, in fact, as an ill-conditioned puppy!"

"Did I say so?" queried Oswald in feigned surprise. "I feel sure you are mistaken, my dear Montague. I spoke generally, I assure you. I would never so far forget myself as to utter disparagements of a fellow member of White's. And to his face! While actually at White's! No, I am sure no one—however ill-bred—would do such a thing. It is impossible; you really must acquit me."

"Aha!" cried Ned, doggedly pursuing. "Now I am ill-bred, am I? Do you expect me to let that pass?"

A friend of Mr. Montague's by the name of Featherstone stepped into the fray at this point. As he was not in Ned's confidence on this matter, he had no idea that he was spoiling the soup. He struggled through the knot of men gathered round the combatants, and tugged furiously at Mr. Montague's sleeve.

"Expect you to let it pass? I go further, Ned—I dashed well expect you to apologize!" announced Mr. Featherstone, incensed. "What the devil do you mean by all this rigmarole? Never saw you in m'life with the malt above the water before noon!"

Oswald turned courteously to Mr. Featherstone. "Mr. Montague is not inebriated, Featherstone," he explained kindly. "He is merely attempting to offer me an intolerable insult, thus forcing me to issue him a challenge. His purpose in doing so, I will admit, has me puzzled. I am hoping he will enlighten me, however."

Mr. Featherstone stared at Ned in the liveliest astonishment. "Well, I call it dashed peculiar!" he exclaimed. "Never knew him to do such a thing before."

"Here, Featherstone, what business is it of yours?" demanded Mr. Montague, harassed. He twitched his sleeve out of his friend's suddenly slack grip. "Just leave well enough alone, can't you?"

"No, that's just what I can't do," said Featherstone unexpectedly. "What I mean is—friend of mine! Can't let you go about making a figure of yourself all over town. Besides, old fellow, Kilverton's the devil of a swordsman, you know. Cool customer, too. You've never been out before, have you? Really, I can't be expected to encourage you to meet him! Stands to reason. And don't go telling me you'd want pistols. I've seen you shoot at Manton's, Ned! I ain't going to let you stand up for Kilverton to blow a hole through you—"

Oswald's shoulders shook with silent laughter. "But I protest, I have no desire to blow a hole through Mr. Montague!"

"Yes, that's all very well—" began Featherstone, but Mr. Montague interrupted him wrathfully.

"Featherstone, I'll thank you to let me manage my own affairs! Do you imagine I am afraid to meet Kilverton?"

"No, upon my honor!" gasped Featherstone, distressed to think his words had been misconstrued. "Nothing to say against your courage, Montague. Pluck to the backbone!"

Oswald Kilverton touched Lord Omberfield's sleeve at this point. "Let us quit the room, my friend, and allow Montague and Featherstone to hash this matter out between them. I perceive I am infinitely *de trop*." Mr. Kilverton bowed gracefully and would have gone, had not Mr. Montague leaped desperately forward to bar the way.

"No, I say! Kilverton, I insulted you—or, rather, you insulted me—" he stopped, exasperated, and turned to Featherstone. "You've muddled me!" he exclaimed. "Where was I?"

Oswald regarded him amusedly, but a sharp gleam of watchful suspicion appeared in his hooded eyes. "I believe you were about to explain yourself, Montague," he said softly, a faint smile curling his lips. "Your conduct is really most extraordinary. I, for one, am unable to account for it. I await your explanation with intense interest."

Oswald's air was languid, his expression weary, but his eyes, half veiled by lazy lids, were cold with intelligence and malice. They never left Mr. Montague's face. "I hope you do not cherish an ambition to meet me on the field of honor, Mr. Montague. I really hope you do not. I fear you are destined to be disappointed. You will never realize that—particular—ambition." His teeth bared in the briefest flash of a smile. "You must appreciate my position, dear boy. I cannot issue—or, for that matter, accept—such a challenge. You are considerably younger than myself, you know, and you are—correct me if I am mistaken—one of my nephew's satellites. His closest friend, in fact, are you not? How shocking it would be for us to quarrel! Whatever else may be said of me, I hope I have never been accused of bad *ton.*"

Mr. Montague stared at him helplessly. "You will not meet me?"

"No, Mr. Montague, I will not."

"I insulted you!"

"Then I forgive you."

"But you insulted me!"

"Then I apologize. Come, Montague, if you continue this absurd behavior you will only be made to appear foolish, you know."

Mr. Montague looked round at the assembled company. Quite a number of avid gentlemen had crowded into the room, and all were regarding him with varying degrees of amusement, annoyance, or interest. Mr. Montague was suddenly assailed by all the embarrassment natural to a man of his upbringing finding himself the center of such attention. His impulse was to bow himself out with whatever dignity he still possessed, but then he thought of Richard Kilverton's danger and a gust of genuine wrath shook him.

"Aye, you're a cold-blooded scoundrel," he growled. "I might have known I couldn't maneuver you into losing your temper. Nevertheless, Kilverton, I warn you to have a care!

Do not grow too confident. I promise you, even if you succeed in your mischief, you will not achieve your ends—for
there are those who will see to it that you are brought to
book!"

An instant hush fell upon the room. Oswald Kilverton's
hand, in the act of raising a pinch of snuff, checked for a moment. The veiled expression left his eyes as his brows flew
upward, startled. Then he regained his iron composure. His
eyes narrowed to slits and his voice became silky.

"Now you interest me extremely, Mr. Montague. Extremely." He deliberately took snuff, and dusted his lapel with
a lace-edged handkerchief. "Is it you, perhaps, who will—
er—bring me to book?"

Mr. Montague's hands clenched involuntarily into fists.
"You may rely on it," he said evenly.

"Ah," mused Oswald pensively. "And of what crime, exactly, will I be accused?"

Oswald's eyes raked Mr. Montague contemptuously, but
Ned thought he could detect an arrested, alert expression in
their depths, almost that of a cat at a mouse hole. This caused
Ned to again become aware of the roomful of spectators, and
he realized with sickening suddenness the danger of his own
position. He could not make a startling and serious accusation
in this extremely public place unless he was prepared to offer
irrefutable proof. He had no such proof. He swallowed, irresolute, and finally said, "You are perfectly aware of your own
plans, Mr. Kilverton, so I fancy I need not explain them to
you. Suffice it to say, your designs have been suspected—and
thus will not bring you your desire. I urge you, then, to recon-
sider! I am persuaded that a little calm reflection will convince you to abandon your fell purpose. That is all."

A flash of anger lit Oswald Kilverton's cold blue eyes.
"That is very far from all, Mr. Montague. You have seen fit to
accuse me of some nameless, but apparently reprehensible,
plot. Kindly divulge, for the benefit of our interested spectators, precisely what scheme you believe me to be hatching.
Otherwise I may find myself in the dock, charged with whatever unsolved crime next comes to light! Do you accuse me
of planning some treasonous exploit? Espionage? Theft?" His

eyes narrowed again, watching Ned carefully. His voice did not alter in pitch or volume, but there was a barely perceptible pause before his next word. "Murder?"

Mr. Montague met his gaze squarely. "I trust you are planning nothing whatsoever, Mr. Kilverton. It will be very much the worse for you if you are."

"Dear me!" mocked Oswald. "Should I tremble with fear? I am desolate, Mr. Montague, to disappoint you yet again. Strange as it may seem to you, your dramatic threats have impressed me as little as your clumsy insults. But I am a phlegmatic creature, I am told, and not easily moved—nor, I may add, am I easily persuaded to abandon my plans. Having determined the course I mean to pursue, Mr. Montague, I pursue it single-mindedly." His gaze hardened, and his lips curled into a singularly unpleasant sneer. "Ruthlessly, if you will."

With this extraordinary utterance, he bowed mockingly and left the room. A buzz of conjecture and exclamation burst out as soon as he had left, but Mr. Montague, much agitated, heard none of it. He escaped Featherstone's clutches, left the club, and returned to his lodgings, berating himself for having made matters—if anything—worse.

Eventually it occurred to him that, whatever Oswald might say, surely it would give him pause to know that his attempts on Richard's life had not gone unnoticed. Ned comforted himself with the thought that he must have done some good, after all, by making the would-be murderer aware that it was impossible for him to avoid the consequences, should he succeed. Why, only an idiot—or a madman—would attempt a murder knowing he was already under suspicion! This was a cheerful thought. Before long Ned was happily congratulating himself on having (probably) saved his friend's life.

He would not have felt quite so sanguine had he been privileged to observe the final effect of his words on Oswald Kilverton.

After leaving White's, Oswald wended his way slowly homeward, apparently in deep thought. His abstracted frown indicated that his cogitations brought him no pleasure. However, although he reached home in the devil's own temper and snapped mercilessly at his valet, his unpleasant ruminations eventually helped him decide upon a course of action. Whatever he may have said to Mr. Montague, the incident at White's did cause him to think furiously—and plot cleverly. It finally occurred to him that certain steps might yet be taken. A grim smile then disturbed the gravity of Oswald Kilverton's countenance.

Oswald was next seen in the company of a small, sharpeyed, closemouthed youth. The boy accepted from him, without comment or surprise, a substantial sum of money and a complicated set of orders.

Ned would have recognized this unsavory individual within the week as Richard Kilverton's new tiger, hired to assist the injured Mullins.

Chapter XIII

For several days after the curricle accident, Caitlin stayed within doors and allowed Aunt Harriet and Emily to pamper her. Her thoughts were in such turmoil she found it difficult to concentrate and almost impossible to sleep, and her listlessness, together with the fairly spectacular bruises she had suffered in the curricle accident, made a sufficient excuse for her to avoid company. First Lord Kilverton, then Mr. Montague and Captain Talgarth, and finally even Sir Egbert sent round to enquire after her health. But it was Emily who appeared downstairs to reply to their kind messages. Caitlin hid in her chamber.

It was most unlike her, but Caitlin had never been so wretchedly unhappy in her life.

She knew it had little or nothing to do with her physical discomfort. It had everything to do with Richard Kilverton. Before he entered her life, she had been tranquilly happy, content with her lot, and enjoying her London holiday. Now she hardly recognized the pale and stormy creature reflected in her mirror.

It was appalling—indeed, it was shocking!—to find herself obsessed with thoughts of a man who was betrothed to another. That went so deeply against her moral code, she never would have believed it possible such a calamity could occur. She was afraid to go among people for fear she would meet him; she was unable to sleep for reliving every conversation she had ever had with him; and she bathed her pillow each night with hot tears, longing for impossible things. Caitlin was furious with herself, distressed by her own waywardness, determined to stop these insane feelings—and terrified that she might feel this way forever.

She was sorely in need of advice, but there was not a soul in whom she could confide. If Caitlin herself was ashamed and confused, she feared Emily would be even more shocked and uncomprehending. Her only other confidante was Lady Serena—and how impossible it would be to tell Serena!

She had heard it said that a green girl invariably fell in love with the man who gave her her first kiss. Well, there could hardly be found a greener girl than herself. Her experience of such matters was less than limited, it was nil. She wondered miserably if that absurd encounter in Curzon Street could really be counted as a kiss. She had nothing to compare it to. She devoutly hoped (however unlikely it seemed to her) that what she felt was, perhaps, just a silly infatuation that would pass as quickly as it came. She had no idea if what she felt was likely to prove lasting. In fact, she was not even sure what it was she felt. Agitation, surely, and melancholy; a strange, terrified exhilaration; and a great deal of misery. The term "lovesick" took on a new meaning for Caitlin—as near as she could tell, what she was experiencing had all the symptoms of malaria!

It would be terrible to see him too soon, before she could command herself. On the other hand, she thought feverishly, perhaps the sooner she saw him the better it might be for her. Perhaps when she met him again she would immediately recover her balance! Her current state of mind might prove to be an unaccountable fit of madness. Not long ago, a friend of Caitlin's had fancied herself head over heels for an absent suitor, and when he reappeared her feelings had instantly evaporated. Such things could happen.

After all, Lord Kilverton was the rudest and most provoking person of her acquaintance! And apart from that, she hardly knew the man! But this train of thought was dangerous. It caused her to recollect everything she did know of him, and that was a painful process. She knew a great deal about him from Serena, of course, who adored him. Caitlin could not help thinking that a sister's recommendation was not to be lightly dismissed. Apparently he was a teasing, but kindly, creature of infinite patience and great good nature, generous to a fault, not above showing his little sister the sights of London or teaching her a few tricks worth knowing before her come-out. Most telling of all, there was no one on earth to whom Serena would rather turn in a fix. Praise indeed! But what did Caitlin herself know of him?

It struck her that she had felt drawn to Lord Kilverton even in their first meeting. She could only ascribe her lack of fear, in what surely should have been a frightening and loathsome encounter, to the instant affinity she had felt for the stranger who had accosted her. The very next morning, long before she knew anything about his identity or appearance—for all she knew he could have been a criminal, or physically hideous—she had felt strangely sad to think she would never know her midnight assailant. How could one be so attracted to a voice in the dark?

It was mysterious, and extremely confusing. She had never considered how many clues one picked up from a voice. There was, somehow, knowledge and intimacy shared in what they had said and how they had said it, in the way her mind and his communicated, even in the way they made each other laugh. She had never realized how irresistibly appealing a shared sense of humor could be.

She was unable to convince herself she was deceived in him, or that it was her own foolish fancy weaving his portrait. She knew enough to the contrary. She felt safe with him, even in the most compromising of situations. She felt sure of his protection, even when he was at his most provoking. Even the quickness of his apology when he knew himself to be in the wrong spoke to her of a gentleman worthy of her regard. Besides, she dimly realized, it hardly mattered to her if he had feet of clay, or if he continued to goad her into losing her temper every time they met. She could not imagine her feelings for Lord Kilverton altering under any circumstances.

This was terrifying.

She must put him out of her thoughts. She must banish his image from her heart. Richard Kilverton was not for her. A portionless nobody from Hertfordshire, a girl no man had ever seriously pursued, raising her eyes to an earl's heir! Why, it was absurd! And to be looking twice at an engaged *parti* was scandalous, whoever he might be! No, she must recover from this appalling greensickness. And, most important, no one must ever know she had suffered it.

Thus it was that when Lady Serena Kilverton paid a morning call on the fourth day after the curricle accident, Miss Campbell smoothed her hair, took a deep breath, and came downstairs. Aside from her wrist, which was still tightly wrapped, she had mostly recovered from the hurts suffered in the accident. She was determined to recover her spirits as well.

As she entered the morning room she checked on the threshold, a little startled to find the room unexpectedly full of people. Lady Lynwood was conversing earnestly with Lady Selcroft over tea, Serena was seated rather stiffly on the edge of a high-backed chair, and Emily and Captain Talgarth were standing together in the window embrasure, oblivious to the world. The expression on her sister's face as she gazed at Captain Talgarth stopped Caitlin in her tracks with a queer little pang compounded of astonishment, joy, sadness—and envy. Events had apparently been moving swiftly during Caitlin's indisposition. Oh, poor Serena!

Her entrance caused something like a sensation. Lady Lynwood dropped her spoon, exclaiming, "Here is our dear Caitlin!" Emily ran forward, crying, "Caitie! I am so glad you are better!" and Serena rose with an overbright smile to greet her friend and settle her in the most comfortable chair. Even Lady Selcroft, in her stately way, gave Caitlin a gentle welcome and said something kind. Caitlin began to feel a bit overwhelmed. When Emily attempted to stuff a pillow behind her back, she laughed and waved her away.

"No, really, Emily, that is the outside of enough! Anyone would think I had lumbago! I am perfectly comfortable, thank you."

After a searching glance at her sister's face and hovering a moment more, Emily seemed satisfied Caitlin was speaking the truth. She gladly returned to Captain Talgarth, completely unaware that their absorption in each other could give pain to anyone. Lady Lynwood and Lady Selcroft resumed their conversation and Caitlin looked worriedly at Serena, whose gaiety certainly seemed a trifle forced.

Serena correctly interpreted her friend's expression of concern, and gave a short, unhappy, laugh. "Well, anyone can see how the land lies," she told Caitlin, tossing her head with a great show of indifference. "I suppose I have been a bigger fool than I had any idea of. But you are the only person I took into my confidence, thank heaven, and you would never betray me."

"You may be sure of that, Serena." Caitlin did not wish to comment on what she feared was the truth of it—that Serena's heart had been so firmly pinned to her sleeve, any number of persons probably guessed her secret. Her own heart, newly awakened to the pain of hopeless love, ached for her friend and she cast about for something comforting to say.

"This comes as a surprise to me, as well," she began tentatively. "I was never more astonished in my life than to discover Captain Talgarth in our morning room, I promise you! I have not spoken with Emily—"

"Oh, I am not imagining a conspiracy," said Serena swiftly. "I am sure this turn of events was completely unplanned. I do not accuse you of hiding anything from me." She smiled crookedly. "The most disagreeable feature of the business, to me, is that I believe they will suit each other admirably. Pray do not think it gives me pleasure to acknowledge it! But to speak truth, although I always thought Captain Talgarth was the perfect man for me, I never quite succeeded in deluding myself that I was the perfect woman for him—try as I might." She could not repress a sigh, and looked so despondent it quite wrung Caitlin's heart.

"Be comforted, Serena. If you are not the woman for him, I am persuaded you will also find he was not the man for you. I am not well-acquainted with Captain Talgarth, but I must tell you I could not picture you happy with him. You seemed to have so little in common, either in temperament or tastes, it could not but strike me how very ill-matched you would have been. You are so lively, and he so grave! Surely some part of you must have wondered if you would not, eventually, have been bored with such a paragon."

"Yes, my incurable honesty!" said Serena, with a shaky laugh. "You are perfectly right, of course. I fell in love with a pretty face and let my imagination run away with me, endowing him with every amiable quality." She gazed wistfully across the room at the captain's handsome profile. "Unfortunately, Captain Talgarth actually does possess every amiable quality, which made it easier to deceive myself. The answer to the maiden's prayer, in fact! But even I can see he is not the answer to *this* maiden's prayer. The more time I spent in his company the more oppressive I found it. What a pity he was such a long time in India! I might have known my heart much sooner, and fallen out of love with him long ago."

Caitlin was glad to encourage this frame of mind, and unburdening herself to a sympathetic ear seemed to help Serena, but eventually Serena stopped in midsentence.

"Never mind about my maudlin affairs! I must tell you the latest *on-dit*. You will never believe it, but the other day Edward Montague tried to force a quarrel onto my wicked Uncle Oswald."

"Good heavens! Are you sure?"

"Perfectly sure! One hears it whispered about everywhere."

Caitlin was mystified. "It sounds very unlike him. Whatever do you suppose he meant by it?"

Serena shook her head. "My dear, I've no idea. Gentlemen are such odd creatures, there's no knowing what they will do next."

And the two girls immediately put their heads together, relieving their aching hearts for a moment in mutually condemning the unaccountable behavior of Men in general and Gentlemen in particular.

Chapter XIV

Wednesday evening arrived, and Lady Lynwood contentedly shepherded her nieces to Almack's Assembly Rooms. She was enjoying this Season enormously, and was in a fair way to thinking it an unqualified success. Little Emily had attracted a substantial amount of attention, and now looked to be safely on the road to making an extremely advantageous marriage—and a love match! Why, it could hardly be better! How pleased Amabel would be! Lady Lynwood had written a lengthy, affectionate, and extremely cryptic letter to her sister, so full of hints, arch suggestions, and mysterious allusions as to be virtually incomprehensible—particularly as Amabel was wholly unacquainted with various persons whom Harriet discreetly identified only by their initials.

Lady Lynwood, unaware that she had written anything obscure, was happy in the belief that her letter had brought unparalleled joy to her sister. If only dear Caitlin could be comfortably established! But alas, it seemed that was not to be. Fortunately, no one had seriously anticipated that a husband could be found for Caitlin, so Lady Lynwood would not repine. On the contrary, the Season had been great fun, and if Emily were to marry Captain Talgarth Lady Lynwood would be very well satisfied with the results of her labors—very well satisfied indeed!

Both girls were looking lovely tonight, thought Lady Lynwood happily. It was exceedingly fortunate that pastels became little Emily so well; she showed to great advantage in her modest, but extremely elegant, ball dress of white spider-gauze trimmed in pale blue. And Caitlin had finally consented to accept, and wear, the sea green silk Lady Lynwood had had made up especially for her. Her resistance to accepting such an expensive gift had vanished seemingly overnight, much to Lady Lynwood's delight, and she looked every bit as stunning as one had hoped she would. Lady Lynwood found it deeply gratifying to have her taste and judgment in matters of dress vindicated by the picture her nieces presented tonight. She swelled with pride to see so many heads turning when they entered the portals of Almack's.

Caitlin was privately suffering from a guilty conscience. She had tried hard (up to now) to avoid accepting the costliest of the garments her aunt pressed upon her as gifts, but lately her resolve had begun to weaken. She had almost convinced herself that it was cruel to disappoint Aunt Harriet by refusing her presents. This was the reason she gave herself for donning the irresistibly luscious sea green silk, but she knew in her heart that she was really wearing it because it suddenly seemed of the greatest importance to look her best in public.

She did not care to examine this newborn anxiety she felt regarding her appearance. Surely it could have nothing to do with her feelings for Richard Kilverton. After all (as she drearily reminded herself for the thousandth time), the man was engaged to Lady Elizabeth Delacourt. Even if Caitlin had the power to attract him, it would be shockingly improper— even wicked!—to do so.

Nevertheless, as she stepped into the ballroom she was conscious of a flutter of nervous anticipation. She was wearing the loveliest gown she had ever owned, in a shade handpicked to complement her coloring, and the silk clung to her figure in a daring and unfamiliar way. The tiny puffed sleeves left most of her shoulders and arms bare, and although she had pulled her kid gloves high over her elbows she still felt rather exposed. She would never have dared to wear anything quite so alluring a few weeks ago, but Almack's patronesses had graciously approved of the Campbell girls by now. Since they were permitted to waltz, Lady Lynwood deemed it permissible for her elder niece to indulge in a little high fashion.

It had been ten days since the curricle accident, so Caitlin had had ten full days to heal her hurts and master her emotions. The bruising had faded in good time, but she feared that

the tone of her mind was far from recovered. Even as she
scolded herself for doing so, she paused on the step and
glanced around the room, her eyes involuntarily seeking a certain gentleman—and just as she was trying to convince herself it was an excellent thing that he was not present, she saw
him.

Richard Kilverton was standing with his mother and sister,
not fifty feet from her, and as their eyes met for the first time
in many days she felt her heart ignore all her mind's warnings
and give a joyful leap. A tremulous little smile wavered on
her lips and, completely unconscious of her surroundings, she
raised a gloved hand in greeting.

Kilverton caught his breath. Miss Campbell, the candlelight
gleaming on her fiery hair, the pale silk clinging to her graceful form, looked magnificent. As if compelled, he instantly
left his party and crossed the floor toward Caitlin.

As she watched his tall person plow heedlessly through the
sea of fashionably dressed people, his eyes never leaving hers,
Caitlin realized with a terrified rush of wonder that he seemed
to feel as drawn to her as she felt toward him. He reached her
side and suddenly her hand was trembling in his clasp as they
stared wordlessly into each other's faces.

It was Kilverton who eventually collected his wits and
spoke. "Miss Campbell," he began hoarsely, but seemed to
lose his train of thought. He tried again. "Miss Campbell—"

An unwelcome tap on his sleeve forced him to drop her
hand and turn. One of the persons from the party he had just
abandoned, a short-sighted old gentleman whose lapels were
coated with a fine dusting of snuff, had followed him.

"I say, Kilverton," this gentleman wheezed. "Can't go
dashing off just now, y'know! Going to get a small party together. Cards in the back room, m'boy, and hang the dancing!"

Kilverton turned courteously. "But dancing, Duke, is the
very reason one comes to Almack's. Miss Campbell, are you
acquainted with His Grace, the Duke of Arnsford?"

Caitlin choked back her surprise and bowed, murmuring
something polite. The duke peered myopically at her.

"Redheaded!" he barked. "What'd you say your name was?
Caldwell?"

"Campbell, Your Grace."

"Ha! Knew a Caldwell once," announced His Grace, thus explaining his brief interest in her. "Shocking little Cit, though. Shouldn't think a daughter of his would be found at Almack's." He immediately transferred his attention back to Lord Kilverton, jabbing him with a pudgy forefinger. "D'you mean to tell me you dragged me here to *dance*?"

A muscle quivered at the corner of Kilverton's mouth. "Not with me, sir."

The duke goggled at him for a moment. "What's that? What's that? Oh. Not with me, eh? Ha, ha! Yes, I dessay! Well, you're an impudent dog. The ladies are always glad to dance. But since Elizabeth ain't here, y'know, *you're* under no obligation to gallop about like some demmed caper-merchant. We can put a snug little table together, boy."

Kilverton's good humor remained unshaken. "I am sure, sir, that many gentlemen present share your preference for gaming. You will find enough like-minded souls without my adding to the number."

The duke shrugged pettishly. "Oh, well—! I'm off, then." And he sauntered away without another word or any acknowledgment of Caitlin whatsoever. She stated after him in astonishment.

"What an impossible person!" she exclaimed, diverted. "Is he really Lady Elizabeth's father?"

"It does seem improbable," agreed Kilverton, with the ghost of a laugh. "Perhaps the duchess played him false."

As Caitlin gasped, he hurried contritely into speech. "No, Miss Campbell, pray do not upbraid me! I should never have spoken so in your presence. There! I have begged your pardon, and we may be friends again." But he turned to find her biting her lip resolutely to keep from laughing, and his face relaxed into a grin.

"What an unusual girl you are," he commented.

Caitlin stiffened warily. "Unusual? How?"

"Arnsford is famous for his incivility, but I never heard anything to equal the shocking bit of rudeness I just witnessed. And you come off from the encounter quite unruffled! Neither the duke's bad manners, nor my own, can rob you of your poise. My hat is off to you, Miss Campbell." He bowed.

She regarded his light brown locks, brushed carefully into a fashionable Brutus, and raised an eyebrow. "Well, your hat is certainly off—but what a goose I should be, to think I had anything to do with it!"

His eyes gleamed, and his mouth twisted quizzically. "You underrate your importance, Miss Campbell," he said softly.

She stared at him, trying to puzzle out his meaning. Hazel, she thought inconsequentially. His eyes are hazel. Suddenly she could not recall what they had been talking about, and cast confusedly about in her mind for something to say. There had been something important stated a few minutes ago; what was it? Oh, yes! Her mind seized gratefully on the thought.

"Did I understand His Grace to say that Lady Elizabeth is not present tonight?" inquired Caitlin politely, not stopping to think that Kilverton might misconstrue her interest. At the arrested expression on his face she blushed furiously, and hastened to explain her meaning. "I hope she is not ill!"

Kilverton's expression became inscrutable. "No, I don't think so," he replied. "I believe she is attempting to teach me a lesson."

Caitlin looked up at him in surprise. His air of candor was unsettling. It struck her that he was treating her with far less formality than their acquaintance warranted. Before she could decide whether she was glad or sorry, he spoke again.

"You appear surprised, Miss Campbell. Do you wonder what I mean? You must understand that I have not seen Elizabeth since our excursion to Richmond Park. I have been inattentive, Miss Campbell. I have neglected my fiancée. Therefore, Elizabeth refuses to accompany me to Almack's tonight—thus paying me back in my own coin. I believe this behavior is supposed to pique my interest. I am expected to arrive on her doorstep tomorrow morning, repentant and eager to make amends." He smiled faintly. "Alas, poor Elizabeth! Her stratagem might have been effective, had my neglect of her been due to thoughtlessness. It was not, however. On the contrary, it was deliberate."

Deliberate! A thrill compounded of hope and fear rushed through Caitlin. Deliberate neglect of Lady Elizabeth! She clutched her fan tightly and, with a great effort, retained her composure, frantically beating back the conjectures seething in her brain. She must not hope, she reminded herself fiercely. She must not hope.

It was difficult to force her voice past the constriction in her throat. "Lord Kilverton, you should not be telling me this. I am not a fit recipient for these confidences."

"Are you not?" He gazed at her with such intensity, she dropped her eyes in confusion. What did he mean? She dared not guess. Before she could speak again, an ivory fan rapped her forearm, recalling her to her surroundings. She turned to find Serena accosting them.

"Richard, you must let me speak to Caitlin!" cried Serena, grasping her friend's gloved elbow and beginning to push her insistently toward the wall.

Lord Kilverton stopped this maneuver by seizing his sister's sash. "Oh, no, you don't!" he said firmly. "Miss Campbell has just met Arnsford, so she has endured enough rudeness for one evening. What do you mean by bursting in and ordering us about?"

Serena opened her eyes at him. "Well! If one can't discard propriety with one's only brother and one's dearest friend—"

"One can't!" he assured her. He looked very hard at Serena's saintly expression. "You're hatching some scheme, Serena. Out with it."

Serena tossed her head. "I mean to come out with it, Richard, but not to you. I must speak to Caitlin—alone!"

Richard groaned and covered his eyes with one hand. "I knew it! She's planning something disastrous. Miss Campbell, I rely on you to dissuade her."

Serena was indignant. "Don't be a beast, Richard," she began—but stopped, regarding her brother thoughtfully. "You know," she said slowly, "it might be a good idea to include you after all."

He flung up a hand in mock horror. "I spoke too soon! Upon consideration, Serena, I believe I would rather know nothing about it."

"But you don't know what it is!"

"No, and I don't want to. Miss Campbell, would you care to be rescued from the hair-raising secrets I am sure my sister is about to pour into your ear? Pray allow me to lead you into the set that is forming."

Caitlin could not help laughing. "What a family you are! Come, Serena, are you really planning something dangerous?"

"Not in the least!" Serena assured her earnestly. "It's a

splendid scheme, I promise you. All I mean to do—and it
won't do a pennyworth of harm to anyone—is flirt *desperately* with Ned Montague. And both of you could help me, if
you only would!"

Caitlin stared at her friend in bewilderment. "Why on earth
do you wish to flirt with Mr. Montague? And how am I to
help you do so?"

Serena turned a little pink, but lifted her chin defiantly. "It
has been brought to my attention that people—*odious* people—have somehow received a—a mistaken impression.
About me. And I wish to correct it. That is all."

Lord Kilverton grinned sympathetically. "Talgarth! Yes,
you needn't look daggers at me, Serena—I am one of the odious people who received a 'mistaken impression.' " His expression hardened a little. "And I believe I can guess who
brought the rumors to your attention."

Serena nodded unhappily. "She meant it for the best. And
of course I am grateful to Elizabeth, because now I shall be
able to do something about it. But somehow—I don't know
why it should be so, but being told something beastly about
oneself by someone who is trying to be kind only makes one
feel worse."

Caitlin's arm stole comfortingly round her friend's waist.
"Never mind. Tonight we shall avenge you, Serena, and right
your reputation in the eyes of the world! One instantly perceives that if you are seen to flirt with Mr. Montague, you will
no longer be suspected of having lost your heart to the dashing Captain Talgarth."

Serena nodded bravely. "Precisely. And Ned is so agreeable to flirt with. He takes one up instantly, and is so amusing! I daresay it will be quite a pleasant diversion."

Richard frowned. "I don't quite see what Miss Campbell's
part is in this game of yours, Serena. Or, for that matter,
mine."

She smiled brightly. "Why, you must see to it that Ned and
I are thrown together, of course."

Caitlin gave a tiny gasp, and Richard stared at his sister in
disbelief. "Do you mean to tell me that you haven't divulged
this little plan to Ned?" he demanded. "Serena, I could shake
you!"

Caitlin was inclined to agree. "Really, Serena, it's too bad!

You mustn't playact when it comes to matters of the heart. What if poor Mr. Montague came to believe you cared for him?"

Lord Kilverton seemed much struck. "Yes, by Jove! You can't suddenly start making sheep's eyes at Ned. What a scare you would give him! Poor fellow might feel obliged to fly the country, you know, or put a period to his existence—"

Serena flushed. "It's all very well for you to laugh. People aren't saying spiteful things about *you* behind your back. All the hateful tabbies, whispering behind their fans—telling one another I've played the fool—thrown myself at a man who won't have me—" Sudden tears sprang to Serena's eyes. "Well, I *will* tell Ned Montague, so there! He won't care a snap of his fingers for anything people may say. He'll help me, even if my own brother won't!"

She turned to flounce away, but Richard caught her hand, stopping her for a moment. He grinned affectionately into the stormy face turned up to his. "Chin up, Serena! You'll come about."

She managed to smile a little, her crossness dissipating. "Shall I, do you think?"

Kilverton flicked Serena's cheek carelessly with one finger. "Yes, I do. Now, head up, and tail over the dashboard! Ned's by the punch bowl."

Serena laughed saucily, and sailed off. Caitlin gazed worriedly after her. "Lord Kilverton, do you think this scheme of hers is wise?"

"Wise? Of course not. I am not even sure it will be effective. The worst of the gossips will see through it. Those who don't will probably talk about her all the more. And it makes my hair stand on end to picture the lengths Serena might go if Ned encourages her—which I'll be bound he will, the rascal! Thank God Almack's serves nothing stronger than negus."

Caitlin was a little shocked. "Surely, if Serena approaches him in friendship, Mr. Montague will not be so lost to all sense of propriety as to take advantage of the situation."

"Oh, will he not? You don't know Ned!" replied Ned's friend. "He's the best of good fellows, of course, but ripe for any mischief! I must have a word with him, or he's liable to— how shall I put it? Embrace Serena's idea—enthusiastically!"

"Oh, dear!" said Caitlin faintly.

There was a stir behind them and they turned to see Captain Philip Talgarth, the light playing beautifully on his gleaming blond head, entering the room. He seemed completely unconscious of the flutter he was causing among a small group of females gathered near the door. Lord Kilverton raised his quizzing glass and viewed Captain Talgarth through it dispassionately.

"When one comes to regard him, he is a rather good-looking fellow. Unfortunate! Is anyone likely to believe, do you think, that Serena's affections *could* be estranged from such a pretty face?"

Caitlin laughed. "Certainly! One does not fall in love with a face, after all."

"I am glad to hear you say so," said Kilverton. His tone was so odd, she looked up at him inquiringly. His eyes held hers. "Now that you put me in mind of it, Miss Campbell, I agree with you. One does not fall in love with a face. In fact, it is possible for people to fall in love without seeing each other at all. I know a case where a man fell in love with a voice, and a manner, and a tiny glimpse of his beloved's soul."

Her mind went swiftly back to a darkened street and a kiss from an invisible stranger who, even then, felt like no stranger at all. Pain caught at her heart. "They do say love is blind," she said faintly.

Kilverton's eyes still held hers, steadily. "The gentleman I speak of was only blind until he met you, Miss Campbell."

She could mistake his meaning no longer. Caitlin stared, transfixed, into the hazel eyes so close to hers. There was a strange roaring in her ears; she could feel her pulse beating in her throat. A mingled rush of joy and sorrow paralyzed her; she could not speak.

The sweet tones of a violin reached them as the orchestra embarked on a waltz.

"My dance, I think, Miss Campbell," whispered Lord Kilverton, and took her in his arms.

Chapter XV

Against the wall at Almack's Assembly Rooms, in a row of chairs reserved for matrons and chaperons, sat one Lady Markham. This lady had once cherished hopes of obtaining an offer from Richard Kilverton for her daughter Anne's hand. Those hopes had proved as vain as they were short-lived, but she bore him no ill will; Anne had not worn the willow long. Lady Markham liked Lord Kilverton, although she did not care for his choice of bride. Hard to believe Kilverton could choose Lady Elizabeth, that colorless shrew, over her own sweet Anne—but ah, well! There is no accounting for tastes, after all.

Lady Markham now sat beside the woman whose maternal ambitions in that quarter had been fulfilled: Her Grace, the Duchess of Arnsford. Elizabeth would be exactly like her in twenty years or so! thought Lady Markham. Heavens, what a fate for that handsome scapegrace, Kilverton!

As if conjured up by her thoughts, Lord Kilverton waltzed gracefully past them with a tall young woman whose flaming hair irresistibly drew the eye. The expression on Lord Kilverton's face as he gazed at his partner was quite unmistakable—and also drew the eye.

The two ladies beheld this interesting picture with various emotions, all admirably concealed. Although deeply shocked, Lady Markham was conscious of feeling a most reprehensible glee. A scandal was brewing, or she missed her guess! She glanced covertly at the duchess, whom she cordially disliked, and thought she saw that lady stiffen—although Her Grace's calm expression never altered.

Lady Markham could not resist. She would speak.

"How well Lord Kilverton dances, Your Grace! Lady Elizabeth is fortunate."

The duchess's thin lips twisted into a perfunctory smile. "Yes, indeed." The two women continued to watch Kilverton and his partner, the duchess with a faintly bored air belied by the muscles tensing in her jaw, and Lady Markham now obviously, and quite frankly, agog.

Lady Markham tried again. "I don't believe I've met his partner. Is she one of your party, Your Grace?"

A spasm of annoyance crossed Her Grace's well-bred features. How much she disliked that gossiping simpleton, Janet Markham! Look at her now, fairly panting with curiosity! What was one to say to the creature? The duchess had been even more shocked than Lady Markham, and far less agreeably, by the sight of her daughter's fiancé waltzing so extremely well with an unknown redhead. Her mind was awhirl with alarm and conjecture, but she was not one to lose her head in a crisis. She maintained her air of indifference and replied repressively.

"I believe that may be a certain Miss Campbell I have heard Elizabeth mention. The Misses Campbell are friends of Lord Kilverton's sister." The duchess placed a slight emphasis on the latter information, and had the satisfaction of seeing Lady Markham's expression lose a little of its avidity.

"Oh!" said Lady Markham, deflated a trifle. "Yes, I think I may have heard Anne speak of her." She gazed thoughtfully at the dancing couple and felt a twinge of sympathy for the pair. Whatever the duchess may choose to believe, Lord Kilverton was not dancing with this girl merely to oblige his sister. He appeared quite spellbound. And the poor girl seemed equally smitten. How sad.

There could be no future in it, of course. One could only hope they would soon recover. If her recollections of what Anne had said were accurate, this Miss Campbell was some connection of that silly woman the late Baron Lynwood had married—in fact, she was nobody at all. Even if Kilverton were free, it would be a most unequal match. And yet Miss Campbell was well-connected enough to be found at Almack's, which certainly precluded Kilverton from setting her up as his *chère-amie*. It was all utterly hopeless.

Meanwhile, the Duchess of Arnsford, behind the mask of her impassive face, was racking her brain to recall what Elizabeth had told her of this girl. Kilverton's unknown partner had to be Miss Campbell. Elizabeth had expressed great concern that her future sister-in-law was being drawn into friendship with a social-climbing, carrot-topped Long Meg possessing no connections of any importance. The duchess instantly recognized this individual in the person now clasped in Lord Kilverton's arms. This naturally made her wonder if Elizabeth had additional reasons for disliking Miss Campbell, but she swiftly dismissed the idea as unworthy of her daughter. However, it clearly behooved Elizabeth's mother to drop a word of warning in her daughter's ear. Her Grace determined to do this before the night was out.

Lady Elizabeth was summoned to her mother's dressing room shortly after midnight. She found the duchess seated before her mirror, leisurely removing the diamond drops from her ears, while Sturby, her dresser, hovered nearby. When Her Grace dismissed Sturby before her usual tasks were completed, Elizabeth knew that whatever her mother had to say to her was of a serious nature. However, the duchess continued her unhurried preparations for bed. Her expression was unfathomable as her steely eyes met Elizabeth's in the looking glass.

"It is a pity you did not accompany us to Almack's this evening, Elizabeth."

One of Elizabeth's finely arched brows lifted slightly. "Indeed, ma'am? I am glad your evening was agreeable."

"I would not characterize the evening I have just spent as 'agreeable,' " said the duchess coldly. "I meant that *had* you made one of the party, we might all have been spared such an evening as I hope never to repeat! I see no reason to mince words with you, daughter. Tell me at once: is it your intention to whistle Lord Kilverton down the wind?"

Elizabeth's eyes widened. "Certainly not! I had a touch of headache tonight—"

"Rubbish!" snapped Her Grace. "Pray do not fence with

me, Elizabeth. When you announced you were staying home this evening, I believed your decision had something to do with Lord Kilverton. Have you quarreled with him?"

Elizabeth gave a tinkling little laugh. "Oh, as to that, ma'am, I assure you there is no cause for alarm! You may have noticed he has been absent from my side of late; I merely wished to give him a taste of his own medicine. I promise you I don't mean to *quarrel* with him! I am only venturing to give him a hint, you know. Kilverton is no fool. I trust his lesson may be learned and he will give me no cause to continue the experiment."

The duchess dropped her earrings into her jewel case with a decided snap. "You would be very ill-advised to continue the experiment! I wish you would discuss these ventures of yours with me before you begin them. You have very little experience in such matters, and it's my belief your conduct has been most injudicious. You are playing a dangerous game, Elizabeth. I perfectly understand your desire to get the upper hand before you are married, but you are correct that Kilverton is no fool. He is also no weakling, and these misguided attempts to lead him by the nose may well prove fatal."

Elizabeth's eyes flashed. "Fatal, ma'am? To what? I beg your pardon, but my position is unassailable. I am securely betrothed to Lord Kilverton, after all! And as to getting the upper hand, I am distressed that you suspect me of harboring such an improper and unfeminine desire."

Exasperated, the duchess turned from her own reflection to face her daughter. "The desire for power is common to both sexes, Elizabeth, and is found inevitably in persons of your temperament! Do not misunderstand me. I do not accuse you of browbeating Lord Kilverton, nor am I afraid you will openly quarrel with him. Such a course would be as disastrous as it would be improper, and I am persuaded you are well aware of that. However, your personality is strong, and your temper has always been your besetting sin. Take care you do not lose it! I believe Kilverton will not hesitate to look elsewhere for a bride if you fly into one of your ungovernable rages before the knot is tied. And I rather fancy he will not have far to seek for your replacement."

Elizabeth's eyes narrowed. "What does that mean, pray?"

The duchess's gaze became searching. "Is it possible you do not know?"

"Know? What is there to know?"

Her Grace compressed her lips into a thin line, and thought for a moment before she spoke. "It is extremely distasteful to me to voice my suspicions to you, Elizabeth. Pray believe I would not do so if I did not believe it to be my duty. You are a sensible young woman, so I trust you will not make a piece of work about the subject I must introduce."

The duchess stared frowningly at her nails, no longer meeting Elizabeth's eyes. "You are aware that marriage, among persons of our order, is the only honorable means for a woman to achieve any position of consequence in the world. Your rank has made it difficult for you to achieve an alliance worthy of your lineage and your personal gifts. We had hoped to secure the Duke of Blenhurst for you—but that was not to be. I will not hide from you that Lord Kilverton's offer removed a great weight from my mind. I have been pleased that in addition to his other advantages, Kilverton appears to have a steadiness of character that I trust will minimize—" The duchess hesitated briefly. Her eyes flicked to Elizabeth's, then slid away. "Minimize, as I say, those unpleasant episodes of infidelity that can be so humiliating. Men's natures are a mystery to us, my dear, and incredible as it may seem, they actually *enjoy*—well, never mind! Should Kilverton indulge in any amorous adventures after you are married, I feel sure you will take care to know nothing about it, as befits your station. However! Any appearance of interest in a female other than yourself while he is *engaged* to you cannot be tolerated."

Elizabeth paled at these dreadful words. "Are you saying—can it be possible—Mother, I beg you to be frank with me! Have you any reason to think—?"

Now that they had returned to safer ground, the duchess allowed herself to look directly at her daughter once more. Her voice was firm, and very cold. "Yes, my love, I am very much afraid your fiancé is finding himself strongly attracted to Another. I put it no higher than that. I trust you will easily be able to turn his mind back to you, where his duty lies. But you must tread wisely, Elizabeth! For Heaven's sake, don't cross him now! You must give him no opportunity to regret his betrothal."

Horrified, Elizabeth sank into a chair and gripped her fingers in her lap, thinking swiftly. Her mother must have seen Richard with someone tonight. She dreaded knowing the girl's identity, but only one name leaped to mind. "Miss Campbell," she whispered numbly.

"From your description of her, I believe so. A tall girl, red-haired. Not uncomely, I regret to say."

"But he would never *jilt* me! It is impossible!"

Her mother waved a hand in impatient dismissal. "Of course it is impossible! He is a gentleman, after all, so naturally his hands are tied. Were he tempted to do anything so outrageous, the thought of how such a scandal must affect his family—why, everyone would cut his acquaintance, and I daresay the unpleasantness would extend to his mother and sister—oh, no! It is indeed impossible. Were you the veriest Nobody, it would be dreadful. Since you are who you are, it is utterly unthinkable."

The duchess rose gracefully, her dressing gown billowing, and laid a manicured hand on her daughter's tense shoulder. "I merely warn you, Elizabeth, so that you may be a little more conciliating. I greatly fear that you are vexing him by continually setting up your opinions in opposition to his—and pray do not waste my time telling me you have not done so! He cannot jilt you, but he may seek to convince you to cry off. It would not astonish me to learn that his recent neglect of you has been part of such an attempt. Take care! You are five-and-twenty, Elizabeth. If you break this engagement, you will wear the willow all your days."

Elizabeth's hands clenched tightly. A terrifying vista opened before her imagination: endless years of spinsterhood; jokes made at her expense; herself and her noble family the objects of pity, ridicule, and scorn; whispers, gossip, scandal! She took a deep and shaky breath, fighting to control the sickening rage that swept through her. It must not be!

She lifted her chin and met her mother's level gaze. Two pairs of ice blue eyes, exactly like each other, locked in perfect understanding. "I am very much obliged to you, Mother," said Elizabeth steadily.

The duchess inclined her head briefly, satisfied with the outcome of the interview. She gave Elizabeth's shoulder an approving pat and returned to her dressing table. Elizabeth curtsied deeply to her mother and exited, closing the door softly behind her.

Her Grace's lips curved slightly as she unpinned her hair. Elizabeth was hot-tempered, but she was not stupid. There would be no breath of scandal attached to the illustrious name of Delacourt. And the matrimonial ambitions of Elizabeth and her mama would be achieved before the year was out.

Chapter XVI

Caitlin drifted awake on Thursday morning with a dreamy sense of well-being. Her eyes still closed, she smiled and stretched, catlike, against the feather pillows. Jane was tiptoeing about the dim room, but when she perceived these signs of life she set down her tray with a clatter.

"There, now! I didn't hardly like to wake you, but your chocolate's hot as hot, miss. Seein' as you're up, you can drink it right off."

"Morning, Jane," murmured Caitlin sleepily.

"And it's a lovely morning, miss!" chirped Jane, crossing briskly to the windows. She pulled back the heavy curtains and flooded the room with light. Caitlin blinked, and instantly came wide awake. As consciousness rushed back, so did memory. The effect was much the same as if Jane had dashed the chocolate in her face.

"Good God!" she cried, sitting bolt upright.

"Miss?"

Caitlin pressed her hands over her eyes, trying to think. Jane clucked her tongue worriedly and pulled the drapes halfway back across the windows. "Oh, I'm sorry, miss! So thoughtless of me! I didn't mean to hurt your eyes."

"What?" Caitlin pulled her hands away and tried to smile. "Oh! Never mind, Jane, it's quite all right." She sank back into her pillows and stared at the canopy over her bed, her thoughts once again in turmoil. Jane clucked and puttered about for a few minutes more, but finally left Caitlin to her own musings.

These were not comfortable. Her mind seemed to have divided neatly in two, and the two halves were arguing hotly.

What have you done! cried one half.

I had the most wonderful evening of my life! replied the other.

Caitlin groaned and buried her face in her pillow. It *had* been a wonderful evening. She smiled mistily as she remembered waltzing with Richard Kilverton—twice!—and the precious hour they had spent talking about everything under the sun, untasted glasses of punch clutched, forgotten, in their hands. She shivered with happiness when she recalled his voice, his touch, the expression in his eyes when he looked at her, the halcyon moments when she had been sure of his regard. Wonderful, magical, beyond anything. An evening she would remember always.

Unfortunately, however, Ruin now stared her in the face. She would have to cling to the memory of that evening, for there would certainly be no others.

"I must have been mad!" Caitlin whispered into her pillow. How could she have exposed herself so shamelessly? As well tie her garter in public! Her cheeks burned as she recalled lecturing poor Serena on the rashness of wearing one's heart on one's sleeve. Excellent advice! Well for Caitlin to have followed it! Instead, she had spent almost an entire evening sitting in Kilverton's pocket—a man whom everyone knew to be betrothed to Lady Elizabeth Delacourt. And to make such a figure of herself at *Almack's*! Almack's, of all the places she could have chosen!

Caitlin writhed, punching her pillow impotently and calling herself every name she could think of. The tale would be all over town by noon. She could count herself fortunate if no veiled references to "Lord K. and Miss C." appeared in the gossip columns. Now, *there* was a thought to make one's blood run cold.

Perhaps the columnists would not dare to offend the powerful Delacourts. She clung to that idea hopefully, until it occurred to her that the press had no hesitation in blackening the names of various members of the royal family. Even the Regent himself received his share of rumor and criticism. It was better to trust to her own obscurity, rather than Kilverton's and Lady Elizabeth's prominence, to safeguard them all from the columnists. The foibles of a mere Miss Campbell might be deemed unworthy of interest.

But nothing, she realized, could save her from the *beau monde*'s rumor mills. If her infatuation with Lord Kilverton had been noticed last night, social ostracism would surely follow. Did she dare to hope that no one had noticed? Or, if they had, could she somehow pass it off as an evening's harmless flirtation?

"Idiot!" she told herself. "There's no such thing as a *harmless flirtation* with a man who is engaged to be married!" No, she must only hope that somehow her behavior had gone unremarked. A rather forlorn hope, she was sure. Especially since (and she could not resist smiling at the memory) Lord Kilverton's behavior had been equally at fault.

Equally at fault? Why, he was *more* at fault than she! Caitlin sat upright as indignation suddenly seized her. What did he mean by it? As usual (she reminded herself), his behavior toward her had been *most* ungentlemanly. Exposing her to spiteful gossip by gazing at her like a moonstruck calf! Remaining at her side virtually the entire evening! Waltzing with her—twice!—when his own sister had already confided to Caitlin that tongues wagged the instant Lord Kilverton waltzed with anyone!

Of course, in fairness, Serena had been referring to the days prior to his engagement. Now that he was betrothed, surely people would not be watching his dance partners with the same keen speculation. No—unless, of course, he *waltzed*! Once a man was engaged, dancing the waltz with someone other than his fiancée was probably improper; Caitlin wasn't sure. It had certainly *felt* improper. In fact, it had felt delicious. Anything so excessively pleasurable had to be wrong. If only she had danced country dances with him instead!

The misty smile returned, unbidden. She was glad they had waltzed. May heaven forgive her! She was *very* glad they had waltzed! She closed her eyes and hugged her knees, imagining she could still feel his arm around her waist, feel his hand clasping hers.

She had forgotten everything when he touched her: their circumstances, their surroundings, the hopelessness of the situation. She had been aware of nothing but his touch, his eyes, his face so close to hers. In the steps of the waltz, the room had whirled out of focus and left her clinging to him as the only stationary object in a tilting, shifting world. She knew he had felt the same. Oh, she knew it.

The sweet music still ran in her mind. Tears stung the back of her eyelids. It was, no doubt, a memory she would carry to her grave. She was seized with a sudden, savage wish that she could remember the feel of his lips on hers with such clarity. The wantonness of such a wish shocked her, but Caitlin was an honest person. And, to be honest, she wished it with all her heart. The encounter in Curzon Street—and last night's waltzes—would doubtless be her only contact with her only love.

Oh, what to do? What to do? There was no help for it. She must strictly hide her unruly emotions in future, and see if she could brazen this situation out. After all, her public conduct had been hardly less shocking the night she ran away from a very exclusive party unescorted. She had survived that fiasco, thanks to Lady Serena's staunch friendship. Perhaps she would survive this as well. Hope stirred faintly.

She would attend Lady Selcroft's soiree this evening, as planned. She would dress with great care—as modestly as she could, within the dictates of fashion. She would appear completely unconcerned. She would treat Lady Selcroft and Serena with affection, Lord Kilverton with civility, and Lady Elizabeth with as much friendliness as she could. She would present herself in the harmless guise of a "friend of the family." And if she could carry it off, it might silence any gossiping tongues.

Thank God she did not have to worry any longer about her own foolishness ruining Emily's chances. Philip Talgarth seemed too besotted to give the snap of his fingers for any faults that might be found in Emily's family. Of course it was Emily's and Aunt Harriet's preoccupation with Captain Talgarth that had prevented them from curtailing Caitlin's indiscretion last night. On the whole, Caitlin was grateful her aunt and sister had been so distracted.

Through the course of several morning visits that day, however, she was surprised—and deeply relieved—to learn that the hottest gossip apparently centered not on Lord Kilverton's conduct at Almack's, but his sister's. Caitlin had steeled herself to meet with coldness, significant glances exchanged when she entered a room, or arch attempts to question her about the state of her affections—and instead she could discern only an eagerness to discover from her what she might know about the state of Lady Serena's affections. In her preoccupation with her own behavior, Caitlin had forgotten Serena's plan to flirt "outrageously" with Mr. Montague last night. Apparently she had achieved her ambition, and the gossips were already busy.

None of the talk seemed malicious. To Caitlin's delight, people seemed, if anything, pleased and congratulatory in their speculations about Ned's intentions. Mr. Montague and Lady Serena were both held in considerable affection by the *ton.* Miss Campbell was known to be Lady Serena's friend, but no one seemed to hold it against Caitlin when she would only laugh and shake her head. Let people read into it what they may! thought Caitlin. Serena had not only stilled the rumors about her own feelings for Captain Talgarth, she had effectively drawn the gossips' eyes away from Caitlin—bless her!

Nevertheless, Caitlin's heart was beating uncomfortably fast when she stepped into Lady Selcroft's drawing room that evening. She had carefully chosen to wear a creamy satin that draped beautifully, but with becoming modesty. Her hair was dressed high, and she carried an ivory fan chosen to match the ivory and pearl ornament in her hair and the pearls clasped round her throat. The effect was elegant, she hoped, but chaste. Tonight she must appear anything but *fast!*

The Delacourt party, and quite a crowd of other persons, was already present when Lady Lynwood and her nieces arrived. They found Lady Elizabeth standing stiffly near the fire, between Lord Kilverton and an imposing woman whom Caitlin guessed must be the Duchess of Arnsford. Elizabeth had also dressed with great care, Caitlin noticed. She looked extremely handsome—or would, if her expression were more amiable. She was wearing a beautiful color that looked magnificent on her: pale violet. Caitlin wondered nervously if

Elizabeth had deliberately chosen a color that Caitlin could never wear.

Lady Selcroft soon drew Caitlin and Emily toward the fire to introduce them to the Duchess of Arnsford. Her Grace proved to be a dragon of a female with a piercing gaze and a hostile attitude. A few weeks ago, Caitlin thought, Emily would have been frightened into imbecility by the duchess. These days, however, Emily's feet barely touched the ground. Mere social terrors could not reach the heights where Emily dwelled since meeting Captain Talgarth.

After bowing to the duchess, Caitlin shook hands with Lord Kilverton as briefly as possible. She did not dare to look him in the face as she did so, but turned immediately to seize Lady Elizabeth's hand before Elizabeth could withdraw it.

"I am glad to see you tonight, Lady Elizabeth," said Caitlin warmly. "I don't believe we've met since the day of the driving party."

Elizabeth bowed coldly, and pulled her hand away. Caitlin, trying not to read anything alarming into this chilly reception, pretended to notice nothing amiss. She summoned a smile, and tried again. "I hope you have been well?"

Lady Elizabeth's upper lip lengthened with distaste, which flared her nostrils as if she had encountered an unpleasant odor. "I have been quite well, Miss Campbell," she said repressively. She then lapsed into silence. It seemed she pointedly refrained from inquiring after Caitlin's health.

Since Lady Elizabeth knew her to have been injured in the accident, Caitlin could not mistake the snub. Misery clutched at her heart, rendering her instantly tongue-tied. Was it possible that Elizabeth suspected Caitlin of cherishing improper feelings for her fiancé? What a fiasco that would be! Caitlin, covered in shame, could neither speak nor move.

Relief came from an unexpected quarter. The Duchess of Arnsford had instantly perceived that Miss Campbell's friendliness toward her daughter was an attempt to scotch any rumors that might have started. This was quite self-serving of Miss Campbell, of course, but it would also serve the ends of the Delacourts. The duchess was as anxious as Miss Campbell could be to squelch any gossip regarding her daughter's engagement. If Elizabeth repulsed Miss Campbell's advances it would confirm the suspicions of such as Lady Markham. The duchess was acutely aware of several glances being furtively cast at their group, and felt a twinge of annoyance. Really, Elizabeth had no notion how to proceed in matters requiring the least delicacy!

Her Grace stepped majestically into the breach, breaking the quelling silence that had fallen. "You refer, I believe, to the driving party wherein Lord Kilverton's curricle sustained an accident," announced the duchess, gently waving her fan. "How thankful I am that Elizabeth was spared! She might easily have been riding in the curricle, you know."

Lord Kilverton's voice entered quietly into the conversation. "It was due to Miss Campbell's intervention that she was not, ma'am. Elizabeth had the headache that day, and Miss Campbell gave her her place in the barouche to spare Elizabeth any discomfort." Kilverton offered the duchess a chilly smile. "I believe you were previously unaware of the debt you owe Miss Campbell."

The duchess was greatly displeased. Impertinent! How dare he suggest that she owed Miss Campbell a debt? She glared at her future son-in-law. "Indeed! No, I had no idea. Certainly I had no idea."

Caitlin saw the struggle it was costing the duchess to accept that she owed a debt of gratitude to her. It seemed very odd to Caitlin. Her Grace was clearly angry with Kilverton; why?

With a shock, Caitlin realized that Her Grace must have been present at Almack's last night. Of course Her Grace had been there! Did I not meet her husband? she thought numbly. Had the duchess witnessed Caitlin and Lord Kilverton's indiscretion?

Color flamed in Caitlin's face. Even if others at Almack's had failed to observe Kilverton's attentions, naturally the duchess would notice something that concerned her so nearly! The realization rendered Caitlin even more acutely miserable. She hoped devoutly that nothing had been said to Elizabeth. But when she stole a glance at her, Caitlin's heart sank further. Elizabeth had turned quite white, save for two spots of color high on her cheeks, and her eyes glittered like blue ice.

This was dreadful. More than dreadful; it was catastrophic. Caitlin hurried into speech.

"Pray do not regard it—really, ma'am, I beg you will not give it another thought!" she stammered, deeply embarrassed. "It was all completely accidental—no one foresaw—no one imagined that anything so unlucky would occur."

Caitlin herself did not know whether she was speaking of the curricle accident or her feelings for Lord Kilverton. Really, it hardly mattered! The disclaimer would do for both.

Chapter XVII

Lady Selcroft was a notable hostess, and her spacious rooms filled rapidly with a glittering throng of fashionables. The musicians she had hired for the occasion struck up, refreshment tables were set out, and the evening progressed flawlessly. Caitlin, however, was not in a mood to appreciate the perfection of Lady Selcroft's preparations.

It seemed that Lord Kilverton was willing to join her in attempting to undo whatever damage they had done at Almack's. At any rate, he assiduously stayed away from her. Odd that she did not find this a relief. In fact, she had to repeatedly remind herself how glad she was that Lord Kilverton had taken her hint and was following her example. Gladness did not seem to be prominent among her emotions when she found herself carefully excluded from his company.

Caitlin gradually became aware that an evening spent in the same room with Richard Kilverton, if one could not speak to him, and if one must be continually on guard never even to *look* at him, was a severe punishment. Whenever she relaxed her guard for an instant, her wayward eyes would seek him out and follow him about the room. She kept catching herself up short and forcing her eyes to turn elsewhere—anywhere. That was how she saw her shy little sister, and that model of propriety, Captain Talgarth, slipping guiltily in from the garden. Caitlin did smile a little when she saw the self-conscious air with which Emily patted her hair into place. The glow in her sister's eyes was as unmistakable as that in Captain Talgarth's. Obviously something excessively improper had just occurred; probably a kiss; perhaps an offer of marriage made without obtaining Papa's consent!

A little laugh, and a pang of envy, shook Caitlin. She turned her eyes away with a sigh, to find Mr. Montague approaching her. He was gorgeously arrayed in dark blue superfine and dazzling white linen. As always, his appearance was precise to a pin—marred only by the indefinable air of rakishness that clung to him.

Mr. Montague handed Caitlin a glass of champagne and nodded wisely, jerking his head in the direction she had just been looking. "Devilish, ain't it? Your sister and Captain Talgarth, smelling of April and May! Enough to give anyone a fit of the dismals. I don't mind telling you, Miss Campbell, the odds are shortening in the clubs."

She stared at him, not sure he was serious. "Do you ask me to believe, Mr. Montague, that gentlemen are placing *bets* regarding my sister's future?"

"That's it." He must have seen her shocked expression, for he added hastily, "Meaning no disrespect to her, of course! But people are bound to talk. Well, only look at Talgarth! Never saw anyone make a greater cake of himself. How long has he known the chit? A fortnight? And here it is, bellows to mend with him already!"

She laughed, but shook her head. "Mr. Montague, if you must employ boxing cant, pray do not expect me to understand you! Are you one of the enterprising gentlemen placing these vulgar bets?"

He waved a graceful hand. "That wouldn't be sporting of me, would it? After all, I'm privy to inside information. Serena's not one to keep her observations to herself."

Caitlin eyed him anxiously. Was he in Serena's confidence on this matter? She wondered if she should warn him that his sudden flirtation with Lady Serena had not gone unnoticed. She began cautiously.

"Until last night, I was not aware of the—the extraordinary degree of intimacy between you and Lady Serena."

Mr. Montague grinned. "Oh, Lord, yes! We've known each other forever. I'm quite one of the family, you know."

That effectively silenced Caitlin. Mr. Montague watched as she cast about in her mind for some tactful way to proceed, and laughed at her. "I believe I know what you are about to

say—in the kindest way imaginable, of course! You would
like to warn me, would you not? I daresay all the biddies are
clucking, and naturally Serena don't know a thing about it.
She never did see past the end of her pretty little nose. Trying
to scotch one rumor, she starts another! It'll be her name
that's bandied about the clubs next—yes, and mine! Going to
ask me not to make a parade of Serena's folly, aren't you?"

Caitlin smiled apologetically. "Well, I wouldn't have put it
quite that way, but I would be glad to know that she stands in
no danger of making a figure of herself. I am very fond of
Serena." She laid a hand on his arm beseechingly. "Mr. Montague, you are a man of the world. I am sure you are aware
how vicious gossip can be. You will take care, won't you?"

Mr. Montague drew himself up indignantly. "Well, I like
that! Is it likely I'd harm Serena? You wound me, Miss
Campbell! Positively, you wound me! You must know I hold
Serena in far too much affection to let her do anything feath-
erbrained."

"You relieve my mind. Thank you! It's not that one expects
Serena to cross the line, naturally—"

"Not with me, at any rate." A hint of bitterness sounded in
Mr. Montague's voice, and Caitlin looked up at him, surprised. His sunny smile instantly returned. "Drink your champagne, Miss Campbell!" he recommended. "You are taking
far too serious a view of things, 'pon my soul!"

As he tossed off the glass in his own hand, Caitlin smiled
and followed his example. Mr. Montague had noticed that she
was not in spirits; that would never do. She had heard it said
that champagne had an elevating effect. She would see what it
could do for her. When a footman passed by with a tray, she
resolutely helped herself to another glass.

Mr. Montague tucked Caitlin's hand companionably into
his elbow. "Let us go and find Serena, Miss Campbell. You
will see for yourself how admirably I hold the line, no matter
how much encouragement I receive to overstep it!"

They found Serena surrounded by a rather noisy group of
admirers. One gentleman was engaged in taking snuff from
her outstretched wrist, while another laughingly protested
against her granting such a favor. Serena, who had stripped

off her glove to allow the foolishness, was flushed with excitement at her own daring. As she perceived Ned and Caitlin
approaching, she tossed Ned a glance full of saucy challenge.
He instantly rose to the occasion.

"What's this!" he exclaimed. "Serena, my love, you pierce
me to the heart! Must I call this gentleman out?"

Serena feigned surprise. "Oh, Neddie, are you here?" she
cooed. "I vow, I had quite given you up."

Ned struck a dramatic pose. "Could you doubt that I would
find a way to your side?"

The snuff-taking gentleman groaned, and the others
laughed good-naturedly.

"Oh, now that Montague is here, we may as well take ourselves off!"

"Farewell, fair Cruelty!"

Serena cried out against this. "No, how can you think of
going? It is only Ned, after all!"

Mr. Montague stared at her with pained surprise, placing
one hand on his heart. "*Only* Ned! But, Serena, what do you
want with these other gentlemen? Trust me, love, it is 'only
Ned' you want—'only Ned,' and no other!"

Caitlin saw the meaningful glances the other gentlemen exchanged while Ned bowed deeply over Serena's hand, and
blushed for her friend. Serena's name would indeed be
bandied about the clubs! How provoking of Mr. Montague!
Had he not just promised he would be careful? He straightened, laughing, and Caitlin threw him a reproachful look. She
quickly found that his fun-loving nature could not resist rising
to this bait.

"Now here is Miss Campbell looking askance at me!" he
exclaimed, covering her with confusion. "What have I done to
earn her disapproval, I wonder? Don't poker up, Miss Campbell, I beg of you! I am such a tender-hearted fellow, you
know, I cannot bear to be in anyone's black books."

Serena looked at her friend, half-laughing, half-anxious. "I
am sure Caitlin will forgive you anything, Ned, if you are
only kind to me!"

He squeezed Serena's hand. "Then I have nothing to fear,"
he said gallantly.

"And what of our black books, Montague? You will soon find yourself there!" cried one of the gentlemen.

"Yes, old chap!" said another. "We wish you will go find something else to do; you are very much in the way."

"Hear, hear!" cried the snuff-taker.

Mr. Montague rolled his eyes heavenward. "If I go, you will begin scraping snuff off Serena's wrist again with that great beak of yours, Crawley. And really, I must reserve that privilege entirely to myself." He pulled Serena's hand into his chest and bent, softly trailing his lips up the inside of her arm until she snatched her hand away, blushing fierily.

"Really, Ned, how can you?" gasped Serena breathlessly. "You know you don't take snuff!"

There was a general shout of laughter. Caitlin finished her second glass of champagne and wondered when she would start to feel better. She decided it was a mistake to surround herself with so much merriment. The more flirtation she witnessed, the more morose she would feel. She set her empty glass carefully on a nearby table, took another, and began to look around the room for an escape.

Serena cast an anxious look at Caitlin and turned up her nose at the assembled men. "I vow, I'll have no more to do with any of you! Come, Caitlin, let us withdraw."

Caitlin was glad to join Serena in bowing to her swains and heading toward the garden door. They had not gone far, however, when Mr. Montague stepped neatly between the two girls and tucked a hand in each elbow. "I hope you ladies don't mean to step onto the terrace without a gentleman in attendance?"

Serena frowned crossly at him. "That is exactly what we mean to do, Ned. I know you are only trying to help me, but I think you've done enough for one night. Pray consider your end of the bargain upheld! You may now go and amuse yourself as you please."

Ned shook his head gravely and assumed a fatherly air. "My dear Serena, I fear you do not understand the complexity of the task you have set me. Convincing the *ton* that you care nothing for Captain Talgarth is a tall order, you know. He is such a pattern-card! But I have some experience with these little *affaires,* and I believe we will succeed—eventually. However, you really must be guided by me on this. You must place yourself entirely in my hands. We cannot hope to squelch the gossip in a single evening, or even two. We must persevere, Serena. We must continue to pursue one another—diligently!"

As the threesome stepped from the brightly lit rooms onto the cool darkness of the terrace, Serena sighed. "I had no notion it would be so exhausting."

Ned abandoned his lecturing mode and grinned down at her. "Confess, Serena! You are enjoying yourself hugely."

Serena giggled, giving a little skip that made her curls bounce. "Well—*some* of it is very agreeable!" she admitted. "But I must say, Ned, the things you do can be a bit shocking. It's all very well to take snuff from a lady's wrist, but when there is no snuff there to be taken—and you know, Ned, you—you went rather farther than my wrist—"

"Beyond the line!" said Caitlin severely. "And you *promised* me you would take care!"

"So I did!" agreed Mr. Montague promptly. "But it's my belief we were doing famously until Serena blushed. Pity! Thing is, Serena ain't a woman of the world."

"She soon will be, if you make her name a byword!" said Caitlin tartly. She stopped, appalled at the raciness of her own remark. An unfamiliar recklessness was stealing over her. The champagne! she realized. Oh, dear!

Serena, meanwhile, was moved to protest. "I never blush, Ned! It's just that you took me by surprise."

An idea appeared to seize Mr. Montague. "You know, Serena, I am persuaded we ought to practice a little by ourselves. If we agree in advance exactly what we shall do and what we shall not, nothing can take you by surprise."

Caitlin regarded Mr. Montague with raised eyebrows. His expression was all innocence, but mischief danced in his eyes. She began to think this entire scenario had been carefully planned by him. The rogue!

Serena looked up at Ned trustingly. "Do you think a rehearsal would help?"

"By all means!" he assured her. "Let us go into the garden and begin."

Caitlin choked. "Mr. Montague, your conduct is quite shameless!"

Serena opened her eyes at her friend. "But, Caitlin, it strikes me as a perfectly sensible suggestion. Only think if Ned were to spring another such scene on me without warning! I am not used to encouraging that sort of conduct. If I am not expecting it I will pull away again, you know, and eventually our tale will be told. I think a rehearsal would be most helpful."

Caitlin tried to keep her countenance severe, and failed. She burst out laughing. "You are both impossible! If you are going off into the shrubbery to practice taking liberties with each other, I shall accompany you—and critique the effect."

"Excellent!" cried Serena happily, but turned to catch Mr. Montague trying to frown Caitlin down. "What is wrong?" she demanded. "Caitlin can be of great use to us, Ned. After all, the effect is the main thing we are trying to achieve."

"It's not the main thing *I* am trying to achieve!" muttered Mr. Montague, but no one paid any heed to this remark.

Caitlin was still laughing. "Come, Mr. Montague, what objection can you have?"

He threw her a fulminating glance, but inspiration struck. "The whole point of rehearsing is that we aren't ready for an audience!" he declared.

"Oh, very good!" cried Caitlin appreciatively. Mr. Montague bowed, his eyes alight with laughter. As he did so, he whispered for Caitlin's ears alone: "Spoil-sport!"

Serena was surveying the garden with a dissatisfied frown. "Our garden in Town is too small. I wish we were at Selcroft. These paths are too narrow for three persons."

"Quite right! What a pity! Well, there's no help for it. Miss Campbell must return to the drawing room, and we two shall stay out here and hone our skills. We will call her as soon as we are ready to demonstrate for a third person, and she may watch us from the terrace."

"To critique your performance?" Caitlin inquired.

"To applaud!" he corrected with an impish grin.

Serena was perplexed. "But I don't wish to abandon Caitlin. Can we not find another person to walk with her?" Her eyes lit up. "Here comes my brother! Now we may be comfortable."

Caitlin turned so swiftly she almost staggered. Lord Kilverton was standing at the terrace doors, his tall form silhouetted against the light. He was alone. Something like panic surged through her. She turned back to her friends and took a deep breath.

"If Lord Kilverton will be so kind as to walk with you, Serena, I will take Mr. Montague's arm—"

"Walk in the garden with my *own brother*?" interrupted Serena, staring at Caitlin in astonishment. "I would never dream of doing anything so—so *Gothic!*" She ran lightly down the terrace steps onto the lawn.

Caitlin could think of nothing to say, and felt remarkably foolish. Mr. Montague bowed briefly over her hand.

"Be comforted, Miss Campbell. Serena will come to no harm under my care," he said softly. "In fact, it is I who am in danger." He smiled a little ruefully at her startled expression, and departed after Serena.

Chapter XVIII

Caitlin watched them disappear down the path together, wondering if she had understood Mr. Montague correctly. Did he believe himself to be falling in love with Serena? Even worse: had he, perhaps, been in love with Serena all along? Pity tugged at her heart. If this were true, she could imagine few fates more horrible than poor Ned's. She tried to imagine how she would feel, if her beloved asked her to flirt with him to mask his feelings for someone else. She shuddered.

"What a strange business it is," she whispered.

"What is?" came a quiet voice at her elbow.

"Love," she replied, without thinking. She looked up. Her last word seemed to echo in the silence. Richard Kilverton was standing so close to her they almost touched.

"Yes," he said unsteadily. "A most mysterious business."

The air surrounding them was instantly charged with tension. Caitlin felt she couldn't bear it. If anyone else came out onto the terrace, her emotions would be in her face for all to read. She dared not speak. She turned blindly and walked away from him, away from the windows, away from the light. The terrace ran the entire length of the building. She thought if she could cross into the darkness she would not feel so vulnerable, so exposed. The moonlight, however, still poured down, and Kilverton followed her. There was no escape. He, at least, would know how she felt.

She stopped, leaning weakly against the cool stone of the Selcroft mansion. Lord Kilverton stood before her, his expression changed to one of concern.

"Are you quite well, Miss Campbell?"

She nodded, still unable to speak. He took the champagne glass from her nerveless hand and held it to her lips. "Drink this," he commanded softly.

Overcome by his closeness, she raised one hand to steady the glass, and sipped cautiously. The constriction in her throat loosened. "Thank you, my lord," she whispered. She sipped again. Both their hands were trembling, and the glass chattered against her teeth.

He turned abruptly, walked over to the balustrade, and set the glass down upon it. He then stood for a moment with his back to her. She watched him take a deep breath and square his shoulders, and knew he was trying to get a grip on his emotions. He would not look at her again until he had succeeded.

She suddenly realized that she did not want him to succeed. A strange, exhilarating rashness swept through her. The champagne tingled on her lips. She remembered how miserable she had felt that morning, thinking she could never have more of him than a paltry waltz or two, and her hands clenched into fists. This might be the last time she would ever be alone with him. Tonight might be the last time she saw him before he married Lady Elizabeth and was lost to her forever. And he was going to try to be *civilized*! No, she did not want him to succeed!

He was turning back to face her again, and this new, savage part of her rejoiced to see that he had failed to master himself. His tormented expression made her shake with love and longing. She felt she would give all she possessed to have the right to comfort him.

Kilverton crossed to her and took her hand. He spoke with a valiant attempt at lightness, but was unable to meet her eyes. He looked, instead, at her hand in his. "Miss Campbell, I—I fear my sentiments cannot be unknown to you." He swallowed painfully. "Forgive me. It was never my intention to—to embarrass you, or put you in a position of—of—"

Embarrass her! Did he think she was *embarrassed*? Among all the emotions swamping her senses, how absurd to single that one out! The instant he brought it to her attention, she banished it. There was no room in her heart for embarrass-

ment; not with everything else she was feeling. Not tonight.
This was the only moment she would have, and she wanted it
filled with a memory she could hold close through the lonely
years that loomed ahead. The sweet new recklessness seized
her; the champagne sang in her veins. A queer little laugh escaped her.

Kilverton's eyes flew to her face in a look of startled in-
quiry. What he saw there made him catch his breath. Caitlin's
eyes were wide and misty, inches from his own, their expression fierce and sultry.

"Kiss me," she whispered.

He stared at her for half a heartbeat, unbelieving. This precious, unattainable girl was lifting her face to his, *asking* for
his kiss! It was the most erotic suggestion he had ever heard.
It would take a stronger man than Richard Kilverton to resist.
To him she seemed impossibly lovely, infinitely dear. He forgot everything but the lips turned up to his.

Caitlin had no time to regret her words, or think better of
the impulse that had prompted them. Kilverton's arms
crushed her to him with a startling ferocity. She found herself
clinging to him, and gasped at the novelty of powerful shoulders beneath her fingers, of his tall, lean body crushed against
her own. Her instinctive response to his very masculinity bewildered her, but there was no time to accustom herself. His
mouth touched hers and she was immediately plunged into a
new flood of sensations.

She was completely unprepared for the totality of this experience. It was impossible to tell where emotion left off and
sensation began. His mouth was softer than she had thought
possible, warmer than she remembered, thrilling in a way she
had never imagined. His lips took hers with a fierce, dizzying
possessiveness. He overpowered her, and she found herself
yielding eagerly. It was astonishing, it was terrifying, it was
glorious.

Her swift response set Kilverton's heart racing. He began to
slow and soften the kiss, knowing this was a mad thing to do.
Warnings sounded in the back of his mind, but he ignored
them. She was so sweet! She tasted like summer, and music,
and the fulfillment of every longing his heart had ever known.

And she tasted of champagne.

It was this that made him eventually, reluctantly, lift his mouth from hers. The sight of her face still turned up to his, eyes closed, her soft lips still parted for him, almost unmanned him. He uttered a sound halfway between a groan and a laugh, and clutched her to his heart. Champagne and moonlight! he thought wryly. I have taken ungentlemanly advantage of a romantic girl's inexperience! Still, he could not resist kissing the top of her head. A sweet, subtle fragrance clung to her hair.

Lord Kilverton had a shoulder very conveniently placed for a tall lady's cheek. Caitlin felt his lips in her hair and sighed blissfully. She wished nothing more than to stand here forever, feeling his strong arms around her, forgetful of everything but the intimacy of this moment. His kiss had left her dazzled, shaken, and utterly content.

Kilverton, however, was far from content. The kiss had aroused more in him than mere emotion, and some time passed before he trusted himself enough to speak. He had no wish to let her go, but finally forced himself to hold her gently away from him. He took a deep breath, his fingers tightening on her arms.

"I should not have done that, Miss Campbell. I apologize."

There was a shocked silence. "What do you mean?" she whispered. He saw the hurt and bewilderment in her eyes and cursed himself silently.

"I mean that—as usual, it seems—my manners deserted me the instant I found myself alone with you."

She pulled herself out of his grasp. He watched as she tried pitifully to collect her wits and regain a measure of dignity. She folded her arms and hugged herself, an unconscious gesture that almost brought tears to his eyes. It was as if she was protecting her heart from further wounding.

She took a ragged breath and managed to smile crookedly. "There is no need to apologize, Lord Kilverton. I believe I—" She stopped, and he saw pain flicker in her eyes before she continued. "I asked for it, did I not? Literally, it seems."

He had shamed her. This was intolerable. Impulsively, he reached to comfort her—then let his arm drop impotently back to his side. She was not his to comfort. "You asked for it very sweetly," he said unsteadily. Memory gripped him, and he thrust it out of his mind. He feared he might ravish her if he pictured again the look on her face, and her voice whispering *Kiss me.* "But it was my part, as a gentleman, to resist the temptation. I had a duty to protect you. I failed, Miss Campbell. Pray do not blame yourself."

The hurt in Caitlin's eyes deepened, and she looked down to hide her shame. How could he *apologize* for what had seemed to her the most transcendent experience of her life? It must have struck him quite differently. She blushed to think how idiotic she must appear to him—how vulgar—how *wanton*! She had disgraced herself indeed.

She did her best to speak lightly. "This is a nonsensical discussion, is it not? I threw myself at your head. It is I who owe you an apology, Lord Kilverton."

"But I began it."

Caitlin looked up at him, puzzled. "Began it? How?" She cast her mind back, in some confusion.

"If you will recall, Miss Campbell, I was on the point of— of making a declaration." He gave a short, bitter laugh. "A most improper declaration, under the circumstances."

Oh, yes. She had been in the grip of so much emotion at the time, she had barely been listening. Now she remembered.

"You were expressing, I think," she said slowly, "a fear that—that your sentiments were already known to me. You believed they had caused me embarrassment." She tried to smile. "Well! Whatever your sentiments failed to do, my own have done—abundantly. It is absurd to stand here and argue about whose fault it was. I suggest we return to Lady Selcroft's soiree and forget what happened here."

She intended to walk away. It was very odd that she found herself pulled back into Lord Kilverton's arms. She wasn't sure how it happened, but once she was there it didn't seem possible to leave.

His voice was low, but charged with emotion. "Can you forget what just passed between us? I cannot."

A rush of relief, joy, longing, and sorrow shot through Caitlin. It had meant something to him, after all. She tried to shake her head, but as it was pressed against his shoulder this was unsuccessful. She found she must lean back against his arms and look into his face. Once she had done this, she found she could not speak. However, it did not seem necessary to speak.

He lifted one hand and gently touched her face. "So sweet," he whispered, and kissed her again. He did not crush her against him this time, but kissed her softly, delicately, as if she might be breakable. She closed her eyes, letting her lips cling to his, willing this moment to never end. When it did, she opened her eyes slowly, feeling dazed and oddly breathless. His hands slid lightly down her arms, and took her hands in a firm clasp.

"Miss Campbell—Caitlin—I must have your answer before I—" He stopped, and took another deep breath. "If I were free to do so, I would lay my heart at your feet. Do you understand that?"

She nodded dumbly, wondering how it was possible to feel wretched and joyous at the same time.

His grip on her hands tightened, and his eyes searched hers painfully. "I must know. If I were free—if I could come to you with a clear conscience—how would you answer me?"

She felt her breath stop. Answer him? How would she answer him? His question shattered all that remained of her defenses. The hopeless dreams she had kept at bay until now suddenly, vividly, materialized in her imagination. She could no longer fight them. Her longing overcame her reason, and a dizzying wave of feelings swept her.

Lord Kilverton's anxious eyes continued to hold hers. "You hesitate! I am answered. Miss Campbell, if I have jumped to the wrong conclusion I beg your pardon—"

It was impossible to think clearly with Lord Kilverton touching her. She snatched her hands away. "Oh, *hush!*" she exclaimed breathlessly. "How can you stand there and talk such fustian to me? You are not answered—I have not answered you. I cannot answer you! Let me think—I have not considered—" Reality returned, and she covered her face with her hands. "This is pointless. You are asking me to consider the impossible."

His voice was salted with bitter amusement. "Miss Campbell, I have done nothing but consider the impossible for many days now."

She shrugged helplessly. "But why? To what purpose? I do not understand."

She felt his arms go round her again with sudden savagery. "By all means, let us have it in plain English! I am sick of this maundering." He pulled her hands away from her face and cupped it firmly with his own, forcing her to meet his eyes. "The idea of marriage with anyone other than your own precious self has become intolerable to me. If it were possible to secure your hand, I would do anything—anything at all—to win it."

Her pulse jumped beneath his fingers, and he smiled tenderly at her. "I am such a coxcomb, you know, that I have come to believe my advances might not be unwelcome to you."

She gave him a tremulous smile. "What an odd idea, my lord."

"Yes, isn't it? I only wish I were free to test the truth of it."

Tears stung her eyes. "I wish you were, too."

He pulled her back into his arms and held her fiercely. "I must break my engagement."

Despair and guilt caught in Caitlin's throat. "You cannot do so."

"I must try. But it will cause a great deal of unpleasantness, I fear, and I cannot tell what the outcome may be. I do not wish to take such a step without some assurance from you."

Her voice was almost inaudible. "What assurance can I possibly give you?"

He sighed. "Why, none at all. You can promise me nothing, and—however much I may wish to—I can promise you nothing. I may not succeed in freeing myself, and until I do, I have no right to ask anything of you. But I have an overbearing disposition, as you have pointed out! I know you have not had time to consider, and it was absurd to think you could give me an answer tonight. But give me some hope, Caitlin." He laid his cheek against her hair. "Only a little hope. Is that too much to ask?"

To his surprise, a chuckle escaped her. "When I consider my behavior during the past half hour, and observe that I am even now clinging to you in a *most* improper fashion, I am astonished you are asking so little."

His laugh rumbled against her ear. "Is that a 'yes'?"

She nodded shyly into his shoulder. "It is as close to 'yes' as I dare go," she whispered.

Despite the seemingly insurmountable obstacles that lay ahead, it was impossible to feel anything at this moment but elation. A rush of optimism caused Kilverton to exclaim, "It is settled, then! I will go to Elizabeth tomorrow morning and we will discuss the matter like reasonable beings. She cannot wish to marry a man whose heart she can never have! Why, nothing but misery could result from such a match. She will release me—and I will come to you—and I will *hope*, Miss Campbell."

Chapter XIX

The next morning, the Duke of Arnsford's second footman presented himself in the morning room to announce the arrival of Lord Kilverton to Her Grace and the young ladies. It was the first time Lord Kilverton had visited the ducal mansion in nearly three weeks, and the footman would have given much to know the meaning of the glance exchanged between Her Grace and Lady Elizabeth. However, Her Grace merely said, "Show him up, William," and so William was forced to withdraw before he could hear anything interesting.

"Gracious!" cried Lady Winifred, a pert and unpleasant child of fourteen. "I vow, I've almost forgotten what Lord Kilverton looks like."

Two of Winifred's older sisters saw fit to snigger at this witticism, but Lady Elizabeth's eyes flashed with anger. Her Grace spoke freezingly before Elizabeth could lose her temper.

"Winifred, Caroline, and Augusta—you will all three go immediately to the schoolroom. Elizabeth and I shall receive his lordship in private."

The nasty smiles were instantly wiped from three faces as the girls chorused, "Yes, Mama," and rose meekly to depart. Augusta appeared somewhat vexed by this dismissal to the schoolroom, as she was nearly twenty years old, but she did not dare to cross her mother—or, for that matter, her sister Elizabeth.

When her sisters had gone, Elizabeth nervously patted her hair and twitched her fichu into place. Richard had apparently not courted Miss Campbell's company last night at his mother's soiree, but neither had he stayed at his fiancée's side. At one point, in fact, he had disappeared for over an hour. She dreaded discovering the meaning of this morning's interview. "Do not desert me, Mama!" she implored under her breath, just before the door opened to admit their caller.

There was a gravity in Lord Kilverton's demeanor, and a martial light in his eye, never before seen by Elizabeth. She carefully ignored these alarming signals and advanced with her hand held out, her face wreathed in smiles.

"Richard! How pleasant this is! What brings you out so early in the day?"

He took her hand briefly and bowed. "The hope that I might claim a fiancé's right to some time alone with you, Elizabeth. How do you do, Your Grace? I trust you will excuse us for a few minutes?"

"How do you do, Kilverton?" pronounced Her Grace, majestically ignoring his request and waving him to a chair. "Your visit is extremely *apropos*. Elizabeth and I wish to request your opinion on several matters. September is not so very far away, you know, and an event of this magnitude requires careful planning. We are expecting several hundred guests at the wedding breakfast. Elizabeth and I had thought to hold it on the South Lawn, but if the weather should be inclement would you object to moving the breakfast indoors?"

Elizabeth picked up her mother's cue and rushed into speech. "Oh, yes! Of course we meant to ask you, Richard. Delacourt has an enormous ballroom. It would certainly hold everyone, but the *decor* is rococo—quite definitely rococo! Do you think it might be too ornate for a breakfast?"

Kilverton was nonplussed. "Well, really, I—"

Elizabeth interrupted him rather feverishly. "There is the gallery, you know! It might be considered odd to serve a wedding breakfast in a gallery, but it is extremely large and all the windows face south, so even on a rainy day the gallery has a great deal of light. I think light gives a cheerful aspect, don't you? Yes, all things considered, I believe I prefer the gallery to the ballroom."

By this time, Kilverton was frowning. "I have seen neither room, Elizabeth, so I can hardly be expected to have an opinion."

Elizabeth uttered a gay and tinkling laugh that made the hairs on the back of Kilverton's neck stand up. "Oh, well, we did not like to make all the arrangements without you, you know! After all, it will be *your* wedding as much as mine."

Kilverton took a deep breath, but the duchess forestalled him. "Very true, my love, but we cannot expect gentlemen to enter into the spirit of planning a wedding with the same interest we do. It will be our place, Elizabeth—yours and mine—to arrange and to execute all the details that will make your wedding day run smoothly. I recall your grandmother saying to me—" And she launched into a lengthy and boring anecdote regarding her own wedding, the only point of which, so far as Richard could see, being that her husband must have been as reluctant a bridegroom as he himself was. For the first time, Richard felt a twinge of sympathy for the luckless Duke of Arnsford.

Courtesy forbade him to interrupt the duchess, but as soon as she paused for breath Kilverton determinedly entered the conversation, no longer caring if he appeared rude. "I fear I cannot spare my entire morning to you ladies. Before I go, I would like to request a few minutes alone with Elizabeth— immediately!"

Elizabeth shot a despairing glance at her mother, but Her Grace was unable to think of any reasonable objection. Once a couple were betrothed, it was absurd to pretend they required a chaperon. Seeing that her redoubtable mother was, for once, at a loss, Elizabeth forced out another high, breathless laugh.

"Well, really, Richard, I cannot imagine why you would need to see me alone. Anything you wish to say to me you may say before my mother."

"You are mistaken," said Richard grimly, striking terror into Elizabeth's heart. "Would you care to step into the drawing room, Elizabeth, or do you prefer the salon? It is immaterial to me." He rose and held the door open for her as he spoke. Thus challenged, Elizabeth felt she had no choice but to comply. She rose stiffly. Kilverton bowed to the duchess and led Elizabeth to the small salon off the entry hall, where he firmly shut the door—greatly disappointing William, who had lingered in the hall hoping to witness just such a scene as was doubtless about to occur.

Once alone with him, Elizabeth faced her fiancé squarely, her eyes now glittering with the light of battle. "What is it you wish to say to me?" she demanded. "I take leave to tell you, Richard, I find your conduct most extraordinary! How dare you absent yourself for two weeks without a word of explanation, and then demand a private interview? I expect an apology, my lord."

This was going to be even more difficult than Kilverton had foreseen. He felt all the guilt and embarrassment natural to a man who was about to do something he feared was not quite honorable, plus a stab of pity for Elizabeth. It cost him an effort to meet her gaze, but he did so, reminding himself that the happiness of three people was at stake—his own, Elizabeth's, and most importantly, Miss Campbell's.

"You have my apology," he said gently. "I am sorry, Elizabeth—sorrier than I can say—for whatever pain I have inflicted, and the pain I fear I am about to inflict on you."

Elizabeth clutched the back of a chair, feeling suddenly faint. He cannot jilt me, she reminded herself desperately. He cannot! Meanwhile, Kilverton launched into a rehearsed speech.

"You have spoken to me repeatedly about the many ways in which our opinions and outlooks differ, Elizabeth. You have pointed out, and carefully explained to me, the gulf that lies between us on almost every issue of importance. I have come to the conclusion that I agree with you on this, if nothing else, and I wish to assure you that I will bear you no ill-will—none whatsoever!—should you wish to be released from your promise. In fact, I will do whatever I can to smooth the way for you and make that decision easier."

Elizabeth summoned up a rather ghastly smile. "You are all consideration, my lord. But I do not wish to be released from my promise. Many couples disagree on various matters and yet live together quite comfortably. I am persuaded you and I will achieve a similar success."

Kilverton almost winced. "You call such a marriage *successful*? I would call it a disaster. Our views are opposed on this, as on nearly everything else." He crossed the room swiftly and took her hands in a strong clasp. "Think, Elizabeth! It is not too late. I beg you, do not force us into this alliance. A marriage between such ill-matched personalities will doom us both to a lifetime of regret."

Elizabeth snatched her hands out of his grasp, an ugly color suffusing her face. Her features contorted with rage. Startled, Kilverton instinctively stepped back.

"So *now* we come to the point!" she spat. "It is you who desires a release from your promise, not I! How *dare* you come to me, mewling and sniveling about 'smoothing my way'? Pretending to consider my feelings! Filling my ears with this Banbury story about a 'lifetime of regret'! I'll show you the meaning of a 'lifetime of regret,' my lord! I'll make you sorry you were ever *born* if you dare to jilt me! You will never live it down! Never! Not you, nor any of your family!"

Kilverton stared in amazement as Elizabeth leaned forward, her eyes narrowing with menace. "Who do you think you *are*?" she hissed. "Viscount Kilverton! What is that? A trumped-up title for the son of Selcroft! And who will you be? The *sixth* earl! Why, the Delacourts were Dukes of Arnsford when the town of Kilverton was a two-horse farm—when your family was nothing but a gaggle of upstart yeomen! If you believe you can offer *me* an insult of this magnitude, you will soon discover your mistake!"

"I have already discovered my mistake," said Kilverton drily. "If you do not desire to become a Kilverton, Elizabeth, you have my heartfelt permission to remain a Delacourt."

Elizabeth realized she had made a tactical error. She struggled for a moment to recover her temper. "I did not mean to speak disparagingly of your family. I beg your pardon! I am afraid I was angry for a moment."

Kilverton laughed mirthlessly. "Handsome of you! But I do not want your apologies. You express nothing but contempt and dislike for me, and yet you propose to live intimately with me for the rest of your life. How can you stomach the idea, let alone insist upon it?"

Confusion flickered in Elizabeth's eyes. "Did you think we

were making a *love match*?" she gasped, her voice and face expressing all the horror she felt at such a vulgar notion.

Kilverton could not repress a shudder. "Certainly not!" he replied. He regarded her gravely. "But did you not hope, Elizabeth, that we would come to love one another—in time? If I had not thought so, I would never have offered for you."

Elizabeth's lips curled into a scornful smile. "I never dreamed you harbored such shabby-genteel sentiments, my lord. I do not consider *love,* in the sense you speak of it, to be either necessary or desirable in marriage. On the contrary, I believe it often leads to unhappiness of the worst kind! Pray do not expect me to hang on your sleeve, my lord, once we are married. I will not willingly provide food for vulgar gossip, or furnish entertainment for others through my behavior."

With a shock, Kilverton realized it was this very quality he had once prized in Elizabeth. He remembered, as if in some distant dream, that he had congratulated himself on acquiring a wife who would enact him no passionate scenes, and expect none from him. The aspect of Elizabeth's character that had most appealed to him a month ago now struck him as repellent. Groaning inwardly, he tried again.

"Elizabeth, believe me, I am doing you a favor in urging you to break our engagement. There must be any number of men who will value your irreproachable conduct. I am not among them! You would do well to look elsewhere. I am willing to play whatever role you assign me in this—to appear villainous, foolish, or licentious—anything you ask! Only set us free from one another, Elizabeth. I beg you."

Elizabeth's angry flush returned, and her voice shook with rage. "I will not! I will not even listen to you! Our betrothal has been announced. The wedding date has been set. How can you ask me to even *contemplate* such a humiliating step? It is far too late for these repinings, Richard! I tell you again, if you play the jack with me I will make you regret it to your dying day!"

Kilverton's mouth set grimly. "Perhaps I have not made myself plain, Elizabeth. What I am proposing is that *you* jilt *me.* I do not share your scruples. You may humiliate me with my goodwill! I will gladly be an object of scorn or pity for a few months, rather than marry where I cannot love. Jilt me, Elizabeth! I will not contradict whatever story you choose to tell to justify the action."

"Very pretty talking, Richard! And what of my reputation? What of my future? What becomes of all the gentlemen who supposedly will value me for my 'irreproachable' conduct? Will these gentlemen still value me, once I have created a scandal? It is preposterous! Who will offer for me, once I have jilted you?"

Kilverton's heart sank. "I have told you, you may place the blame for it squarely on my shoulders."

"Yes? And what am I to say? Why did I cry off, Richard? Are you a drunkard? Odd that no one else has noticed it! Did you, perhaps, strike me? Is that more likely?"

"Yes, it is," agreed Kilverton promptly.

Elizabeth was not amused. "It is not at all likely, and that is precisely my point! No one will believe any tale wild enough to justify my taking such a drastic action." She faced Kilverton squarely, her eyes glittering.

"In the interests of our future harmony, I have decided to forget this conversation ever took place. I believe it is natural to feel some degree of nervousness before one's wedding. I consider that you have expressed to me nothing more than natural misgivings, and that we have now dealt with them satisfactorily. My sentiments have undergone no change, Richard, and I contemplate our future alliance with every expectation of happiness. I will be glad to take your hand in church on the second of September. Good day, my lord!"

Kilverton regarded her bleakly for a moment. "I will leave you," he said quietly. "But I hope you will carefully consider what I have said."

"Good day!"

"If you change your mind at any time, Elizabeth—"

"Get out!"

Kilverton bowed ironically and flung open the salon door, thinking savagely what a gudgeon he had been to believe Elizabeth would never enact him any emotional scenes! His rapid exit greatly discomposed William, who had been hovering directly outside. All expression instantly vanished from the footman's countenance and he stared impassively into the middle distance. Kilverton took no notice of him, however, but strode purposefully toward the front door. William watched his lordship's departure with covert interest. Furious sobs and the crash of flying ornaments seemed to be emanating from the salon. He wondered if this would be the last the ducal staff might see of Lord Kilverton.

Lord Kilverton, meanwhile, went directly to Half Moon Street, inadvertently beginning a train of speculation in the mind of Lady Lynwood's butler.

Stubbs would never so far forget himself as to betray either his suspicion or his disapproval, of course, but it was uncommon odd for his lordship to be visiting at all—and to be asking for Miss Campbell, rather than her ladyship—well, it was hard to put an innocent construction on that, wasn't it? Not to mention that the gentleman had A Certain Look about him, as Stubbs confided later in the privacy of the housekeeper's office.

"Crossed in love, Mrs. Hopper, or I miss my guess!" said Stubbs impressively.

"Go on with you, then!" chided Mrs. Hopper, pouring the butler a second cup of tea. "You never saw this Lord Kilverton above twice in your life, Mr. Stubbs, and for all you know that's his natural expression."

"Well, then, he's mad as a hatter," averred Stubbs. "And pale as a panada, to boot! No, Mrs. Hopper, I know a gentleman what's been crossed in love when I sees one. Had you seen him, you'd say the same."

"And do you ask me to believe Miss Campbell has encouraged Lord Kilverton to dangle after her? Why, his lordship is engaged to the Duke of Arnsford's eldest!" Mrs. Hopper was an avid reader of the society columns. "I'll never believe such a thing of Lady Lynwood's own niece, Mr. Stubbs, and I'm ashamed of you for thinking it."

"Well, I've got nothing against the gel," said Stubbs, aggrieved. "But what am I to think when a strange gentleman arrives all in a pother, hammers on the door like one demented, and instead of enquiring for her ladyship, as he *should* do, asks to see this Miss Campbell? I put it to you, Mrs. Hopper:

'How does it look? And does she refuse to see the gent? No! Ties on her bonnet and steps out with him, if you please! And off they go, a-walking to the Green Park!" Stubbs shook his head slowly. "It don't look right, Mrs. Hopper. That's all I'm saying!"

The housekeeper stirred her tea, pondering this information. "Perhaps Lady Serena had an important message for her particular friend, and sent it through her brother."

Stubbs gave a snort of derision. "Why should they step out together like it's a great secret? A deuced long message, that! They were gone above an hour!"

Mrs. Hopper was incredulous. "Well, I never—! Are you sure, Mr. Stubbs?"

"Above an hour, I say, and very nearly two! I let them out, and I let them in. Well above an hour, or my name ain't Bob Stubbs. Which it is!" He leaned forward meaningfully. "And the way he looked when he arrived wasn't nothing to the way he looked when he left! Blue as megrim, Mrs. Hopper!"

"Then you may depend upon it, Miss Campbell gave your fine gentleman his comeuppance." Mrs. Hopper nodded comfortably. "Left with his tail between his legs, did he? That'll teach him to come sniffing round a respectable female!"

Stubbs scratched his chin thoughtfully. "Well, it didn't strike me that way. Not quite that way. In fact, if you was to ask me, Miss Campbell herself looked as queer as Dick's hatband. She sent him off, all right and tight, but she didn't look any too happy to see him go, Mrs. Hopper. She went to the parlor and watched him walk away. Sat at the window, she did. Watched him all the way to the end of the street. I stepped away for a bit, and when I come back, there she was, still a-sitting at the window and a-staring down the street. And him gone for ten minutes or more! I says to her, 'Can I get you anything, miss?' and she says to me—"

They were interrupted by a pattering knock on Mrs. Hopper's door followed by the breathless entrance of Jane. She bobbed a nervous curtsy when she saw Stubbs closeted with her supervisor.

"Oh, I'm sorry, Mrs. Hopper—Mr. Stubbs—"

Mrs. Hopper beckoned her forward. "That's all right, Jane. What is it?"

Jane's eyes were big as saucers. "It's Miss Campbell, mum! She's asking to have her trunks brought down from the attic. She's going back to Hertfordshire, mum! Did you ever?"

The housekeeper's startled eyes met Mr. Stubbs's over their teacups. Mr. Stubbs nodded with great satisfaction, forgetting in the excitement of the moment to maintain his dignity before Jane.

"There, now! What did I tell you?" he exclaimed. "Crossed in love, Mrs. Hopper—the both of them!"

Chapter XX

Lady Lynwood was not fond of rain under the best of circumstances. All Saturday morning it rained, and she found herself feeling more and more cast down. Caitlin's abrupt departure had thrown a pall of gloom over the household, and now the weather trapped her ladyship in the morning room with Emily. She tried to recruit her spirits with a novel from the lending library, but Lady Lynwood had never been much of a reader. The heroine's improbable adventures completely failed to divert her attention from the cares and disappointments pressing upon her. When she realized she had been reading the same sentence over and over for several minutes, she gave up. Emily looked up from her needlework as her aunt flung the book down with a sigh.

"I do not understand why Caitlin left us!" exclaimed Lady Lynwood pettishly, for perhaps the twentieth time.

"She felt she could not stay, Aunt."

"Yes, but *why*? It's nonsensical! Pretending Amabel needs her to help with Nicky—such stuff! I have two boys of my own, and it's my belief they're all the same. When James broke his arm, do you think he would let us cosset him? Well, he wouldn't! And no more will Nicky, you mark my words. She'll go home to find she's not wanted in the least. And if she *was* wanted, wouldn't Amabel have said so in her letter?"

Emily's lip trembled. Caitlin had confided to her the real reasons for her departure. It was difficult—and rather dreadful—to keep secrets from Aunt Harriet, but Emily had to agree that it was better to hide all knowledge of Caitlin's illicit romance from their aunt if they could. Aunt Harriet would be so distressed!

Emily sincerely pitied her sister. She had herself recently learned something of the power of love, and knew how inexplicably it could bind two people together. Emily tried to imagine what she would have done, had Captain Talgarth been betrothed when she met him. The idea made her shudder.

The butler stepped into the morning room, and Lady Lynwood brightened. A visitor was just what she needed. She believed she would welcome Bonaparte himself on a day like today! However, Stubbs' announcement, although not so dramatic, caused her ladyship's face to crumple into an expression of dismay. Lady Serena Kilverton had arrived, asking for Miss Campbell. Ought he to show her up?

"Oh, dear! Yes, of course—at once, Stubbs." As Stubbs bowed himself out, Lady Lynwood straightened her cap distractedly. "How excessively provoking! I wish Caitlin had left a note for Lady Serena. I do think she might have thought of that. Whatever are we to say to her?"

Emily had paled a little, but replied with composure. "We have only to tell her what happened, Aunt." Emily devoutly hoped she would have the presence of mind to reveal nothing of the truth to Lord Kilverton's sister. Somehow it struck her as a very different matter, and much more difficult, than keeping the secret from Aunt Harriet.

Serena entered the room with her usual briskness, bringing the smell of rain with her. Her cheeks were pink with cold. "Oh, what a lovely fire!" she exclaimed, rubbing her hands with delight. "This rain is delicious, though, isn't it? I do love a cold snap after it's been so warm."

Lady Lynwood was so very far from agreeing that she was thrown even further into disorder. She clucked and fluttered vaguely, leaving Emily to shake hands and settle their visitor on the sofa.

Emily picked up her needlework again, blushing a little as she spoke. "I am sorry Caitlin is not here to receive you, Lady Serena. She will be so vexed to learn that you ventured out in all this weather to call on her, only to find her gone."

Serena paused in the act of brushing raindrops from her sleeve. "Gone! How is this? She said nothing to me."

Emily found it difficult to meet Serena's gaze, and bent quickly over her sewing. "Well, it was quite sudden, you see. Our brother, Nicholas, has broken his arm and Caitie felt she could be useful to Mama."

"Do you mean she has gone to *Hertfordshire*?" demanded Serena, astonished. "In the middle of the Season?"

"I daresay she may return before long." Emily blushed at her own untruthfulness, but tried to speak lightly. "After all, Rosemeade is only half a day's journey from town."

Lady Serena's sentiments now seemed to coincide so exactly with her own that Lady Lynwood's sense of ill-usage returned in full force. She rushed into agitated speech. "You are thinking how excessively odd it is, Lady Serena, and I must say, I perfectly agree! I thought she was fixed here for another three or four weeks, at the least. Why, *everyone* is! And it isn't as if she went to Brighton, or even Bath. She's gone off, all in a quack, to Hertfordshire! Well! It presents a very off appearance if you ask me—which, however, nobody did. Anyone would suppose Nicky to be on his last legs, and it's nothing of the kind! In fact, it's not his legs at all, it's only his arm—but that's all of a piece! Or, rather, I suppose it's not all of a piece, because it's broken—but that's neither here nor there! Well, of course it's *there,* actually, but it certainly isn't *here,* and now Caitlin is *there,* when she ought to be *here,* and I, for one, simply cannot understand it."

"Yes, but it all sounds like a hum," objected Serena, as soon as Lady Lynwood stopped for breath. "After all—"

"Oh, no, Lady Serena, I'm afraid it's not a *hum,* although I am not precisely certain what that signifies. I would be very glad to believe it is all a hum, but I daresay Nicky *has* broken his arm, for what purpose could Amabel have in deceiving us all? And I cannot believe they would be mistaken about such a thing, for a broken bone is nothing like a sore throat, which could be anything at all, but my point is: what does Caitlin mean to do about it? She's not a surgeon! And even if she *were,* which, as I say, she is not, I daresay everything was done that could be done for Nicky a week ago, and very likely more!" Lady Lynwood began ticking the days off on her fingers. "Amabel wrote on Wednesday, you know, so I suppose Nicky broke his arm last Monday or Tuesday, or even earlier than that, because the house would have been at sixes and sevens when it first happened and I cannot imagine Amabel sitting down to dash off a letter in the midst of a domestic crisis. We had her letter Thursday morning, and Caitlin left yesterday afternoon, and of course today is Saturday, so Nicky would be—"

"Forgive me, but I don't perfectly understand you," interrupted Serena. "If you received the letter Thursday morning, and Caitlin considered the news to be so grave, why did she not leave until Friday afternoon?"

Lady Lynwood's jaw dropped. "That *is* odd!" she exclaimed. "Most extraordinary! Why, she was completely calm when we read the letter, was she not, Emily? She never said anything on Thursday about wanting to go home, did she? Fancy! She didn't say anything Friday morning, either—although she did look a little peculiar. Do you recall that, Emily love? We both remarked on it. She wasn't herself at all. And then all of a sudden, that afternoon, she decides she must go home. I wonder if that was what she was discussing with Lord Kilverton? You know, I often feel the lack of male advice in my life these days, and I suppose Caitlin does, as well. Men have such excellent, practical notions! I fancy she discussed it with him, and he advised her to go."

Now it was Serena's jaw that dropped a little. "You think she discussed it with *my brother*?"

Lady Lynwood nodded, pleased to find herself understood. "That must have been it. For why else would he call? He had certainly never called here before."

Serena, thoroughly mystified, turned to Emily for enlightenment. The state Emily appeared to be in increased Serena's bewilderment. She was plying her needle with an assiduousness belied by her trembling hands, and the face bent over her work was scarlet.

"Emily, what on *earth*—"

"Oh, pray, Serena, do not ask me!" gasped Emily, pressing her hands over her burning cheeks. And to the amazement of both Serena and Lady Lynwood, Emily rose and fled.

A short time later Serena burst into her father's library in high dudgeon. Just as she had guessed, her brother and Mr.

Montague both were present, poring over the racing forms. They looked up in surprise as Serena flung open the door and glared at them, her small hands balled into fists. Mr. Montague unconsciously touched his cravat and straightened in his chair, but these telltale signs were lost on Serena. She was far too angry to notice, and she was not looking at him.

"Richard, what have you done to Caitlin Campbell?" she asked fiercely. "Has that *poisonous* fiancée of yours finally succeeded in driving her away? I know perfectly well what Elizabeth has been saying, but it's all utter *rot,* and at any rate I won't have you repeating it to Caitlin!"

Ned rose to his feet with aplomb, bowing gracefully. "Serena, my dear, how delightful to see you! Do come and join us," he suggested. "Do you fancy Jack-Come-Tickle-Me or Mother Goody in the fourth?"

"What? Oh, sit down, Ned, for heaven's sake," Serena said, but her lips twitched and her expression lost a little of its heat. He obeyed her solemnly.

The *Weekly Dispatch,* meanwhile, had slid from her brother's grasp. "What happened?" he demanded. "Is Miss Campbell all right?" The intensity in Richard's voice caused Ned's eyebrows to fly up in surprise, but although he cast a rather searching glance at his friend, he said nothing.

Serena flung her gloves onto the library table with much the same gesture as one issuing a challenge. "She has gone home to Rosemeade, and I know perfectly well she had no plans to do so. You may as well tell me the truth, Richard! She decided to leave only after speaking with you yesterday, so I am certain it was something you said that caused her to go. She told her aunt some farradiddle about her mother needing her. Well, I wasn't deceived! It's my belief Emily knows why Caitlin left, but she won't say anything—when I tried to tax her with it, she ran out of the room! Now, why on earth would you call on Caitlin? And why would she consent to see you alone? There's some mystery here, and I will *scream* if you don't tell me what it is!"

"Can't have that!" said Ned promptly. "Bradshaw would summon the watch, and we'd all end up in the roundhouse. Beg you will sit down, Serena!"

Serena tossed her hat to join her gloves, and sank into a chair across from the two men. Her anger muted into anxiety.

"I cannot believe Caitlin would leave town without a word to me." Serena gazed solemnly into the hazel eyes so like her own. "I'm sorry if I offended you by calling your fiancée poisonous, but I'm afraid my first thought was that she's done something to drive Caitlin away. You must be aware that Elizabeth has taken Caitlin in dislike for some reason. She has tried for weeks to persuade me to cut the acquaintance. I can't begin to tell you how vicious she's been, how persistent! And Caitlin has done nothing whatsoever to incur such enmity."

Serena leaned forward earnestly, placing a beseeching hand over her brother's. "Caitlin is a perfectly *splendid* girl, Richard. I wish you knew her! It is impossible to believe anything bad about her once one is truly acquainted with her. I can't bear it if Elizabeth has used my own brother to hurt Caitlin in some way."

A queer little laugh escaped Lord Kilverton. "You need not seek to convince me, Serena. I am perfectly ready to believe Miss Campbell a paragon among women." He rose suddenly and walked to the window, apparently struggling with some strong emotion. "I wish I could offer you an explanation," he said at last. "The truth is, I did not know Miss Campbell would leave the metropolis. I promise you, Serena, that was not my object in speaking to her yesterday."

"Then why did she go?" demanded Serena.

Kilverton turned to face them, his face suddenly haggard. "I do not know."

"What a rapper! It's clear you know *something*."

"What I do know, I am not at liberty to divulge."

"Well!" gasped Serena, affronted. "Anyone would suppose you were employed in espionage!"

However, all her urgings failed to induce her brother to confide in her. Mr. Montague eventually escorted Serena from the room, recommending her kindly not to tease Richard to tell her a secret that anyone but a peagoose could see involved someone other than himself. Serena took exception to this, declaring her conviction that if it was Caitlin who had a secret, she herself would be in possession of it. But she finally con-

sented to go, having expressed the opinion that when she lay
on her deathbed—in Bedlam, no doubt—Richard would be
Excessively Sorry that he had not trusted her!

Ned followed her, but paused with his hand on the latch.
"You'll be wishing me at the devil, old fellow, so I'll take
myself off. No, no, do not apologize! I've no wish to intrude
on what is clearly not my affair. But if you think of a way I
can assist you—or Miss Campbell—you'll find me at my
lodgings in Clarges Street."

Kilverton's shoulders relaxed a little. "Much obliged to
you, Ned." He smiled faintly. "As you have no doubt guessed,
I am in the devil of a coil."

Mr. Montague nodded, keeping his face carefully neutral.
"I have guessed what the trouble is, of course—but, for your
sake, I hope I am wrong." And with that Parthian shot, he exited.

Kilverton spent the greater part of the afternoon cudgeling
his brain in a futile attempt to decide what was best to do. His
immediate inclination, sternly suppressed, was to post instantly to Hertfordshire. He knew that would be useless, however, In fact, the longer he thought, the more he understood
Caitlin's course of action. It was depressingly clear to him
that unless he prevailed upon Elizabeth to change her mind,
Miss Campbell's company would be torture and the pursuit of
her acquaintance folly.

An evening spent staring into the fire, and a sleepless night,
resulted in a decision. Kilverton would post off to Hertfordshire after all—to seek the advice of his maternal grandmother, Lady Colhurst. Lady Colhurst was a needlewitted,
sharp-tongued octogenarian with a great fondness for him. If a
way out of his difficulties existed, her shrewd common sense
would find it.

Lady Colhurst resided year-round at Hatley End, a country
house near St. Albans. Kilverton knew his grandmother was
old-fashioned enough to disapprove of any visitor arriving on
the Sabbath, so he contented himself with sending her word to
expect him on Monday. He informed Jamie, his new tiger,
that he would require the tilbury to be brought round Monday
morning.

The tilbury was ready betimes, Lord Kilverton's valise was strapped onto the back, he gave his horses the office to start, Jamie jumped nimbly up behind, and they were off. Kilverton skillfully threaded his horses through the metropolis, and the scenery soon took on a more rural aspect. The traffic dwindled and eventually disappeared.

They had reached a stretch where his lordship's tilbury was the only vehicle in sight, when Kilverton was roused from a brown study by a sound of galloping behind him. He pulled obligingly off the crown of the road, creating space for whoever was in such a hurry to overtake him.

It almost sounded as if the thundering hooves were drawing too near for safety. Kilverton turned to glance behind him, intending to call out a warning.

Then something struck him a powerful blow on the back of his head and he knew no more.

Chapter XXI

On Monday afternoon, Miss Emily Campbell, tortured by guilt, set out to pay a call of apology on Lady Serena Kilverton. She was taking the first possible opportunity to explain, if she could, her strange and hasty exit during Serena's Saturday visit. Her plans were soon hindered somewhat by an unexpected encounter with Philip Talgarth. Captain Talgarth, through a combination of luck and design, met Emily *en route* to Mount Street and offered to escort her to her destination. Once she had Captain Talgarth's arm to sustain her rather than Lady Lynwood's footman trailing in her wake, Emily's progress slowed from a businesslike walk to a dreamy stroll. By the time they reached the Earl of Selcroft's town home it was nearly two o'clock and she had all but forgotten the purpose of her visit.

Serena received the two of them with great fortitude, although it was certainly a little off-putting to feel oneself a third wheel in one's own home. Besides, it still annoyed Serena to see Captain Talgarth dancing attendance on anyone other than herself. Desperate to distract her visitors from their absorption in each other, Serena had just rung for tea when Mr. Edward Montague was announced. Serena brightened perceptibly.

Before Serena could tell Bradshaw to show him up, however, Ned shouldered past the affronted butler and fairly ran to her, seizing both her hands in his. "Serena, where is Kilverton?" he demanded.

"Three miles from Selcroft Hall," she replied promptly.

"Not the town, you little wretch! Your brother!"

Serena, laughing, struggled to disengage her hands. "He

drove out this morning to Hatley End, I believe. We don't expect him back before evening, and perhaps not until tomorrow. Really, Ned, how can you burst in here in this hurly-burly fashion? Do you not see I am engaged?"

"Beg pardon!" said Mr. Montague hastily, favoring Emily and Captain Talgarth with a sketchy bow. He turned back to Serena at once, however, regarding her with painful intensity. "Serena, did Kilverton have his tiger with him when he left?"

Serena stared at him. "Yes, of course. Whatever is amiss? You look as if you'd seen a ghost."

Ned swore under his breath and took a swift turn about the room. "What I have seen is your brother's tiger!" he flung over his shoulder at Serena. "Leaving messages all over town for your Uncle Oswald!"

Serena caught Ned by the arm. "Sit down, Ned, for pity's sake! You are giving me the fidgets. Now, pray, what are you on about? Why should Richard's tiger be leaving messages for Uncle Oswald? What sort of message is he leaving?"

Ned perched obediently on the edge of a settee, but gave the appearance of being poised for instant flight. "Well, you've hit it, Serena. Why *should* Richard's tiger be hunting high and low for Oswald Kilverton? Oh, and skulking about with the greatest secrecy imaginable, let me tell you! Leaving discreet little messages at White's, and Boodle's, and the Lord alone knows where else. I discovered it by the merest accident. I was just coming out of White's when I saw him— what's his name? Jimmy?"

"Jamie. But, Ned, you must have been mistaken! Jamie is even now with my brother—"

"No, he is not, I tell you! Unless—Serena, is it possible Richard has returned to town for some reason?"

Serena looked doubtful. "He has certainly not returned here, at any rate."

Emily's soft eyes widened. "Oh, I do hope Lord Kilverton has not met with another accident!"

Ned's mouth hardened into a grim line. "I hope not, indeed."

It was clear he placed no dependence on this hope. Serena's fingers tightened on the arms of her chair, but she took a reasonable tone. "Ned, if some accident befell Richard, Jamie would be with him. He would certainly not return to London without my brother! If Richard were injured in any way, Jamie would fetch a surgeon. Or at the very least he would return to Mount Street with the news, not go off to tell my uncle, of all people!"

Ned leaped up as if goaded, and took another turn about the room. "Yes, except that he has not returned to you, and he *has* gone off to search for your uncle! And where is Richard? There's something devilish havey-cavey afoot!" he exclaimed. "Your brother has met with too many accidents lately, Serena. And I'd stake my last groat your uncle's at the bottom of 'em all!"

Having stunned the company to silence, Mr. Montague then delivered a pithy outline of the suspicions he had voiced to Richard in Lord Selcroft's library not so long ago, and ended with: "There will be the devil to pay, if that new tiger of Richard's was somehow bribed by your uncle to—" He broke off, swallowing hard.

Serena, who had grown noticeably paler during Ned's summation of the dangers he saw threatening her only brother, pressed a shaking hand over her mouth. Emily flew to her side and placed an arm around her. "You must not be alarmed, Lady Serena," she said gently. "We do not know that anything bad has happened, after all."

"There may be an innocent explanation for these things you have mentioned, Montague," said Captain Talgarth bracingly. "And there may be an innocent explanation for Lord Kilverton's servant seeking out his uncle. Kilverton may have sent him to do so."

Mr. Montague gave an expressive snort, and Serena shook her head, whispering, "Impossible!"

Captain Talgarth lost none of his calm authority. "Well, if Mr. Montague suspects foul play, we certainly must take steps to discover the truth. It does seem unusual that Lord Kilverton's tiger, after driving off with him as recently as this morning, should have returned to town."

"Aye!" Ned growled. "Without Richard! And searching eagerly for that scoundrel, Oswald Kilverton! Daresay they've

connected by now. Even as we speak, Oswald may be congratulating Jamie on a job well done."

Serena uttered a squeak of fear and bounded up out of her
chair. "Why are we all standing about? We must do something!" she cried.

"So we shall." Captain Talgarth, accustomed to command,
was not surprised to find three pairs of eyes turning expec-
tantly to him. He cast an appraising glance at Mr. Montague.
He had been in the habit of thinking Edward Montague a frippery fellow, but Ned was returning his gaze with a level, con-
centrated attention that caused the captain to hope he had been
mistaken. He reserved judgment until he could determine how
well Mr. Montague followed orders.

"Mr. Montague, do you go back to White's and discover
what you can. Someone will know of Jamie's whereabouts, or
Oswald Kilverton's. With luck, Lord Kilverton himself may
be there, or someone may have seen him, and the mystery will
solve itself. In the meantime, I will pay a short visit to the
Duke of Arnsford. It may be that Lord Kilverton has, in fact,
returned to town and is even now with his fiancée. It is con-
ceivable he would go there first, rather than here. Regardless
of what we find, we shall reconnoiter here within the hour."

This demonstration of the captain's masterful ways caused
Emily to glow with admiration, but Serena bristled at such
high-handedness. "And what am I to do?" she demanded. "I
cannot sit here waiting tamely for your return!"

The captain regarded her, considering. "I believe you
should ensure that horses are waiting for us when we do return." He bestowed a reassuring smile upon Lord Kilverton's
anxious relative. "More than likely, we will have no need of
them," he said soothingly. "But if we fail to find Lord Kilverton—or at the very least, Jamie—Mr. Montague and I will
ride out in search of your brother's tilbury."

As soon as the men were gone, Serena jumped to ring the
bell and plunged into a flurry of activity. The tea for which
she had rung earlier arrived, and while Emily poured, Serena
arranged for the requested horses to be saddled and brought
round. She also sent for her abigail, ordering her to instantly

pack a bandbox with all items necessary for an overnight so-
journ at a country house.

"Mind you, Sarah, it must contain only the bare essentials!
Everything must be included in one bandbox. But, stay—do
pack extra linen, if you please, and my pink muslin."

Sarah hurried off to do her bidding, and Emily turned bewildered eyes upon her hostess. "Lady Serena, I do not understand. Why must your abigail pack a bandbox?"

Serena struck a small fist into a determined palm. "If Ned
and Captain Talgarth go in search of Richard, I go with them!
He is my brother, after all. I cannot stay here, fretting myself
to flinders while others ride to his rescue! Mama would see
me and instantly know something was amiss, and I do not
wish to frighten her when there is nothing she can do." She
clasped Emily's hands beseechingly. "You will go with me,
will you not? Pray do not desert me—for I very much fear we
will not return before dark, and must stay with my grandmother Colhurst one night. I have directed Sarah to bring
extra linen, and my pink muslin will suit you beautifully."

"Go with you!" gasped Emily, shrinking. "Oh, Lady Serena, I cannot—"

"Yes, indeed you can!" urged Serena. "We may easily send
a note round to Lady Lynwood. And oh, Emily, if you do not
go, how can I?"

Emily instantly saw the force of this argument. She was
very much in sympathy with Serena's desire to join in the
search for her beloved brother, but it would, after all, be a
shocking thing for Lady Serena to ride out of Town with two
single gentlemen, unaccompanied by any female. If she did
not return until the morrow, that would be more shocking still.
However, neither Emily's regard for the proprieties, nor her
strong inclination to accompany Captain Talgarth wherever
he might go, could immediately persuade her to set down her
tea and dash off the requisite note to Lady Lynwood. Serena
spent the better part of an hour pleading with her. Emily had
just seated herself reluctantly at the tambour-topped writing
desk when they heard Mr. Montague's excited voice raised
once again outside the drawing room door: "Thank you, I'll
announce myself!"

Ned burst in and Serena ran to him, thoughtlessly clutching at his elegant lapels and crushing them in her anxious fists. "Ned, what has happened? I thought Captain Talgarth would return before you! Did you find Richard?"

"No, I did not." Mr. Montague's sustaining arms came up to steady Serena, and he grinned down at her. "No need to pull my coat about, Serena! We'll find him, all right and tight."

There was a reckless, angry glitter in Mr. Montague's eyes, and although he kept one arm around Serena his concentration was clearly elsewhere. "I take it Captain Talgarth has not returned? Well, we may still hope he found Kilverton in Lady Elizabeth's drawing room."

Serena, unaware that she still clung to Mr. Montague's willowy form, turned a shade paler. "No, for if Richard were there, the captain would have returned or sent word by now. I was convinced you would find him at White's!"

"No, neither Richard nor his tiger. White's had nothing to tell me but that they had sent Jamie to Mr. Oswald Kilverton's lodgings. So off I went, hot-foot, to knock on Oswald's door. Had to grease that butler of his in the fist, but I found out a few things worth knowing." Ned uttered a short, ugly laugh, and his arm tightened around Serena. "Jamie had been there less than an hour before me, and had private speech with Mr. Kilverton. Your precious Uncle Oswald then instantly ordered a hack sent round. When last seen, Oswald was riding out of town—north! With your brother's tiger to show him the way, Serena."

Both girls gasped, and Mr. Montague ground his teeth. "The worst of it is, I didn't even have to describe the rascal to Oswald's butler—he knew Jamie's name; knew him quite well, in fact! Your brother's tiger was a bootblack and kitchen boy in Oswald's own household until very recently!"

Serena gave a little scream of fright and flew out of Mr. Montague's arms. "What can be keeping Captain Talgarth? We must set out for Hatley End immediately!" She rang the bell violently and sent a startled footman to fetch the bandbox from her abigail.

Mr. Montague, whose appetite was unaffected by emergency, had discovered the tea cart and was refreshing himself with a generous slice of cake. "Here, I say!" he spluttered. "What do you want with a bandbox, Serena?"

Emily, pale but resolute, laid a gentle hand on Mr. Montague's arm. "Pray let me hand you a dish of tea, Mr. Montague! Lady Serena and I will naturally accompany you on any search for her brother."

Mr. Montague choked. "Will you, by Jove? I think not! No, Serena, do not argue with me! Captain Talgarth and I are not setting off on an expedition of pleasure! If you are picturing a gentle canter across a meadow, you're fair and far off, my girl! Neither of you has the stamina to join us on this venture, and I'll be da—I'll be *jiggered* if we slacken our pace to suit a couple of sidesaddled demoiselles bogged down with baggage!"

"Very well, then, Emily and I will not ride. We shall go in my phaeton!" said Serena staunchly.

Mr. Montague groaned, but Serena nibbled her finger, thinking swiftly. "Driving the phaeton will not be as tiring as riding. We must not attempt to keep the parties together, of course; you and Captain Talgarth should ride ahead—although the phaeton will probably keep up with you regardless, because we will not stop for any reason. Emily and I shall drive directly to my grandmother Colhurst. You men must halt from time to time to ask if anyone has seen my brother's tilbury. If you encounter any news—*any* news, Ned!—you must either find us on the road or catch us up at Hatley End."

"What, two girls alone, bowling down the open road in a park phaeton?" objected Ned. "For one thing, it ain't safe, and for another—"

"Then you and the captain may take turns escorting us! But I can't and I won't be left behind!" cried Serena vehemently, and pulled the bell yet again to order the phaeton. Lady Serena and Mr. Montague were still arguing when Captain Talgarth arrived. To everyone's astonishment, Lady Elizabeth Delacourt walked in with him.

Captain Talgarth, in the mistaken belief that Elizabeth was suffering the alarm and tender emotions he knew Emily would feel in a like situation, had kindly brought her to Mount Street so she might have the comfort of her future sister-in-

law's companionship while he and Mr. Montague searched
for Lord Kilverton. However, in the cacophony of excited
voices that followed his entrance with Elizabeth on his arm, it
became abundantly clear that Lady Serena was refusing to
stay quietly in London, either to comfort her brother's fiancée
or for any other reason. When he learned that Emily intended
to join Serena on this foolish and dangerous exploit, the captain was genuinely shocked. His vigorous protests found a re-
ceptive ear in Lady Elizabeth, who (to Serena's dismay and
Emily's relief) instantly proposed to go in Emily's stead.

"For whatever Serena may be willing to risk in this preposterous escapade, she must not risk her reputation!" pronounced Elizabeth. Captain Talgarth honored her for this
noble sentiment, until he realized that Lady Elizabeth's resolve stemmed largely from her belief that Emily's inferior
social standing rendered her chaperonage inadequate. He instantly took umbrage at this offensive notion. Serena, half
wild at any delay, and Emily, anxious to escape the necessity
of leaving her aunt alone, managed to soothe the captain's irritation before much time was wasted in a fruitless attempt to
convince Lady Elizabeth of her error.

Emily was soon safely despatched back to Half Moon
Street, Mr. Montague and Captain Talgarth were adequately
mounted, Lady Serena and Lady Elizabeth were handed into
Serena's phaeton, and the party set off in search of Lord Kilverton.

Chapter XXII

L ord Kilverton was struggling with a difficult decision: whether or not to open his eyes. He was lying on an extremely hard and uncomfortable surface, and a pounding sensation at the base of his skull interfered with his ability to think clearly. He reluctantly concluded that he was, in fact, awake. He reached this conclusion several times, each time forgetting that he had pondered the question before. His thoughts flew away like startled sparrows whenever he reached for them.

Something had happened; that much was clear. Something odd. Something bad. It seemed important to recall what it was, but his memory, like his wits, floated above his grasp. A vague feeling of dread seized him through the fog. Perhaps it would be better to clutch the remaining shreds of unconsciousness round him and slip back into oblivion. He slept.

When he drifted back into consciousness the pounding in his skull had lessened, but his body felt stiff and sore. He tried to stretch his limbs and discovered they were bound. Startled, his eyes flew open. As the light stabbed into them he groaned, and thus discovered he had been gagged. A rough cloth was stuffed into his mouth, and apparently tied round the back of his aching head. Somehow this infuriated him more than the tying of his hands and feet. He struggled and kicked impotently for a few seconds, trying to loosen the restraints enough to get his hands to his mouth and remove the gag. It soon became apparent that any exertion would cause him to pant, and panting was an uncomfortable proposition with his mouth tied up. He lay still again, and forced himself to think.

He was lying on the floor of a very small, and exceedingly

dusty, room. It had every appearance of belonging to an abandoned cottage. How he had come there was beyond his ken. He was completely alone. The fireplace looked as if it had not been used for months, possibly years, and there was no furniture of any kind. The dimness of the light filtering through a dusty casement in the stone walls indicated that the cottage's exterior must be overgrown with some kind of foliage. Certainly no one lived here.

He recalled that he had been on his way to visit his maternal grandmother, to ask her advice on how one might gracefully extricate oneself from an unwanted betrothal. He reflected wryly that there was nothing like having one's hands tied literally, to make figurative snarls seem trivial.

He remembered now that a man—or was it two men?—had ridden up behind him and that something had then struck him a tremendous blow. It did not require a powerful leap of intellect to deduce that whoever had ridden up behind him had struck the blow. He strained to recall the face he had just glimpsed over his shoulder before turning back to his horses. Certainly a stranger. He could recall nothing of his appearance except that he had worn a brown coat, and had a muffler round his neck. Not a very useful description.

His mind was still moving too sluggishly to make sense of it all. He ceased to ponder the whys and wherefores, and bent his mind to the more immediate task of freeing his hands. He rolled rather painfully onto his side. This caused his head to swim sickeningly for a moment, but he lay quietly and waited for the sensation to pass. He could now discern footprints in the dust, and a clean swath cut from the door to where he lay. This indicated he had been tied by the door and then dragged to the center of the room. He promised himself that he would contemplate the implications of this in a moment. It might be important. Meanwhile, he would close his eyes.

Time passed. He might have slept again. When he opened his eyes once more, it seemed the light had subtly altered. It occurred to him to wonder if it was still Monday. His thoughts were sharper now, but his discomfort had increased. A raging thirst consumed him. He burned to rid himself of the gag. Now that his wits were returning, it occurred to him that whoever had brought him here, and for whatever purpose, he must free himself before he (or they) returned to finish their business. Richard stared at the marks on the floor with new concentration. Why had he been dragged to the center of the room?

The walls of the cottage were very rough. Light showed dimly through chinks between the stones. Was it possible the villains who had tied him thought he might sever the ropes by sawing them against a sharp stone? Was that why they did not leave him against the wall? He would test that hypothesis. He began to inch himself across the floor, back along the trail where he had been dragged.

It proved to be extremely difficult to move across the filthy floor to the wall. Not only were his feet and hands bound, but the separate loops round his feet and hands had been connected with a third rope, neatly trussing him like a Christmas goose. Urgency drove him. He half rolled, half squirmed, his head pounding, dust filling his nostrils and gritting in his eyes. He eventually reached the wall and tried to catch his breath. Sure enough, several of the stones close to the floor had sharp protrusions. Working his way up to a sitting posture seemed impossible, so he felt along the base of the wall behind him until he found a likely edge, and began sawing against it with grim determination.

It was exhausting work. He did not have much play in the ropes, and could only guess at where the knot must be. The muscles in his forearms began to cramp and he still could not gauge if his efforts were having any effect whatsoever. Then he suddenly felt something snap, and heart flowed back into him. He rubbed and sawed with renewed persistence, and soon felt the bonds give way. Rejoicing, Kilverton eased his stiff and cramping arms up and untied his gag, working his jaw and groaning with relief. He had just finished untying his legs and was trying to massage some life back into his limbs when he heard the unmistakable sound of someone approaching on horseback.

Cold fury gripped him. Quick as thought, he grabbed his bonds and repositioned himself in the center of the room, looping the ropes back around his feet and reluctantly replacing the hated gag. He put his hands behind him and lay on the floor. The daylight still seemed strong outside, and he hoped whoever entered the dim cottage would be dazzled enough to not immediately perceive the telltale marks on the floor or any change in the way he was tied. He feigned unconsciousness, but lay facing the door, his eyes not quite closed.

Appearing helpless, but with every sense on the alert, Lord Kilverton awaited developments.

The door opened, flooding the room with blinding daylight. Kilverton's eyes closed in earnest for a moment. Someone was pausing on the threshold. He cautiously opened his eyes just a slit.

With a strange sense of inevitability, and an utter lack of surprise, Richard recognized his Uncle Oswald. It is terrible, he thought, to discover such a monstrous thing and feel no amazement. Sadness mixed with his anger. But Richard did not move, and his slack expression did not change.

He watched his uncle's elegantly shod feet take a few cautious steps toward him. Still he did not move. Oswald paused again, then advanced and bent over him. Instantly, Richard sprang up with a snarl and knocked Oswald Kilverton to the floor. His loosened bonds and gag went flying. Oswald gave a startled cry as he hit the floor, and Richard sent a crashing right to his jaw.

"Let's give you a taste of your own medicine, you conscienceless bastard, and see how you like it!" Richard gasped, ripping the starched cravat from his uncle's throat and stuffing it into Oswald's mouth. Oswald's eyes widened in pain and fury, but in his white-hot rage Richard paid no heed. He gagged his uncle quite thoroughly. As Oswald struggled, his eyes burning with hate over the folds of the gag, Richard tied him with his own discarded bonds and finally sank back, panting, to regard his handiwork.

"Well, that's turned the tables rather neatly," he remarked, wiping the sweat from his brow with a shaking hand. "I'll think what to do with you in a moment. Faugh! I'm as weak as a kitten." Richard leaned against the sharp stone walls and closed his eyes against the light pouring through the door, fighting to regain his breath. Through the haze of fatigue that gripped him he was dimly aware of the sound of carriage wheels. To his considerable astonishment, it was his cousin Egbert's voice he heard raised in anxious query as this equipage pulled to a halt outside the cottage.

Sir Egbert's "Holloa!" was followed by a great sound of creaking and puffing as he obviously clambered down from the carriage unassisted and hastened across the yard. Richard turned his head against the wall and regarded the opened doorway in bemused weariness. In due time, Sir Egbert's portly form appeared in it. An almost comical amazement was writ large across his features.

"I say!" exclaimed Sir Egbert. "What's toward? Richard, by Jove! Is everything all right?" His eyes traveled to where his father lay, and nearly popped from his head in dismay. Richard laughed faintly, partly at the picture of Egbert goggling at the scene, and partly with relief.

"Well, Egbert, I don't know when I've been more glad to see anyone," said Richard gratefully. "Give a fellow a hand up, won't you?"

Egbert, turning to stare in bewilderment at his cousin, perceived his disheveled state and at once crossed to help him stand. "Yes, but—how comes it that you are here? And with my father! God bless my soul! What can this mean?"

"I should like to know that myself," replied Richard as Egbert, striving for respectability even in this extremity, dusted his cousin ineffectually with a handkerchief.

"But have you been set upon by thieves? Were you kidnapped? For God's sake, let us untie my poor father!"

"No!" said Richard sharply, reaching out to stay Egbert's hand. "I feel rather safer with him bound, thank you."

Egbert's jaw worked soundlessly for a moment. He stared first at his father, then at his cousin. "Never tell me my father has offered you a mischief!" he finally uttered, wringing his hands. "Oh, I feared it! I feared it! But I never thought—oh, surely this is impossible! It cannot be!"

"Apparently it is possible, and it can be. Come, help me think! We must extricate ourselves from this tangle with a minimum of scandal. What lucky chance brought you here? I must say, it's a stroke of good fortune. Who better than Oswald's son to tell me how I can render Oswald powerless without causing irreparable harm—either to his person, or our family?"

Sir Egbert was not much given to the exercise of swift thought, however, and his character was neither decisive nor masterly. He had turned quite pale with horror and perplexity, and stood in the center of the room, uttering disjointed exclamations for several minutes. His confusion was so evident, Richard took pity on him.

"I fancy we need not decide immediately what is best to be done. Let us take my uncle up in your coach and convey him to Hatley End. My grandmother Colhurst will look after all three of us while we talk the matter over like civilized beings."

But Egbert shook his head, distressed. "No, Richard, dear old boy. I fear our only course is to take my father directly to Bow Street, or the nearest roundhouse, or—or somewhere where he might be incarcerated. It is very dreadful, but how much more dreadful if he should escape us somehow! A dashed clever fellow, my father. We must give him no opportunity. I have no more wish for a scandal than you, coz, but we must do what is right. My father must repent of his actions. He must suffer for his designs. He must pay the price of his iniquity. He must—"

"Yes, yes, I daresay!" interrupted Richard. "But not, I think, immediately! Here, assist me. I cannot lift him alone. Let us get him into your carriage, where we may argue about our next step in comfort."

Richard bent over his uncle's prostrate body, Egbert still clucking and muttering behind him. Just then there was a tremendous crash and a shout from the casement. A small body hurtled through the open door. Richard turned and straightened in surprise, just in time to see his tiger, Jamie, leap onto Sir Egbert's back with a bloodcurdling whoop. Egbert staggered, overbalanced, and went down with a startled "Oof!"

"What the—" Richard began, but got no further. The Honorable Edward Montague and Captain Philip Talgarth burst ferociously into the room, effectively robbing him of speech.

Lord Kilverton blinked at these unexpected arrivals in the liveliest astonishment.

Jamie, in the meantime, had jumped off the prostrate Egbert. He sprang to one side with his fists purposefully clenched, but Sir Egbert did not rise. "That's done 'im, then!" he exclaimed shrilly.

"Good work, lad," pronounced Captain Talgarth. "You may safely leave him to our devices."

It dawned upon Richard that his friends were brandishing pistols in a manner that struck him as theatrical in the extreme. He was seized with an overwhelming longing for his quizzing glass. Lacking this necessary article, it was difficult to properly express his emotions upon this occasion. His lips twitched.

"Er—I beg your pardon, but is this a rescue party?" inquired Lord Kilverton politely. "How very much obliged to you I am! Really, one does not know quite what to say. I had hoped you might arrive a little sooner, of course—prior to my disposing of the danger myself—but after all, it is the thought that counts."

Mr. Montague, much moved, strode forward and clapped Lord Kilverton on the back so heartily that Kilverton winced. "Aye, you wouldn't believe me, would you? But I wasn't far wrong."

"My dear Ned, you were not wrong at all—hit the nail squarely on the head, in fact."

"No, no—for I thought your uncle was behind all these attempts on your life!"

Kilverton's brows lifted. "And so he was. At least—one assumes, naturally—" He glanced round the room in surprise, and took in the meaning of the scene for the first time. Captain Talgarth's pistol was leveled not at Oswald, but at Sir Egbert, who was still lying facedown upon the floor.

Kilverton pressed a hand to his brow. "I see," he said slowly. "I think—yes, I really think I had better sit down for a moment." He waved a hand faintly toward Oswald. "And perhaps someone should untie my good uncle."

Chapter XXIII

Lady Colhurst, expecting a visit from her grandson Richard, suffered a vague sense of ill-usage when her granddaughter and prospective granddaughter-in-law were announced. Her habits were regular, and her mind was not elastic. The unexpected never failed to annoy her. She peered suspiciously at her footman and thumped her cane in irritation.

"What's that? Serena and Lady Elizabeth? Alone? Fiddle! You can't have heard properly. Richard must be with 'em, although why he brought two girls along, without a word to me, is more than I can say."

The footman, a long-suffering individual, bowed. "I h'apprehend, madam, that, so far from h'accompanying or even h'expecting his lordship, the ladies are h'unaware of his precise whereabouts."

Lady Colhurst gazed balefully upon her servant. "Ought to buy you an ear-trumpet!" she announced. "You may expect one for Christmas, Addison! Well, I'll soon get to the bottom of this. Did you leave my granddaughter kicking her heels in the hall? Show her up, man, for heaven's sake! And the Delacourt chit, of course. Can't abide her, nor any of her family, and I'm not likely to change at my time of life. Still, if she's to marry my grandson I suppose I'll be doing the pretty to that mackerel-backed Arnsford and his whey-faced daughters for the rest of my life. May as well begin now."

Serena and Lady Elizabeth, ushered into Lady Colhurst's tiny, but formidable, presence, looked a little the worse for wear. They had not had an agreeable journey. By the time they arrived at Hatley End both were hanging on to their tempers by the slenderest of threads. Serena's indignation at having Elizabeth's company forced upon her did not augur well for the expedition at the outset, and the natural differences in the two girls' temperaments and opinions made their confinement together in the phaeton extremely trying to both of them. The drive had been dusty, long, and excessively warm, and the strong sunshine had given Elizabeth her usual headache. Serena was frantic with anxiety about her brother; Elizabeth, irrationally but unshakably convinced that danger could not possibly threaten persons of Lord Kilverton's rank, was growing increasingly waspish. Elizabeth could scarcely have been more annoyed if Richard had engineered his own disappearance expressly to embarrass the Delacourts. Her air of exasperated martyrdom naturally infuriated Serena, and something very like a quarrel was brewing between them. Lady Colhurst's sharp eyes perceived hostility in the air the instant the two girls, tired and travel-stained, walked through her drawing room door.

"Good day to ye both," said Lady Colhurst. "You'll forgive me if I don't rise. I'm not as spry as I once was, more's the pity. To what do I owe the honor of this visit?"

At the sight of her beloved grandmother, sudden tears stung Serena's eyes. She affronted Elizabeth's already lacerated sensibilities by immediately rushing forward with a little sob, and falling upon her grandmother's neck. This gratified Lady Colhurst extremely, but she spoke with her accustomed sharpness even as she patted Serena comfortingly with one arthritic hand.

"Well, what's all this? Serena, you always were a widgeon! Stop behaving like a watering pot and give us a proper kiss."

With a shaky little laugh, Serena kissed her grandmother's cheek. "I beg your pardon, Grandmama. But it's been the most dreadful day—you don't know! I was sure we would find Richard here, and now we see he has never arrived, and oh, Grandmama, what if something terrible has happened to him?"

Lady Colhurst gave a derisive snort. "Nothing more terrible than a lame horse, or a broken trace, I trust! La, child, why should anything terrible have happened to Richard?"

Serena sank down at her grandmother's feet, clutched the

black silk of Lady Colhurst's old-fashioned skirt, and launched into a tangled and agitated narrative from which Lady Colhurst with difficulty picked the main threads of information. Once she was in possession of a few facts, however, she gave it as her decided opinion that although she would not put much past Serena's Uncle Oswald, kidnapping the Heir was where one drew the line.

A cynical gleam lit Lady Colhurst's eyes. "Bad *ton*," she pronounced crisply.

"Oh, would he think so?" said Serena breathlessly. "How I hope you are right! Uncle Oswald would never do anything he considered bad *ton*."

Lady Colhurst chuckled. "You may depend upon that! Oswald was always full of starch. Men of his stamp don't give a fig for morality, and they snap their fingers at the Law, but they care a great deal about 'the done thing.' Beneath him! You mark my words."

Serena impulsively jumped up to hug her grandmother again, thanking her over and over. Elizabeth's sharp voice shattered this affecting scene like the crack of a whip. "Forgive me, ma'am, but if we may descend from the heights of melodrama now, I would be grateful for a dish of tea!"

Lady Colhurst fixed her unwelcome visitor with a basilisk stare, then recalled her determination to treat Elizabeth with civility. She bit back the crushing snub she longed to utter, and instead gave a gruff nod. "Ring the bell for me, if you would, Lady Elizabeth. I daresay you each would be glad of a chance to wash your face and hands as well, eh? Meredith shall see you upstairs and bring you hot water."

Elizabeth gave a peremptory tug on the bell rope. "I own, I should be glad to lie down for a few minutes. Such an enervating journey! Forgive me if I seem uncivil, but really, I am completely unaccustomed to so much *adventure*."

"Well, I can't think why you came!" said Serena with asperity. "Emily would have satisfied the proprieties just as well, and wouldn't have driven me to distraction with complaints and crotchets all the way."

Elizabeth's upper lip lengthened. "Miss Emily Campbell is a very good sort of girl, I daresay, but hardly a suitable companion for Lady Serena Kilverton. As well take your maid along, like an eloping schoolgirl! It is my duty, Serena, to impress upon you that these wild starts of yours are beyond the line of being pleasing. But this entire situation is outrageous! I intend to speak to Richard on this head before I am much older."

Serena's eyes filled with tears. "Indeed, Elizabeth, I hope you may. I hope any of us may speak to Richard before we are much older!"

Elizabeth's brows snapped together. "There is no occasion for these lurid flights of fancy, Serena. Pray calm yourself!"

Lady Colhurst possessed herself of one of Serena's fluttering hands and pressed it warningly, hoping to forestall the fury she saw kindling in Serena's eyes. "Lady Elizabeth is in the right of it, child. You are tired, and you have been badly frightened, but there's no need to despair. Go wash your face! When you come back down we will consider what's best to be done."

When the girls had gone, Lady Colhurst's clawlike hands clutched the arms of her chair. She stared fiercely into the drawing room fire and thought about Serena's tale. Like most of her generation and rank, she had a fine distaste for singularity and an abhorrence of scandal. What a muddle the children have made of it! she thought irascibly. Gentlemen galloping all round the countryside, asking after Richard's tilbury! As well send to Bow Street and set the runners on him! St. Albans will talk of nothing else for a fortnight. The disappearance of Viscount Kilverton! Fine food for an evening's gossip!

A commotion in her hall eventually disturbed these ruminations. Lady Colhurst's limbs may have been twisted with arthritis, but her hearing was as good as ever. A voice she instantly identified as Edward Montague's was raised in something perilously close to a shout. She had no trouble distinguishing Mr. Montague's ebullient words.

"Addison, you old pigeon-poacher! Still gainfully employed, eh? Where's her la'ship? We've brought her grandson to her in one piece, as you see, but we've had the devil's own work to bring it about!"

Lady Colhurst's lips twitched. She had always had a soft spot for that merry rascal, Ned Montague. Her drawing room door then burst open to admit a rather large party of persons in various states of dishevelment. Her grandson Richard was certainly among them, but Lady Colhurst's brows lifted in astonishment at his appearance. He looked pale and worn, his expression was unusually grim, and he was covered from head to toe with dust and cobwebs. Her brows climbed higher when she saw that he was accompanied by Oswald Kilverton, of all people, whose clothing and demeanor were in the same sorry state as Richard's. Mr. Montague strolled in behind them, neat as wax and in fine fettle, followed by two complete strangers: a small, grimy Cockney and a stalwart young man of unmistakable military bearing, so excessively handsome he made one blink.

"Well!" said Lady Colhurst, with great relish. "What a delightful surprise, to be sure! Richard, I suppose you will explain the meaning of this to me in your own good time. For pity's sake, don't sit on the ottoman! It's silk! Addison, set two of the wooden chairs for my grandson and Mr. Kilverton before they ruin my furniture. And tell the kitchen to increase the covers for dinner."

Mr. Montague stepped forward and saluted Lady Colhurst's hand with rare grace. "Beg pardon, Lady Colhurst—infamous of us to intrude! Such a ragtag crowd as we must appear, too. Permit me to present Captain Philip Talgarth, and—ah— Jamie." The captain bowed, and the Cockney nervously tugged his forelock, muttering something unintelligible. "As Richard and Mr. Kilverton appear disinclined for conversation, pray allow me to explain—"

But at that moment, Serena flew into the room, laughing and crying together. She flung her arms round her brother's dirty neck. "Richard, thank God you are safe!" she cried. "I heard you arrive. But what on earth happened to you? You're all over cobwebs! Are you hurt? Were you kidnapped? Good gracious, if it isn't Uncle Oswald! What are you doing here? I thought—that is, Ned thought—well! And here you are, looking for all the world like—why, you're almost as dirty as Richard. What can this possibly mean?" Serena placed her small fists against her hips. "Will someone *please* tell me what is going on?"

Mr. Montague took Serena firmly by the shoulders and seated her on Lady Colhurst's silk ottoman. "Willingly, if you stop prattling like the shatterbrained little bagpipe you are—"

"Shatterbrained?" Serena gasped.

Ned's eyes twinkled. "Shatterbrained, gooseish, and enough tongue for two sets of teeth." Serena lapsed into offended silence and Ned turned back to Lady Colhurst. "As I was saying, ma'am—"

The door opened again, this time to admit Lady Elizabeth, who was looking, and feeling, extremely put out. Elizabeth had washed the travel stains from her person, but there had been no time to lie down and her headache had not abated. In contrast to Serena, Elizabeth greeted the assemblage punctiliously, and very correctly. Addison beckoned to Jamie, who ducked gratefully out to be taken to the kitchen. Serena fairly danced with impatience. Eventually Elizabeth completed the rituals her upbringing demanded of her, and requested that she be put in possession of the facts. Richard waved a weary hand, deferring to Ned. This time, Lady Colhurst interrupted.

"One moment, Ned! My grandson is completely done-in. Oswald, you don't look much better than he, if you'll forgive my saying so. We keep country hours here at Hatley End, and I can't sit down to dinner with you two looking like you've spent the day wrestling pigs in a byre! I'm sending you both upstairs for a wash and a lie-down. Now, don't argue with me! Dinner in forty-five minutes, gentlemen, and it won't wait for you. Ned and Captain—Talgarth, is it?—will tell us anything we need to know while you are gone. Be off with you!"

Oswald had been completely silent. He now rose, and, despite his dirt, executed the bow that had made him famous in a younger day. He spoke with a palpable effort. "Lady Colhurst, I will be glad to obey you, but will not then trespass upon your hospitality further. When you have heard the story Mr. Montague is about to pour into your ears, you will have a tolerable understanding of my reasons. I am grateful for the opportunity to compose myself a little before departing, but I cannot stay for dinner. Forgive me. I must return to London post-haste." His smile was a trifle forced, but he quitted the room with his usual panache.

Richard crossed to his grandmother and kissed her withered cheek. "You're a rare one, Grandmama," he told her. "Thank you! I will be right as a trivet in half an hour, I think, and only too ready for my dinner. Forgive me for foisting all these people on you. It really was not my intention, you know—but Ned will explain." He followed his uncle out the door.

Lady Colhurst fixed Ned with a grim stare. "Well, sir? Begin, if you please!"

Ned scratched his head in perplexity. "Now we come to the point, though, I'm dashed if I know where to begin!" he said. "I feel deuced sorry for Oswald Kilverton, I must say! Why, here I'd thought for months he was the worst kind of unprincipled villain, and all the time—well, I was wrong, that's all. It makes a chap think. Shouldn't leap to conclusions, y'know. Mustn't judge by appearances, and all that. I made a cake of myself; I admit it. That is, I daresay Oswald may be a thorough-going rotter—well, everyone says so! But he's sure as check not a *murderer*. Shouldn't blame him if he called me out for that. Ugly thing to say of a fellow, after all."

"My head is going round and round!" complained Serena. "Do you mean to tell me Richard was in no danger after all?"

"I told you as much," said Elizabeth tartly.

"Oh, he was in danger, all right and tight! But not from your Uncle Oswald," explained Ned. "In fact, the only good thing I achieved in this bumble-broth was when I issued that silly challenge at White's. Put the wind up your uncle, proper, but not for any reason I ever dreamed of! The very circumstances that sent me haring after Oswald put Oswald squarely on the scent. He instantly knew there was a scheme, knew who was behind it, and knew it was going to be laid in his dish if he didn't act sharp to prevent it! Once he knew what was toward, Oswald did all he could to keep Richard safe. I say, that was neatly done! Your uncle's one of the tightish clever sort, Serena! Sent one of his own servants round— that's Jamie—got him hired on as Richard's tiger, and paid him to keep his eyes open. Told Jamie to report back to him if he saw anything suspicious. That's why Jamie wasn't with your brother today. Jamie came hot-foot back to Town after the ambush, to report it to Oswald just as he was hired to do."

Serena's eyes widened. "Ambush!"

"Yes, a couple of ugly customers rode up behind your brother and coshed him—but never mind that!" added Ned hastily, as Serena gasped. "Wasn't going to mention it. Forgot. But there was no harm done, after all! Jamie took one of Richard's horses and escaped, hid long enough to see where the villains stashed your brother's tilbury, and then followed them at a distance so he could discover their hiding place. When the fellows left Richard in an abandoned cottage and set off again in search of Jamie—they knew Richard's tiger had gotten away, of course—Jamie galloped off to find Oswald. Intrepid little fellow! The silly clunches wasted so much time searching for Jamie, they made it possible for him to find your uncle and lead him to the cottage *before* Sir Egbert could get there."

All three of the women exclaimed at this. "Sir Egbert!" cried Serena and Elizabeth in concert.

"Before Sir Egbert could get where?" demanded Lady Colhurst testily. "None of this makes a particle of sense to me!"

"Well, once they had Richard secured in the cottage, the blackguards were supposed to bring Egbert there—in Oswald's traveling coach, no less—how's that for a nice touch? But, as I say, they didn't get word to him soon enough. By the time Egbert arrived at the cottage, Oswald had come on horseback and was there to greet him. Or, rather—well, I suppose he *would* have greeted him, if Richard hadn't put a gag in his mouth."

Captain Talgarth, seeing three bewildered faces, took pity on the ladies and stepped forward. "Forgive me," he said, "but I fancy your skein has gotten tangled, Montague. Allow me to tell the rest."

Lady Colhurst gave a short bark of laughter. "We'll be mightily grateful to you, sir! Ned could never tell a story straight."

Serena shot Ned a provocative look through her lashes. "Shatterbrained," she murmured.

Mr. Montague grinned down at her appreciatively. "Anything you like, Serena!" he whispered. She blushed, and attempted to concentrate on Captain Talgarth's summation.

The captain, now with four expectant pairs of eyes upon him, cleared his throat a trifle self-consciously. "You see, it was Sir Egbert, not Oswald Kilverton, who had been making these attempts upon Lord Kilverton's life."

"And so we might have known," interrupted Mr. Montague. "For if ever there was a clumsy fellow, it was Egbert! Why, if Oswald had been behind it all, the deed would have been done months ago—with no one the wiser!"

Serena knitted her brows. "I do not understand," she said. "Why would Egbert take such a risk? My brother's death would not profit him—at least not for many years. It is Uncle Oswald who would become the heir, not he."

Ned leaned forward enthusiastically, ticking the points off on his fingers. "Yes, but don't you see? Why, that was the only piece of cleverness your curst cousin showed! He knew perfectly well that his father was the only man in England with a clear motive for murdering Richard. He knew everyone else would think so, too! That was the reason he took his father's traveling coach—wanted the corpse to be discovered in it, I have no doubt! Who would look for further proof? Oswald has too many enemies, and his reputation would hardly stand him in good stead. He might protest his innocence all the way to the scaffold. No one would believe it!"

Vociferous exclamations, questions, and arguments broke out, until Captain Talgarth finally made himself heard once again. "Please—if I may clarify this confusion." The ladies turned back to him in relief. "What Mr. Montague is trying to explain to you, Lady Serena, is that Sir Egbert did, indeed, have much to gain from your brother's death—if he could pin the murder onto his *own father*. For Oswald Kilverton's place in the succession would, naturally, come to Sir Egbert instead."

"Oh!" gasped Serena. "Of course! If Richard dies without an heir—and if Uncle Oswald were *also* out of the way—oh, but it's—it's dastardly!"

"Yes," said Captain Talgarth. "But dastard or no, Egbert Kilverton would surely become the sixth Earl of Selcroft."

Between Ned and the captain, the ladies eventually heard the entire story. The two gentlemen had been riding down a side road in search of the tilbury when they suddenly spied Jamie galloping toward them on a lathered horse. Ned had recognized Jamie and uttered a furious shout. But Jamie, instead of exhibiting the fear and guilt Ned expected, appeared delighted and relieved to meet Mr. Montague, and pulled his horse up, waving frantically. When they cantered up to him, Jamie poured an excited and urgent tale into their incredulous ears. He earnestly pleaded with them to accompany him back to the cottage, where he greatly feared his master (Oswald) was in need of reinforcements—for from the top of the last hill he had seen Sir Egbert approaching on another road in Oswald's traveling coach. The threesome then made all possible speed back to the cottage.

Just as Jamie had feared, Oswald's coach was parked in the cottage's dirty yard. Sir Egbert was nowhere to be seen, but the door of the cottage was ajar. At Captain Talgarth's command, they had dismounted at a distance and crept cautiously forward on foot to spy what they could through the casement. As they approached, Jamie saw he would be too short to see through the casement. He immediately disobeyed orders and stole round the front to peep through the open door. From there he saw Lord Kilverton bending over Oswald's bound and helpless form, and, standing directly behind Lord Kilverton, Sir Egbert fumbling with something in his pocket. When he realized Sir Egbert was pulling out a knife, Jamie did not hesitate. He rushed in and leaped upon Sir Egbert's back. Simultaneously, the captain reached the same conclusion. He smashed the casement with his pistol, but by then Jamie had knocked Egbert to the ground and away from Lord Kilverton.

"Mercy on us!" cried Lady Colhurst. "Do you mean to tell me that little stableboy who was just here saved my grandson's life?"

"That's it," nodded Mr. Montague. "Pluck to the backbone, that Jamie! I've a mind to hire him away from Richard."

"Well, you won't do so!" declared Serena, much moved. "I mean to see that Jamie leads a life of ease from this day forward. Think of it, Grandmama! We might never have seen

Richard again! I'll send him to school, perhaps, or turn him into a gentleman's gentleman."

Ned regarded her doubtfully. "I shouldn't think it would suit him, Serena. Not school. And I'd go bail Jamie wouldn't like the life of a valet, either. Only think of my man Farley! Why, he never sleeps. It ain't natural."

"Very well, I'll set Jamie up in a stable somewhere. The point is—"

"The point is," interrupted Lady Colhurst, "what has become of Egbert? You never left him on the floor of that cottage!"

Captain Talgarth and Mr. Montague exchanged uneasy glances. "No, ma'am," said the captain soberly. "Mr. Montague and I—ah—conveyed Sir Egbert to a nearby inn."

Serena was puzzled. "An inn? Why an inn?"

Mr. Montague took one of Serena's hands and placed it comfortingly between his own. "There was a surgeon at the inn, Serena," he said gently. "When Jamie knocked him down, Sir Egbert fell on his own knife."

Serena gazed up at Ned uncertainly. "Will he be all right, do you think?" she asked.

There was a short silence. Then Captain Talgarth spoke in his usual measured tones. "Sir Egbert is dead."

Chapter XXIV

At ten minutes to six, Oswald and Richard Kilverton rejoined the company in Lady Colhurst's drawing room. Both had bathed and rested—Lord Kilverton, in fact, had even slept a little. Jamie had had the foresight to snatch his lordship's valise from the tilbury. Lord Kilverton, therefore, was the only gentleman present who was arrayed gorgeously, and very correctly, in evening attire.

Oswald Kilverton had not had the luxury of a change of clothes, but his riding clothes had been cleaned with a damp cloth and pressed. His appearance was as neat as ninepence, but he moved slowly and seemed to Lady Colhurst to have aged ten years this day. She pressed his hand in silent sympathy when he bowed over her own. Children were a trial and a tribulation, she thought sourly.

Lady Serena was the only visitor besides her brother who had provided herself with luggage. She had extracted a silken gown from her much-maligned bandbox, and was looking extremely fresh and pretty. This was a circumstance which gratified Lady Colhurst and Mr. Montague, but chafed Lady Elizabeth. Elizabeth could not resist voicing her opinion that Serena's dressing for dinner, when Elizabeth could not, showed a lamentable want of conduct. Mr. Montague shot Lady Elizabeth a look of disgust, and promptly removed Serena to the other end of the drawing room.

"You know," he confided, "the more I am around that Delacourt chit, the less I like her. What is this bee she has in her bonnet about you, Serena? She's forever trying to thrust a spoke in your wheel! Slap me if I don't speak to your brother about it."

Serena squeezed his arm with real gratitude. "Thank you, Ned, but I doubt it will do any good."

Ned's brows shot up. "Bound to! He'll soon send her to the right-about. Nothing niffy-naffy about Kilverton."

Serena shook her head despondently. "Elizabeth will listen to no one. She believes it is her duty to correct my behavior, and nothing can convince her otherwise. Richard tells me he has already spoken to her on the subject. Intolerable, that he finds himself forced to apologize to me for something that is in no wise his fault!"

Mr. Montague studied Serena's unhappy face with consternation. Indignation welled in him. "If that don't beat all!" he muttered. "She feels a duty to correct *your* behavior, does she? And won't listen to Kilverton? I've a mind to speak to her myself! Why the deuce don't you correct *her* behavior, Serena? She could take a few lessons from you on—"

He broke off. Serena's eyes, shining trustfully up at him, somehow caused him to lose his train of thought. Her unaffected gratitude at finding a champion in her brother's friend was touching.

"Lessons on what?" asked Serena hopefully.

Mr. Montague's throat tightened. Serena's small hand still rested on his arm. On impulse, he reached up and covered it with his own. "On charm, and spirit, and sweetness, and everything dear."

Serena stopped breathing. Rich color flooded her cheeks. "Oh," said Serena faintly. She swallowed, and transferred her gaze to Mr. Montague's cravat. The oddest sensation of shyness gripped her; as if she hadn't known Ned all her life! As if he were not her dear friend! As if he were something else to her entirely.

Ned's cravat, although very nattily tied, gave her no clue to his thoughts. She lifted her eyes back to his. They were gazing at her with such painful anxiety, and such tenderness, she again forgot to breathe.

"Oh," she whispered once more. It sounded foolish, but foolish was how she felt. Foolish, in fact (she suddenly realized) was what she had been all along. Her eyes widened in wonder. Why, she had looked at Ned a thousand times, and never really *see* him.

Across the room, an entirely different scene was unfolding. Lady Elizabeth had requested private speech with Lord Kilverton.

He had bowed, and accompanied her to the portion of the room farthest from the fire. Once out of earshot of the others, Elizabeth bestowed a glittering, angry smile upon her fiancé. "You are wondering, no doubt, at my presence here in your grandmother's home."

Kilverton's voice remained neutral. "I own, it did surprise me to find you here."

"I came with motives of the purest altruism, believe me! When I heard of your preposterous disappearance, I intended to await your return—and your explanation—in Mount Street. Imagine my emotions when I arrived there to find that your sister was determined—in the most headstrong manner!—to actually *join* in what I deemed a totally unnecessary search for your person—well! I naturally made it my business to accompany her."

Kilverton sighed wearily. "Naturally."

"Serena intended to set out in an *open carriage,* Richard, on the *public highway,* with no other chaperon than Miss Emily Campbell! I could scarce believe my ears! Of all the foolhardy, improper, hoydenish starts—I could not allow her to expose herself so dreadfully. I therefore—"

Kilverton held up one hand, stopping her. His appearance of weariness had vanished. "Let me understand you, Elizabeth! Did you accompany Serena because you believe your presence in her carriage preserved her from censure? Are you telling me that my sister lacks enough credit on her own, or with some *lesser* figure at her side, to protect her reputation?"

Elizabeth flushed. "Well, I certainly would not express it in quite those terms—"

"But that is, in fact, a tolerably exact picture of your sentiments!" Kilverton's voice became almost savage with anger. "Elizabeth, pray allow me to inform you that you are, and have always been, an insufferable, fault-finding, ill-tempered *snob*—and I will no longer tolerate your criticisms of my sister, my family, my friends, or myself!"

Elizabeth recoiled, almost as shocked as if Lord Kilverton had struck her. "Do you dare speak to me of what *you* will or will not tolerate? And *now,* of all times! When your family has become entangled in the most sordid, shameful scandal I have heard in many a year!" She pressed her shaking hands together. "I have tried to make allowances—I have refused to be drawn, on many topics—I have overlooked many instances of what I can only term—oh! So often I have *longed* to tell you exactly what I think of your manners, your morals, and your conduct! I have shown a forbearance toward you which you do not deserve! In the interests of our future domestic harmony—"

Kilverton uttered a crack of mirthless laughter. "Pray do not let *that* consideration weigh with you, Elizabeth! You and I will never enjoy domestic harmony, try as we might!"

"It needed only that!" she cried, white with fury. "I have been grossly deceived in you, Lord Kilverton! You are a frippery, vulgar, care-for-nobody! What I have learned this day covers me with shame. I am *mortified* at the thought of allying myself with you—embroiling my family in this scandal of your cousin's making! Merciful heavens! How could you think I would view with equanimity a situation which promises to drag your name—and, therefore, mine—into every newspaper in the land? In connection with a *murder plot*? Every feeling is offended! I would give *anything* to find myself well out of it!"

Kilverton's eyes gleamed. "Would you, indeed? That is easily done."

"Yes!" cried Elizabeth wildly. "And I will do it! Pray accept my sincere regrets, Lord Kilverton, but I find I cannot, after all, accept your obliging offer! I will *not* marry you!"

The words were no sooner out of her mouth than she regretted them, but Kilverton gave her no opportunity to retract. He seized her hand and wrung it enthusiastically.

"I honor your decision, Elizabeth—I accept it with the greatest goodwill imaginable! Thank you! I am sure you will live to bless this day." He turned to walk away and found that the room had gone silent. Everyone's eyes were upon himself and Lady Elizabeth. As their conversation had grown more heated, their volume had increased, and had eventually attracted the attention of everyone within earshot.

The awkwardness of the moment was broken by Oswald Kilverton, who stepped forward and bowed with his usual aplomb. "Lady Elizabeth, if you would care to return to London rather than dine in—er—present company, I will be happy to offer you a seat in my coach."

Elizabeth, stiff with mortification, bowed her acquiescence. She found herself unable to meet anyone's eyes. She took Oswald's proffered arm and swept from the room with what dignity she could muster, barely nodding to Lady Colhurst on her way out.

After the door closed behind Oswald and Lady Elizabeth, Lady Colhurst's sharp eyes turned back to her grandson. "Hm! We couldn't help overhearing, Richard, so I hope you don't expect us to feign ignorance. Are we to offer you our condolences, or our congratulations?"

Richard smiled affectionately at the anxiety underlying his grandmother's gruff tone. "Now, how shall I answer that home question?"

"Truthfully, if you please."

He grinned at her. "I beg your pardon, Grandmama, but I must decline to answer you truthfully. I fear I cannot do so without appearing rag-mannered. As a gentleman, I am sure it is incumbent upon me to contain what I truly feel—a relief so overwhelming, in fact, that it borders on joy."

Lady Colhurst's lips twitched, and she visibly relaxed. "Congratulations, then! I am glad."

Serena ran forward and seized her brother's hand, peering anxiously into his eyes. "Richard, are you sure? I am so afraid it is all my fault! I would not for the world have made you unhappy. If you like, I will call on Elizabeth tomorrow and—"

"No, no!" said Richard hastily. "You will do no such thing, Serena! In fact, I depend upon everyone here to stand as witnesses, if Elizabeth tries to deny she cried off! Now, *there's* a thought to keep a man awake nights."

Ned strolled over to them. "He's right, Serena. Dash it all, haven't we just been saying they wouldn't suit? And besides—not your affair! Leave well enough alone." He took

Richard's hand from Serena and wrung it in a brief, painful grip. "Daresay it's not the thing, but just between ourselves—well! I congratulate you, too, old man. I can't say I'm sorry to see the last of her."

"No," agreed Richard. "Neither can I."

An idea seemed to strike Mr. Montague. "You know, if it hadn't been for you getting coshed on the head, and Egbert falling on his knife and all that, you'd still be engaged to that harridan. Reminds me of a piece out of Shakespeare. Can't recall precisely—not bookish; never was! Something about 'all things working to the good.' "

Lady Colhurst snorted. "It's from the Bible, you ninny! 'All things work together for good, to them that love the Lord.' Well! If Arnsford and that hatchet-faced duchess of his taught their daughters to love the Lord, this is the first I've heard of it."

Ned nodded sagely, unperturbed by her ladyship's characterization of him. "Proves my point."

These waters were getting too deep for Serena. She shook her head impatiently. "But, Richard, you have wished to be married for the past two Seasons."

Richard smiled quizzically at his sister's worried expression. "I still wish to be married. Not, however, to Elizabeth."

"But now I am afraid no respectable female will accept an offer from you. If Elizabeth portrays you as a jilt—"

Ned shouted with laughter. "Not accept an offer from Viscount Kilverton? Heir to the title *and* the fortune? My dear Serena! The matchmaking mamas will be thrusting their daughters in your brother's path before the week is out!"

"To no avail, however," said Richard calmly. "I hope to be engaged again before the week is out." His grandmother, sister, and best friend stared at him. Lord Kilverton's eyes lit with laughter. "What, have I astonished you at last?"

Ned frowned severely at his friend. "Stop bamming us! The only female besides Elizabeth I've ever seen you take an interest in was some incognita you met in Curzon Street—"

"You will forget that incident, if you please!" interrupted Richard.

Ned's jaw dropped. "What! Don't tell me you *found* her?"

"Very well, I won't."

Serena, bewildered, pressed her hands to her cheeks. "What on earth are you talking about? Richard, do you mean that you have *fallen in love?*"

Kilverton looked a little sheepish. "Well—in a word, yes."

Lady Colhurst and Mr. Montague exclaimed at this, but Serena glared at her brother in gathering wrath. "Oh! If that isn't *just* like you, to fall in love and never say a word to me! Who is she?"

Kilverton's color heightened. He grinned apologetically. "You will be furious with me, Serena, but really—consider my position! How could I say anything? I was betrothed to Elizabeth! In fact, I still cannot say anything; pray remember that I have not spoken to the lady in question since the end of my—er—entanglement."

Serena's eyes narrowed in speculation, but before she could begin guessing aloud, Kilverton's eyes lit with a sudden idea. He turned impulsively to Captain Talgarth, who had been silently watching all these events from across the room.

"Talgarth! What a stroke of good fortune that you are present—the very man who might know!"

The captain was mildly surprised to find himself addressed. "What might I know?"

Kilverton gave an odd little laugh. "Where, exactly, is Rosemeade? And how far is it from Hatley End?"

"Rosemeade!" cried his sister. "Why, that is where—*oh!*" Serena's voice choked in midsentence. She turned pink with indignation. "Oh, Richard, you *wretch!* And Caitlin! I would never have believed she could use me so! Why, I had nary an *idea*—"

But her brother was no longer listening. Lord Kilverton and Captain Talgarth had plunged into earnest conversation with Lady Colhurst. The two men were making plans to leave directly after dinner for Rosemeade, which the captain believed they could reach before dark if the captain drove them in Kilverton's tilbury. Lady Colhurst was complaining of their rudeness, but it was clear that no matter what she said, she found the situation vastly entertaining.

Overcome, Serena sank onto the ottoman. Ned watched her, his expression growing grave as he saw various violent emotions chasing each other across Serena's face. He would have given a great deal to know whether it was Richard and Caitlin's perfidy in keeping secrets from her, or the fact that Captain Talgarth was about to pay a visit to Rosemeade, that had temporarily robbed Serena of the power of speech.

Addison arrived to announce dinner, and Richard and the captain, still engrossed in their plans, together escorted Lady Colhurst from the room. Serena rose without a word, and took Ned's arm.

Mr. Montague looked down at Serena's woebegone little face. He suddenly felt a burning desire to choke the life out of Captain Philip Talgarth. "Do you mind it so much, Serena?" he asked in a low tone.

She gave an uncertain little laugh. "Well, it is just so odd. To think that Richard said nothing to me—and what is worse, that *Caitlin* said nothing to me—and that I never guessed!"

Ned stopped in the passage. He lifted Serena's chin with one finger and gazed searchingly at her. "Is *that* what is bothering you?"

Her eyes met his, genuinely puzzled. "Why? What else is there?"

Ned took a breath, and struggled to find words. "I thought—I thought you were distressed because—well, Talgarth going off to Rosemeade, you know! I daresay he means to speak to Mr. Campbell. And I thought—" He stopped.

Serena blushed hotly. "Oh. That. I see."

"Yes, that! I am afraid—Serena, you must put on a brave face. The captain will offer for Emily, sure as check."

Serena looked thoughtful. "Yes, I am sure you are right," she said slowly.

Ned looked at Serena's downcast eyes, his heart wrung. "I am so sorry, Serena," he said gently.

"Are you?" asked Serena, addressing his waistcoat in a small voice. "The odd thing is—I am not sorry in the least."

"By Jove!" whispered Mr. Montague, much moved.

Serena looked up at him, shy but hopeful.

There's no knowing where this scene might have ended, had Addison not opened the door at that moment. Edward Montague, normally a man of action, was forced to quell his impulses and usher Serena sedately into the dining room.

Chapter XXV

During the soft glow of a June twilight, day lingers well into the evening in Hertfordshire. Caitlin closed her eyes and breathed in the warm, still, golden air. It was beautiful. How strange that beauty, these days, only made her heart ache.

She had hoped that coming home to Rosemeade would cure her. She had expected, once she removed herself from places where everything reminded her of Lord Kilverton, and where she was forever on tenterhooks with the possibility of actually meeting him, that she would instantly recover her spirits and be cheerful, practical Caitlin again.

She sighed. I must give it some time, she reminded herself. After all, home was very dear to her. It was lovely to be back with Mama and Papa and the children. And it was, in fact, a great relief to be freed from all possibility of seeing Richard Kilverton. She could rise in the morning and put on whatever first came to hand; it no longer mattered to her what she wore or how she looked. She could spend her mornings doing whatever needed to be done, feeling no compulsion to linger in rooms where she might listen for the knocker. Evenings could now be spent quietly sewing or reading by her own fire—rather than being pinched and pushed and crimped and perfumed to stand about in lady So-and-So's drawing room, watching the door out of the corner of her eye and wondering Who might come through it next. Oh, the fever of hope and fear and excitement and misery! And the sleepless nights! It was all behind her now.

Well, perhaps not the sleepless nights. But those would pass, too, she promised herself firmly. Someday soon her appetite would return, her peace of mind would be restored, and life would no longer seem to be a dreary and meaningless affliction.

There was enough light to afford one more walk before evening closed in. Caitlin's spirits lifted faintly. Walking was the only thing that brought her solace these days. Tramping about the beloved countryside, every byway familiar to her feet, she could give herself over to her tumbling, chaotic thoughts and find some measure of relief in the combination of exercise and solitude. No need to hide her emotions, no need to make conversation, no need to do anything but think and dream if she wished—or, more often, not think at all. She longed to walk herself to exhaustion, but of course that was an absurd idea. Still, she could not help thinking it would be lovely to be really tired. Too tired to think, too tired to grieve, tired enough to sleep the night through. She pushed open the garden gate and headed for her favorite path.

A worried voice called after her. "Caitlin, dear! Are you going for another walk? You mustn't forget your shawl, my love, with the evening setting in."

Caitlin stopped, turning courteously toward her mother, framed in the doorway behind her. From where Caitlin stood, looking at her mother across the garden, it seemed as if Mama's form was rising from waves of roses; a plump little Venus with an absurdly anxious expression.

"Mama, you know I never catch cold. And I will be back directly, I promise—long before it grows damp."

Amabel hesitated. Caitlin was wearing a long-sleeved woolen dress, which had privately distressed her mother very much at dinner—heavens, the child cared so little about anything, she came down to dinner in her morning dress!—but if she planned to walk, her arms were covered just as surely as if she wore a shawl. Caitlin's strained expression and haunted eyes wrung her mother's heart. Oh, let the poor child do as she wishes; there's little enough she enjoys these days, thought Amabel. She forced a wavering smile to her lips.

"Very well, Caitlin, I won't tease you. But be careful, my dear, and don't be too late."

"No, Mama."

Amabel walked slowly back to the parlor. Her husband was idly flicking over the pages of a London periodical, but held out his hand to her as she entered.

"Well, my love! This is cozy, to have you all to myself. Where are the children?"

"Agnes and Nicky are upstairs, and Caitlin has gone for another of her walks."

Mr. Campbell raised an eyebrow. "Caitie is very fond of exercise since she came home."

"Yes," agreed Amabel absently. He pulled her down beside him on the settle.

"What troubles you, my dear? Is it our Caitlin?"

Amabel clutched her husband's comforting hand and nodded vigorously. "Oh, John, I am so worried! What can have happened to her, do you think? I'm glad to have her home, of course—but I was never so astonished in my life as when she came back from London so suddenly, with never a word of warning. It's unlike her to behave impulsively; she has never done so! Something terrible must have occurred, to send her home like that. And do not tell me it was Nicky's broken arm that brought her, for I don't believe it! She is so unhappy— what on earth can be troubling her? I can see how she tries to support her spirits, and tries so hard to behave as if nothing is wrong, and, oh, John, it is *pathetic*! And the way she picks at her food—the expression on her sweet face when she stares out the window and thinks no one sees—why, it would make a cat weep! She has yet to say one word to me about it. I hardly like to ask her—I don't wish to force her confidence— but do you think I ought?"

John frowned thoughtfully, playing with his wife's fingers. "I don't know," he said slowly. "Like you, I have been much struck by the changes in our little Caitie. But she has just spent many weeks in her aunt's household, you know, with nothing to do but amuse and indulge herself. I hope she is not pining for what we can never give her."

Amabel sat bolt upright with an indignant gasp. "Our Caitlin? Pining for *wealth*? Why, it's nonsensical!" she declared. "How can you indulge such a thought for even an *instant*?"

"Well, of course I don't mean it in any mercenary sense—"

"I should hope not!"

"But you know, my love, life here might seem very dull to her, compared to London in the height of the Season."

Amabel sniffed. "Pooh! Caitlin isn't bored, John. She is unhappy."

Their *tête-à-tête* was suddenly interrupted by a knock at the front door. Mrs. Campbell jumped hastily out of her husband's arms, patting her hair into place. "Heavens! Whoever can that be? Why, it's nearly nine o'clock."

"I daresay it is Isabella and Tom; did not Isabella tell you they would stop on their way home from the vicarage? Only family would pay a visit at such an hour," replied John, rising leisurely from the settle. "I'll let them in."

Amabel brightened. "Perhaps they have brought the baby!" she said hopefully. She was curled comfortably on the settle with her feet tucked beneath her when her husband returned with a rather dazed expression on his face and two complete strangers in tow. One of the strangers was the handsomest man she had ever seen, and the other the most elegant. Mortified, Mrs. Campbell leaped to her feet and threw her husband a look of reproach wholly wasted on that bemused gentleman.

"My dear, two of our daughters' friends from London have arrived to make our acquaintance," said Mr. Campbell. "I have the honor to present Lord Kilverton and Captain Talgarth to you. Gentlemen, my wife."

Mrs. Campbell was favored with two beautifully executed bows. Not by the flicker of an eyelash did she betray the painful train of speculation racing through her mind. She seated the gentlemen and managed to make small talk with them for nearly a quarter of an hour without betraying the various emotions surging within her heart. Was one of these gentlemen the author of Caitlin's unhappiness? And, if so, which of them? And had he come to make amends, or to make her cherished daughter even more unhappy? She hardly knew whether to be glad or sorry when Captain Talgarth asked very soberly if he might speak with her husband in private.

This sounded serious. The captain's heightened color and self-conscious air was not lost on Amabel. It was all she could

do to keep her tongue between her teeth. She exchanged a
Speaking Glance with her husband as he bowed Captain Talgarth out of the room. This must be He—Caitlin's unknown
heartache!

Impossible to know if John understood her silent message.
He still appeared dazed by the extraordinary and unprece-
dented arrival on his doorstep of two completely unknown
Corinthians. The door closed behind her husband and the captain, leaving Amabel alone with Lord Kilverton.

Mrs. John Campbell was not in the habit of entertaining
persons of rank. However, after weathering the anxiety and
mystery of the past few days, she felt herself equal to anything. At any rate, she would make a push to discover who
these gentlemen were and what their errand was. If the happiness of her beloved daughter was at stake, why, she didn't
give two pins for their consequence—she would show them
the door, and out they would go!

Amabel cast a speculative glance at his lordship, who was
staring abstractedly out the window. His aspect did not strike
her as particularly villainous, but one never knew with persons of rank. She had heard it said, often and often, that many
a charming nobleman possessed the heart of a scoundrel.

"Do you make a long stay in Hertfordshire, Lord Kilverton?" she inquired politely.

Kilverton turned courteously to answer her. "Not long, I
think," he said. A rather disarming smile lit his features, and
he met her gaze frankly. "In truth, madam, my plans—and all
my future plans, for that matter—depend upon what I find
here at Rosemeade."

Amabel stared at him. "What you find here?" she repeated.

"Well, yes." Lord Kilverton's neckcloth appeared to have
suddenly become too tight. He swallowed, and cleared his
throat.

But before he could speak again, Amabel struck her hands
together in dismay. "Is it you, then, and not Captain Talgarth
who—oh, dear!"

This was dreadful. Her gaze traveled unconsciously to the
door. If only John would return and rescue her! This had all

the makings of an extremely ticklish situation. But he was off with Captain Talgarth; she must brazen this out alone.

Amabel Campbell turned to face Lord Kilverton, her spine very straight and her cheeks very pink. "My lord!" she pronounced awfully. "I cannot pretend to know why you have come here, or what you may mean by your 'future plans'—"

"That is easily explained, at any rate," said Kilverton. "At least—" He paused, seeming at a loss to continue. "Well, perhaps it is not so easily explained." The disarming smile lit his features again. "In fact, it's the deuce of a coil! But explain it I must." He took a deep breath, and began.

Ten minutes later, Lord Kilverton strolled down a charming country lane where his kind hostess had, in the end, directed him with her blessing.

The gathering darkness was muting the twilight's glow from orange to purple. Stars glimmered in an umbrella of night sky that had opened above the still-glowing horizon. A nightingale's song and the distant lowing of cattle were the only sounds to punctuate the fragrant hush of the warm June evening.

Just as Mrs. Campbell had told him it would, a solitary figure soon appeared on the crest of a low hill before him—a slender form that checked its approach when it saw him. The girl took a few steps more, then halted completely. A smile disturbed the gravity of Kilverton's features. He had been recognized, then! He continued toward the motionless silhouette at a leisurely pace.

Caitlin, wrapped deeply in her own thoughts, was nearly home when she saw him; a tall man strolling toward her—improbably, but indisputably, clothed in immaculate evening dress. This was an incongruous sight deep in the country, but not startling enough to pull her out of her reverie. Her thoughts had been conjuring just such a figure; he might have stepped out of her imagination. A pleasant sense of dreamlike unreality swamped her, watching the man's graceful, athletic stride as he advanced, his white shirtfront pale against the gathering gloom. He very much resembled Richard Kilverton. Ah, but then, he would. If only it were he . . . Caitlin's stride faltered; she paused. This was no figment of her imagination. The man was real.

Oh, madness! She must be dreaming, she told herself. She took another step forward, and stopped again. Her hand crept to her throat. Her heart seemed to have leapt there, and was pounding crazily beneath her fingers. The eerie sense of having stumbled into a dream seized her again. She watched, utterly still, as her fate approached.

Kilverton strolled up to her, the picture of nonchalance. His manner was as formal as his attire; they might have been meeting casually in a London drawing room. He executed a graceful bow. "Good evening, Miss Campbell," he said pleasantly. "Delightful weather, is it not?"

She stared, unbelieving. A thousand possible rejoinders jostled each other in her brain, but she found herself unable to utter any of them. After struggling for a few seconds to regain the power of speech, she managed only to blurt out: "What are you doing here?"

The ghost of a laugh shook Kilverton, but he managed to raise an eyebrow at her as if suffering pained surprise. "I am walking, Miss Campbell," he said gravely. "Walking. One of the principal forms of healthful exercise enjoyed in the country, I believe." He waved a graceful hand to indicate the surrounding woods and fields. "How lovely the evening is, with the moon beginning to rise! You perceive me rapt, Miss Campbell, in contemplation of nature's majesty. A charming spot! I am glad I came."

All the heartache Caitlin had suffered in the past week came crashing in on her. To her annoyance, she found herself fighting back angry tears. Impossible man! Why had she been longing to see him? He never failed to put her out of countenance! The shock of this meeting was too much. She was not prepared. She could not maintain her composure. She was tired and unhappy and life was a miserable affair. When she spoke, her voice quivered. "If you have come here—I know not how—merely to make a May game of me, I wish you will go away!"

Kilverton smiled down at her, an oddly tender light in his

eyes. "I never play May games in June. Look at me, Caitlin! Can you not guess why I have come?"

Caitlin found she was trembling. She took a deep breath and achieved something like an air of cool amusement. "Yes, I see—to admire Hertfordshire, and to comment upon our weather."

"I will be happy to discuss the weather with you, or anything else you like—if you will first hear me in another small matter."

Her eyes searched his, bewildered. She saw no mockery there. "What have you come to say to me?" she whispered. "What is there to say?"

"Only this," he replied, none too steadily. He took her hands in his. "In all my life and in all my searching, I never met a female other than yourself who could brighten my life merely by walking into a room. You haunt me, Miss Campbell. You fill my thoughts when I am awake and my dreams when I am asleep. When we are apart I long every moment to be with you, and when we are together I feel I have come home. I want you, and only you, for my life's companion. I have never been more certain of anything in my life."

Caitlin stood very still. She looked down at her hands in his. She looked back up at Kilverton's face. She forced a wavering smile to her lips. "I cannot help feeling glad to hear these words from you," she said, with difficulty. "You must be aware that I feel the same. But we must forget we ever said these things."

Kilverton looked startled. "Must we?" he asked. Then he dropped her hands with an exclamation. "What a clothhead I am!" he remarked. "You must forgive me, Caitlin; pray chalk it up to inexperience! I have proposed marriage before, but, as you must know, I have never before offered it to a woman I actually love."

Caitlin felt that her head was swimming. "Marriage?" she choked.

Kilverton grinned at her affectionately. "Why, yes! But in my anxiety to get to the heart of things, I forgot just now to mention to you, my darling, that I have recently rejoined the ranks of eligible bachelors."

"Oh," said Caitlin faintly. "You have?"

"Yes," said Kilverton cheerfully. "The Polite World is about to offer its condolences to me. My suit has not prospered."

"Not prospered?" repeated Caitlin. "I do not perfectly understand—"

Kilverton assumed an air of gravity. "Shocking, isn't it? That one so well-born could behave so shabbily! But Lady Elizabeth, of all people, has—er—played the jack."

A crease appeared between Caitlin's brows. "Done what?"

"Played the jack. Played nip-shot. Turned short about. Cried off. In a word, Caitlin, I have been jilted."

Caitlin suddenly wished very much that it were possible to sit down somewhere. Her knees felt like they were turning to water. Fortunately, Kilverton took her hands once again in a sustaining clasp. She clung to them gratefully.

"Miss Campbell, I have not spoken to your father yet for two very good reasons: one is that I rather fancy you are of age. The other is that Captain Talgarth stole a march on me and has been closeted with him for the past half hour."

"Merciful heavens! Captain Talgarth is here as well?"

"I had to bring him, you know; you neglected to inform me of Rosemeade's whereabouts. Your sister Emily was not so remiss. Captain Talgarth was given your parents' direction."

Caitlin choked. "My sister Emily was being *courted* by Captain Talgarth—an experience I have yet to enjoy!" she reminded him.

"An experience you will, alas, never enjoy," said Kilverton firmly. "You will not be courted by Captain Talgarth, or any other man! Unless, of course, you reject my offer of marriage. In that case, I will court you myself—assiduously, ardently, and persistently—until I change your mind."

A mischievous smile played at the corners of Caitlin's mouth. "You tempt me, Lord Kilverton. I would very much like to be courted by you."

She was immediately seized in a pair of strong arms, and Kilverton's breath stirred her hair as he embraced her fiercely. "And I would very much like to court you, Caitlin! The suspense would be hard to bear, but I could dance attendance on you for the remainder of the Season—make you the envy of the *ton,* if possible—God knows you deserve it!—and wait until autumn to ask for your hand. Shall I do that, my dearest heart? Would you rather we did things properly, for once?"

Caitlin sighed blissfully. Standing in the middle of a twilit lane with Richard Kilverton's arms around her, it was simply too difficult to make decisions. "It does sound wonderful," she admitted happily.

His chuckle rumbled against her ear. "What, to have me dancing attendance on you for a few paltry months? If I promise to dance attendance on you for the rest of our days, will you give me your answer now?"

Her arms stole shyly around him. It felt every bit as marvelous as she had dreamed it would. She smiled mistily. "That sounds even more wonderful."

She felt his lips in her hair. He murmured, "Then do not make me wait, I beg of you. Will you be my wife?"

Caitlin closed her eyes. In that halcyon moment she felt her life reach its most eventful corner, turn it, and flow forward.

"Yes," she whispered. "With all my heart. Yes."